# THE PALAZZO SHIMMERED AND BLAZED LIKE THE VERY GATES OF HELL

↔

The screams were terrible; he could see nothing but fire in all directions. Then, despite the danger, he froze. In this room. Yes, somewhere near. To the left.

A presence.

His body prickled, all senses on alert. All he saw was row upon row of fiery eruptions, shooting up like fountains. All he smelled was fire and death.

He waited, scanning. His eyes watered. The other was nearing. Close now, very close.

A black-cloaked figure on a rope swooped down on him, blade extended. Easily, MacLeod ducked, then sprang with his scimitar extended in an attempt to inflict some damage. The tip of the scimitar caught the hem of the cloak; he pulled hard. The hood yanked back and slipped off the head. The figure was masked; MacLeod pulled harder.

If all he had seen was the hatred in the eyes, he would have known it to be Ruffio.

↔

ALSO IN THE HIGHLANDER SERIES:

*The Element of Fire*
by Jason Henderson

*Scimitar*
by Ashley McConnell

*Scotland the Brave*
by Jennifer Roberson

Published by
WARNER BOOKS

# HIGHLANDER™

## MEASURE OF A MAN

# NANCY HOLDER

ASPECT®

WARNER BOOKS

A Time Warner Company

*For dearest Brenda, our guardian angel,*
*and for Alyson, who led us to her.*

WARNER BOOKS EDITION

Copyright © 1997 by Warner Books, Inc.
All rights reserved.

"Highlander" is a protected trademark of Gaumont Television. © 1994 by Gaumont Television and © Davis Panzer Productions, Inc. 1985.
Published by arrangement with Bohbot Entertainment, Inc.

Cover photo by Ken Staniforth

Aspect is a registered trademark of Warner Books, Inc.

Warner Books, Inc.
1271 Avenue of the Americas
New York, NY 10020

W A Time Warner Company

Printed in the United States of America

First Printing: May, 1997

10 9 8 7 6 5 4 3 2 1

# *Author's Notes and Acknowledgments*

The first part of *Measure of a Man* was inspired by Ashley McConnell's HIGHLANDER novel, *Scimitar*. My thanks to her and to authors Jason Henderson and Jennifer Roberson, and to all those who created and have subsequently enriched the universe of Duncan MacLeod and his kinsman, Connor.

Very special thanks to my researcher and friend, Hodge Crabtree, Jr. Any errors in this book are mine. Mythenos is a fictional colony, although the Venetians were indeed hard put to maintain their Greek colonies, and Crete was always a thorn in their sides. The six-month celebration of Carnival developed gradually and reached its culmination in the eighteenth century. In 1655, Venice had a terrible reputation for its torture chambers, but historians tend to agree that the Republic was relatively mild in this regard. Also, the Inquisition tended to slap the hands of accused witches rather than execute them.

I used the Thomas Cleary translation of *The Art of War* and the John Stevens translation of *The Art of Peace*. The unattributed quote about samurai in the epilogue is from *The Art of Peace*. There are dozens of good books about chess; one is *The World's Great Chess Games*, edited by Ruben Fine. There is absolutely no historical evidence to support my fictional explanation for Machiavelli's "will to power."

Without Maryelizabeth Hart, this book would not have been written. My deep thanks to her for her generosity and friendship. I would certainly be the poorer without them.

I'm very grateful to executive producer Bill Panzer and to staff writer Gillian Horvath for saying yes. They and script coordinator and Watcher Chronicle CD-ROM author Donna Lettow worked hard to help me find the right story to add to Duncan's chronicle.

Thanks to my Warner editor, Betsy Mitchell, for being everything an author dreams of. Thanks also to Wayne "Zelig" Chang for his assistance. And to you both for walking, and walking, and walking.

To my terrific agent, Howard Morhaim, *mahalo and aloha nui nui.*

To Jeremy Lassen, Elizabeth Baldwin, Patrick Heffernan, Jeff Mariotte and Christopher Golden, my thanks for their wonderful imaginations and their support.

Also, my sincere thanks to all the fans who have built HIGHLANDER web sites. To Queen and Roger Bellon, thank you for the evocative music I have listened to all day, every day, for months. *Memento mori*, Freddy Mercury.

My everlasting gratitude to my husband, Wayne, whose love makes me immortal. To everyone at Reproductive Sciences, bless you: Samuel Wood, M.D., Ph.D.; David Smotrich, M.D.; Lila Schmidt, M.D.; Elaine Epperson, Ph.D.; Steven Chan, Ph.D.; Catherine Adams, Ph.D.; Vickie Stocker, R.N.; Becca Hansen, Cindy Miller, Jennifer Bantle, Janell Terry, R.N., Amie Baldwin, and Linda Anderson.

Finally, I would like to thank Mssrs. Christopher Lambert and Adrian Paul, and the casts of *Highlander: The Series* and the films, for creating a kind of magic that has made me, quite simply, lose my head.

# Prologue: The Kata of the Adversary

═══

*"When you want to fight, do not face an enemy near water. Watch the light, stay in high places, do not face the current...."*

—Sun Tzu, *The Art of War*

Here we are,
Highlander.
Princes.
But there can be only one king.
So, listen. Listen to my voice that stretches across the universe and tells you a story of once upon the end of your time:
This is how it will be when you die,
Bonnie Prince Duncan.
And this is the nature of the life you will lose:

Into the misty Highland dawn you come, (or you believe that you did), and as any wee, trusting bairn, you smile and reach out your chubby fingers to faces that croon and hearts that embrace. You are held within the band, the tribe, the clan. You belong. You have rights, privileges, duties, and obligations.

Then, slashing deep, lightning upon a battlefield, the sword hacks into body, heart, and soul. You are not the longed-for son, the mother's mirror, the prayers of your grandparents.

You are no one.
You are outcast.
Although your body heals, your soul and spirit are forever maimed, and will never again be whole.

From this moment on, you are alone inside yourself for the rest of time.

And alone, you are abandoned, driven out to hunt your own kind, who hunt you in return. You may love fiercely for centuries, but at the Gathering, your beloved may take your head. You may protect, but your student is a hunter, too, and there can be only one.

The mortals you love will prove their fragility, and you will mourn in darkness over their rose-strewn graves.

If you attempt to stop loving, you will be more alone than ever. And of everything in the world, you are the most alone already.

Forever apart, forever waiting, forever watching, and Watched.

But no, not forever.

For imagine the heartbeats of your days and nights, pulsing endlessly like star bursts. Is there a limit to the heavens?

Infinity is a mortal dream.

Is there a limit to eternity?

There can be only one.

And so you go through your life a being unlike any other, even the ones who are of your kind. A lifeless object—*katana*, scimitar—is more vital to your existence than your blood or your breath. You are a secret, a cipher, a legend even to yourself. Since you do not know the who and why of yourself, you must cling to what you have become. Motherless, fatherless, a family dynasty of one.

Who wants to live forever?

You do.

Because this is how it will be when you die.

You'll start out, of course, in battle. The particulars don't matter, but for the sake of argument, let's say you're challenged at a beach in the south of France. Of course, you could be confronted on the ravaged Russian plains, or in a Chinatown warehouse, or along the shore of the Pacific Ocean. And then there are museums, castle ruins, and secluded rural cabins. Terrible battles can take place in antique store showrooms. Have taken place.

But imagine that it's a warm, sunny day at this remote French beach. By some lucky chance, few locals know of its existence, and no tourists at all. You've arrived not half an hour before with a lover, a mortal woman who has no idea what's in store for her.

As you unpack your Citroën, you satisfy yourself that you are, for the moment, safe. There are no other Immortals around.

Your adored one looks to you, sees that you are satisfied, and reveals her relief in a quick smile. She is in your care; though she doesn't grasp it, she is your responsibility. If harm comes to her, you will try to forgive yourself, but you know from experience that you will never succeed.

While you fold your duster around your sword and pull off your shirt, she spreads a blanket, takes off her top, and puts on her sunscreen, chatting to you of the things that are still important to women: her friends and perhaps a new hairstyle and wondering what she should do about her career. She is clever and witty, and never ceases to fascinate you intellectually as well as physically.

Ah, physically.

You help her oil her back, making slow, teasing movements as you cup the sides of her breasts with your hands. So firm. So yielding. Your women are always beautiful, MacLeod. Even your bitterest enemies, if they are female, want you. And this one stretches like a pampered cat. She loves you, loves it when you fondle her. A man who has lived for centuries knows much of pleasing women.

She turns her head for a kiss, and then she is in your arms. You lower her to the blanket. She smiles. You take off your boots and stand barefoot in the satiny sand as she raises her hips to pull off her shorts and bikini bottoms. Your jeans come next, and she knows that you're hungry for her, and that you must have her.

When you lie on top of her, holding your weight above her, she lightly scratches your back and arms, traces the whorl of hair on your stomach that plummets to places you reserve for her touch only. When you enter her, she arches her back and cries out with animal pleasure, feral, lusting joy. Her fingernails dig into your back, your hips. You kiss her as you move, slowly at first, and then faster, faster, taking her to the heights of ecstasy. When she cries out, you allow yourself release.

Your eyes tightly shut, you feel the warmth of her contented sigh against your ear and kiss her hair. She wears a perfume you buy for her. You've never bought it for anyone else, and you never will.

After a time, she returns to her previous conversation. She asks for your opinion; drowsily you give it, feeling yourself drift away into memories of other good days long past. Wandering cobbled streets that now are car parks. Supping on the flesh of animals now extinct. Hearing music no one knows how to play, not really, not anymore.

Wondering if this day will melt into your parade of memories, and knowing that if it does not, it will be because today you died.

"What do you think, Duncan?" asks your love, and you pull yourself back to the present and apologize. You know Immortals who laugh at you for your preoccupation with mortals, even with other Immortals. The Game insists that every man be for himself.

But you know others who don't accept that. Methos, the oldest Immortal, once offered his head to you so that you could beat Kalas. Rebecca allowed herself to be slain to save her aging, mortal husband, who would have died soon anyway.

You would do the same for this woman, and you know this can be used against you.

Now, as your beloved sighs at your silence—she accuses you on occasion of being too closed and brooding—you open your eyes and stare out to sea. The water is a deep, azure blue Mediterranean, beckoning. You kiss her deeply and tell her that you're sorry, you're preoccupied, and suggest you both take a dip.

Softening, she shakes her head, says it's too chilly. But she urges you to go because she loves you, and she wants you to enjoy yourself.

Nuzzling her firm, flat belly, you rise and walk through the sand as the sea rolls gently toward you. The uneven ground is soft and stretches the muscles in your feet in a pleasant way.

You reach the water's edge. The rippled flow is cool but not cold. It will be good for swimming. Again you glance at your duster, at your woman. You look up and down the deserted coastline.

You walk into the water.

A breeze laps at your skin, tickles the hair on your chest, legs, and arms. The water swirls around your ankles, your shins, your thighs. You crouch forward and push off, swimming toward the horizon. The water is colder now. She calls, asking how the water is. You mimic shivering. She laughs and tells you she will warm you when you come back.

You ride the waves as they take you farther out, the color changing from deep blue to blue-gray. The sun shines brightly overhead. A seabird whirls above you, flies away.

The waves rock you up, down, and you swim with long strokes. You swallow sandy salt water, throw back your head to slick your hair away from your face. A piece of seaweed brushes your thigh. You grab at it. Not seaweed, but a small fish. It submerges perhaps another five centimeters; the water is too dark to watch the little creature's escape.

Then, in one instant, you feel a *presence*. The prickling of your skin; for some—but not you, you are too seasoned—a disorienting vertigo. Another Immortal is nearby.

And you are naked, and unarmed.

Your blood floods from your face. As you have done for centuries, you quickly look around. You concentrate. You feel.

There is a shadow behind your lover, who is innocently pouring herself a glass of wine.

You wave your hands, call out. She does not hear you.

You begin to swim with all your strength, swearing at yourself, swearing at the shape, willing it to be a friend who has sought you out for some good reason.

But you know you mustn't waste your time with idle thoughts. You must assume the worst. You must begin to prepare your assault on the beach. You play out various scenarios: if he holds your woman hostage; if she runs away; if she grabs your sword; if she is killed.

It is taking too much time and too much strength to get back to shore. Dimly you realize you were probably caught in a rip current that carried you out to deeper seas. Today you might have drowned once, twice, three times; no matter now. No matter at all.

You are closer. You must stop to survey the scene. The shadow stands alone, farther back, sword drawn.

Your beloved lies inert on the sand. For a panicked moment you see her head a meter away; then you realize it's the picnic basket.

You charge the beach. There is nothing else you can do.

And while I have already sensed your presence, it did not dawn on me to look for your sword. And so you surprise me, I give you that, as you grab up your duster and extract your sword. So we are on a more even footing, you and I, but I know my gods are with me today.

I know that I will kill you, Highlander.

You are fierce. You have always been fierce. Though you cast away your warrior's role, you have never cast away your warrior's heart. You fly at me; you thrill and terrify me. Unclothed, you are more vulnerable than I, and I take every advantage. I slice your chest, I pierce your shoulder socket; you stagger back, chancing a glance at your sweet darling. You know she's not dead. You know that if you look at her again, you will be.

For I am on you. I slash and slash, impressed by your lightning parries, your riposte, your lunge. You are relentless. Everything they say of you is true. I almost begin to doubt myself, but you have been in the cold water, and you have worked harder than I this day.

You cuff me with the hilt of your dragon blade. You hit me with your fist, you knee me. You push me backward and leap on top of me. You are a savage. You have never left the heather forest primeval.

You are hitting and punching and I hear the bones in my face crunch and shatter. I see the sun on your blade as you raise it; I hear your grunt as I throw sand in your eyes and slam you with the full force of my upper body.

Mortals never fight like this. Their guns do the work. If they use knives, they are cautious. They hold back. We do not. Every hit, every thrust, produces noise and pain. Sweat flies; we heave with effort. Mortals may battle to the death, but we battle to the Death. We, who have fought for centuries, who have survived, do so because in our ferocity we are fearless. It is as if we are possessed. There can be only one. It is our *kata*, our mantra, the consuming drive that controls our muscles and arteries and nerve endings: Survive, survive, survive at any cost.

At any cost.

But you are weak: You want to protect your love. I love no one. You want to maintain your honor. I have no honor.

I am stronger.

And I am winning.

I see nothing of defeat in your face. You cannot know it yet, cannot accept it. But I have you.

*Hidari-do*, blow to the left; *migi-do*, blow to the right. *Ryote*, sword in both hands, *katate*, in one hand. You are skilled in *Iai-jutsu*.

As soon as I answer your *kata*, you switch to another school—*Ichiden-ryu*. Then to pure Highlander fury.

But you misstep.

You smack backward against a boulder and slide to the sand, the rough rock ripping the skin off your back. Oblivious, you charge. Bloodlust burns in your eyes. Your teeth gleam, bared, and there seems to be no mind to you, no thought to you. You dervish like a machine, like the energy of a hurricane.

For me: survival, survival.

For you: survival, tempered by the need to protect.

I know you. I know that in your soul you believe you will never die. You think you are the one.

I thought the same about you. But today something told me to take you. Today I knew I could beat you.

Only today.

And what mythic power compelled me, what force of nature or supernatural being whispered in my heart, *"Today,"* I may never know. It is not important.

All that matters is that it was telling me the truth.

And you die, Duncan MacLeod. You see the blade, you see the flash and shine of it colliding with your future. You feel the first tissues of your neck separate from your head.

You whisper a name I cannot hear. The name of a love, perhaps. Or a teacher. Or the parents who cast you out.

And is there relief? Is there the knowledge that, at last, the Game is over and your burden is lifted?

Or is there only terror and despair?

I cannot say. Your dark eyes are hooded; I half suspect a trick. But then your head comes off, so cleanly, so easily, and falls upon the sand. I am almost sorry, but I have come so close to dying that I cannot spare the confidence necessary to have such a thought.

The Highlander is dead.

I have killed Duncan MacLeod.

And your Quickening? The violent death of a legend?

The earth shakes; the waters rise up in a tidal wave and engulf and overthrow the beach. Lightning shrieks down the breakers, down the blackened sky. I writhe and shatter and roar out your name and remember with your life force the lives you led: I am Duncan MacLeod of the Clan MacLeod. I am MacLeod.

I lose myself utterly in your spirit. I am you; I am consumed. Such a heart! Such a mind.

We roll into the sea; we are whisked by the undercurrent as we sizzle and explode.

And then, it is a baptism. I am myself again.

And you are dead.

I will stand over your grave and laugh. *In pace requiescat.*

Rest in peace, Duncan MacLeod.

And that is how it will be. And, more or less, how you will die. Oh, it may not be at a beach, or in a museum, or an antique store showroom.

But you will die.

By my hand. And by my name, which today is one thing, and tomorrow another, but remains this: your last adversary. The one who is stronger. Down through the centuries, I will come to you one day, and you will surely leave this world to me.

There can be only one, Scotsman.

And I am coming.

It was almost dawn when Duncan MacLeod completed the first of the bare-hands forms of the Seven Star Praying Mantis kung fu style, Secret Force. Frowning, he bowed to his imaginary adversary and slowly exhaled. He had hoped a good workout with the soft southern Chinese style would calm him, but he was more charged up than before he had begun. Adrenaline coursed through his body as if preparing for a fight, not ending a training session. But better to hone his body and his reflexes than stay in bed, tossing and ruminating, and watching the sun rise.

He grabbed a towel off a wooden chair, dried off, and pulled back his hair. On light feet he crossed to a Chinese lacquer table containing a large glass of water, a café au lait, a croissant slathered with marmalade, and the certified letter he had received late yesterday afternoon. Again he took the letter from the envelope, though he had done so at least a dozen times already, and reread the cryptic message, inked in a swirling hand:

*P-K4.*

The advance of a pawn. The opening move in a chess game.

He had no idea what it signified, but there was no question who had sent it.

"You old devil," he murmured. "I shouldn't be surprised that you're still alive, but I am."

He turned the letter over with his left hand as he downed the water and looked at his own name and address in a nondescript, typed font. The postmark was Tokyo. The water gone, he sat on an ornately carved bench beside the table, picked up his café au lait, smooth and pungent, and took a small sip.

*P-K4.* A very standard opening for a thousand different potential games. But not sent, he knew, by a standard opponent. How long since the two of them had played? More than three hundred years. How long since he had received an opening move in the mail? Perhaps sixty years. He counted backward, and was startled to realize it had been precisely one hundred. Was this some sort of anniversary, then? Or was the ancient Italian merely bored?

"Or up to something," MacLeod said, and put the letter down. Like the others, he would not answer it.

And as with the others, the memories flooded back:

*Italy, 1655.*

Venice, to be precise.

Niccolo Machiavelli, the deceiver, the murderer, who wore a smile as easily as a dagger, whose every gesture of friendship cloaked a carefully planned scheme of betrayal.

One of the most dangerous Immortals MacLeod had ever crossed swords with.

MacLeod crumpled the letter and aimed it at the trash can. He pitched it; the shot fell short, and the letter tumbled like a head to the wooden floor.

MacLeod grunted in disgust, reached for the croissant, closed his eyes, and remembered it all, as clearly as if it had happened yesterday . . . which in some ways, it had, for time for an Immortal is not what it is for mortals. It is compressed, expanded, distorted, and put in compartments so that one does not go mad with so much remembering.

But these memories, the memories of Machiavelli, were brilliant and vivid, like gaudy and desperate Venice herself. As shimmering and unforgettable as the beautiful women he had loved with the brute energy of youth in those early years of eternal life: Debra, Terezia, Maria Angelina.

Maria Angelina . . .

# OPENING:
## King's Gambit
### Venice, 1655

# Chapter One

===

*"... for a man who strives after goodness in all his acts is sure to come to ruin, since there are so many men who are not good."*

— **Niccolo Machiavelli,** *The Prince*

*The Protector* was a fine, well-armed brigantine decorated at the stern with the coat of arms of its master, Lord Arthur Burlingame. She was given her name to flatter Oliver Cromwell, the Great Protector of England, who had lopped off the head of the rightful king and sent his son and successor scurrying to France. The world was in a deplorable state: kings murdered; wars lasting for thirty years; Turks growing beautiful women like tobacco on farms to placate their savage sexual appetites; plagues that killed more than all the century's wars and the incompetent, small-minded men who sat on most of the thrones of Europe combined.

On top of all that, the *poseur,* Cromwell, wanted to readmit Jews into England. Burlingame snorted with disbelief.

But a man could count on safe passage. Honor still existed. So, while Lord Arthur's ship plied the perilous Mediterranean on a peace mission sanctioned by the Signory of the Most Serene Republic of Venice, he kept his safe-passage confidently locked inside the strongbox beneath his bed.

Nevertheless, in the dead of night and without warning, the Venetians attacked him.

"MacLeod!"

His name was a shriek as the Highlander awoke; he was but an hour off the late watch and, as usual for him on a seagoing vessel, very sick.

Nevertheless, decades of training leaped to the forefront of his consciousness, and he was instantly, fully alert. Wearing nothing but his loincloth, he grabbed his scimitar and leaped up the companionway, taking the steps two, three, four at a time.

There were shouts and the clash of steel, but MacLeod saw nothing in the blackness. Then a man cried in Italian, "Halt, Turk!" and made for him. MacLeod thrust forward, upward, sideways. Since his unseen foe assumed he was an Ottoman, he employed the classic French fencing style to throw the Italian off-balance. He spun around and lunged left, right, using his curved scimitar like a saber.

A sharp cry told him he had hit his target. There was the thump of a body on the deck.

"To arms! To arms!" an Englishman shouted. MacLeod thought it might be Burlingame, but he couldn't be sure.

Chaos stormed around him. Steel clanged loudly in his left ear; his cheek was sliced open and blood gushed freely as he threw his weight to the left and rammed his attacker. The other man snarled at him like a dog and punched his stomach. MacLeod took a single step backward and heard the loose-sack sound of contact with the deck.

Then lanterns blazed and arced like fireworks as Venetian seamen catapulted themselves onto the deck of the *Protector*. The English officers ordered the mixed crew forward. General Mustapha Ali's towering Ottoman bodyguards needed no prompting. The Turks ululated and leaped at the boarders, slashing and hacking with the abandon of holy martyrs. The complement of ship's officers was fenced in from the fray as the English crew joined the Turks, knives between their lips, cutlasses flashing.

A lantern hit the deck, and there was a shout as a Venetian's leather boot caught fire; the flame rushed up his leg as if it were made of gunpowder. He jumped over the side, arms and legs flailing.

A dozen battles raged. The growing flames climbed the rigging and danced like St. Elmo's fire along the yards. By the red, flickering light, MacLeod disarmed a man and ran him through. Whipping around, he held his sword over his head in fifth position, then sliced at an angle across another man's throat. The man's sword clattered to the deck; he clutched the gaping wound and fell to his knees. Gurgling in his own blood, he crumpled in death.

"General Ali! Ali, where are you?" MacLeod bellowed.

"No, I am an envoy. A special envoy. I was promised safe passage by your ambassador, Giorgio Battista Donado," Ali insisted from the forecastle. "Duncan!"

"An envoy, 'General'?" someone asked mockingly.

Two Venetians dragged Mustapha Ali amidships, an arm's breadth away from MacLeod. Blood stained his now-filthy white robe and jeweled ankle-length sleeveless coat. His kaffiyeh had been knocked askew, revealing his gray hair. He was a tall, imposing man, muscled and scarred from battle, and it was a shame to him to be held by two dirty, ill-kempt men wearing little more than rags. MacLeod thrust out his left hand and grabbed Ali's shoulder, an offense in Arabic Algiers, but here, an act of heroism, for one of the Venetians brought down his sword and nearly severed MacLeod's hand from his wrist.

"He's on official business!" MacLeod shouted, as if shouting would make the invaders believe him. "He was promised his safety, ye loutish curs. We—"

"Be silent or die, Turk." The man fingered the jewels on Ali's coat and looked cryptically at his comrade.

MacLeod replied in heavily accented Italian, "I'm no more a Turk than you. We have safe passage, guaranteed by the Doge. In writing," he added, for he respected the written word, having little ability in that area himself.

"I have seen it. It's clearly a forgery. What odd Italian you speak." The man laughed and thrust his sword beneath MacLeod's chin as his comrade hustled Ali away. "You speak it worse than the Turk."

Ali and the other Venetian disappeared into the smoke. "He's on his way for a private audience with your Doge, Francesco Molin," MacLeod insisted.

"He's dead." The man cuffed MacLeod with the hilt of his sword. "Carlo Contarini is our Doge now, and he knows of none of this."

Though dizzy from the blow, MacLeod took a threatening step forward. A large block of wood rocketed past him, barely missing his head. He hazarded a quick glance up. Both masts blazed like crosses at an auto-da-fé of the dreaded Holy Inquisition; the fiery sails luffed like giant bellows, blowing more air into the conflagration.

MacLeod said to the man, "'Twere better we settled this elsewhere. She's sure going to sink, if she doesn't burn all to hell first."

"Silence!" But the man was startled; he looked around as if it were the fist time he'd noticed the fire. It was whipping into an inferno. The boards of the deck beneath his feet creaked ominously and he blinked rapidly, shocked speechless.

"Give me your hand," MacLeod urged.

"By the bones of St. Mark," the man said, staring at him as the deck bowed. "I'm going to die."

"Nay. Give me your hand!" MacLeod leaped forward and threw the man to the deck just as the section they had been standing on buckled and disappeared.

MacLeod's feet jutted over the chasm and, as flames shot up, he cried out with pain. The man began to kick at him as if to push him into the hole, but MacLeod gripped him fiercely and glowered at him. "You owe me, on your soul." He clenched his jaw and spoke through his teeth. He was furious. "Though I canna trust that, can I, from a bastard who would kill the man who just saved his life."

"*Si,*" the man rasped, shamefaced. "*Si.* I do owe you my life. I swear to St. Ursula that I will protect yours when God sees fit to test my honor."

"Then know my name. I'm Duncan MacLeod of the Clan MacLeod." He wondered if it were wise to announce himself so publicly. He had been in Venice only two years before. He wasn't certain if the family of Terezia d'Allesandro, captured by the corsair ibn Rais, had been ransomed, or if they knew that she had willingly become one of the pirate's many brides. "If I ever have cause for your aid, you're bound to give it to me. Do we understand each other?"

The man's eyes widened. MacLeod frowned at him and began to rise. Was his Italian so bad, or did this man deliberately pretend ignorance because he was untrustworthy?

"*Signor, signor,*" the man babbled. "*Signor,* behind you."

Too late, MacLeod turned. The blade was through his body before he saw his attacker. Blood spewed from his chest like white water through a breach in a ship's hull.

"I am discharged from my vow," said the man, scrabbling from beneath MacLeod as he collapsed.

"Aye, ye are," MacLeod replied. "And I am dead." His eyes began to close; he could feel his heart struggling, his lungs capitulating. Och, he'd been so stupid. Thank God his Immortal kinsman, Connor MacLeod, was not here to see how badly his former pupil fared.

Though blinded by death's skeletal fingers, he felt himself lifted, swung, contracted in the iciness of the water and blinked at the accompanying splash as he shattered the surface of the deceptive Mediterranean, an ocean promised to be warm and calm and filled with comely sirens. He sank rapidly. Large, slimy masses examined his body as the blood poured out of it; sharks would soon gather, of that he had no doubt. They might pose a problem even for him. But for those now joining him in the water, their bodies smashing into him like cannon balls, sharks and drowning would be their final ends indeed.

*Damn you, we had safe passage,* MacLeod thought, enraged, and felt his life go.

# Chapter Two

===

*"Those who become princes by virtue of their abilities . . . acquire dominion with difficulty but maintain it with ease."*
—**Niccolo Machiavelli,** *The Prince*

Carnival began in Venice on the first Sunday in October and ended with Lent, with a short resting period from Christmas Day until the Epiphany. That made six months of festival, and pretending that the Republic wasn't a nation kneeling at the block. Crisis? Decay? How could that be? It was Carnival, and Venice was the most beautiful city in the world!

Yet above the bunting and the crowds that reveled twenty-four hours a day, swords of a dozen nations dangled by threads: French, Portuguese; those of former colonies frenzied with the thirst for vengeance; the endless struggle for Crete.

But the heaviest and largest sword was a scimitar curved and sharp like a smiling tiger. It belonged to Mahomet IV, sultan of the Ottoman Empire. After centuries of warring, the Ottomans had seized the advantage, and all that remained was to deliver the mortal blow. Then the Most Serene Republic would be dead.

But Venetians would not, could not, think like that. So during Carnival, virtuous wives who for six months prayed daily at St. Mark's, donned concealing hooded garments called *chaperones* and bird-beak masks in the silvery night and lay with soldiers and prelates like licentious whores. Prostitutes dressed like harem girls and Smeraldina from the *commedia*. They danced half-naked in the taverns and in the firelight beside the bridges, gave the general populace, from the fiercesome *condottieri*, or mercenaries, to the gondoliers, the even more fiercesome "French disease." (Which the French called the "Italian disease.")

Priests stole money for drink from the poor boxes and merchants filed their gold pieces for more profit. The Doge and the Signory lied to the people and told them there was nothing to fear from the Turks while they themselves made contingency plans for escape. What did it matter who lied and who died? The world was ending, and at the Devil's Masque, no one knew, or cared.

MacLeod, sopping from the well water he had used to clean himself, put on his black mask and peered through a chink in a whitewashed balcony. One could not stroll through Venice naked—not even at Carnival—so he had with regret lightened a drunken reveler of his costume. He was now dressed as a swashbuckling corsair in red satin pantaloons, a white silk shirt, and a turban. The wide-topped boots almost fit, a miracle for which he was most grateful.

Remarkably, the man had been carrying an authentic scimitar, not a beauty such as MacLeod had carried in Algiers, but something merely serviceable. It hung now at MacLeod's side, and while he doubted it would ever become part of him, at least he was armed again.

Overflowing with partygoers, most masked and many cloaked against the October chill, the fairy-tale Piazza San Marco sprawled before him. The cathedral, with its golden domes and white and gold facades, was a roar of noise and color. The Campanile, where the church bells played, rose like a red-hot sword from the cobbles.

At MacLeod's left, the Doge's magnificent palace lay before him. Drunken revelers had managed to climb atop the bronze horses along the balustrade and were making great show of urging them to war. He remembered the interior as an ornate and splendid combination of grand *palazzo* of the most powerful aristocrat in Venice, as well as functional seat of government. Besides the grand apartments and private quarters of the Doge, it was bulging with warrens of council chambers, administrative offices, and guard rooms overpowered by beautiful Byzantine mosaics, priceless Greek statues, and exquisite Veronese paintings. During his last Carnival in Venice, he had witnessed no fewer than six trysts in one evening, atop the desks of mid-level bureaucrats, in his simple quest to find a privy in the cavernous building.

Over the water spanned the Bridge of Sighs, through which prisoners entered the dreaded New Prisons. Trials were swift in Venice. Punishment was swifter. If he was lucky, Ali languished there, but he doubted Ali would count himself lucky. Or that the great general was simply languishing. The Venetians had a reputation throughout the world for their vicious torturing of suspects. There were three prisons in the Doge's palace—the *piombi*, the *torresella*, and the *pozzi*,—and two in the New Prisons, the Leads, on the top floor, and the Wells, at the water level. None of them was a place a man wanted to be.

MacLeod scratched his cheek as he contemplated his next move. With a grappling hook, he could hie himself up and over the—

"Breathe, and you die," growled a man behind him. The razor-sharp end of a knife penetrated MacLeod's silk shirt and pierced the skin between his shoulder blades.

One swift backward kick would free him. But it would not be the quietest way. So he bided his time.

The blade pierced more deeply. By the man's guttural chuckle, it was clear he enjoyed inflicting pain and fear on those he considered defenseless.

Angered, MacLeod whirled around and grabbed the man by the forearm. He smashed his own hand into his attacker's mouth as the man began to bellow in pain. "Shut up!" he whispered violently, and pulled up and forward on the arm. The man fell to his knees. With a swift chop to the back of his neck, he crashed face forward onto the dirt.

MacLeod waited a moment, then checked the pulse at the man's neck. He was unconscious, but not dead. His coarse clothes and start-up boots identified him as a peasant, a man of no account in the glittering city that worshiped wealth. A thief, no doubt. That was good; MacLeod feared discovery from the guards, not the inconvenience of simple robbery.

MacLeod exhaled and felt in the man's pocket. He found a large leather purse jingling with coins. A thief, indeed. And a busy one.

He looked left and right again, checking for the man's mob. Then he began to climb the wall.

The moon blinded him as he reached the top. Straddling the stonework, he blinked rapidly to regain his sight, pushing off for the other side just as he felt

*another*

*a presence.*

*More than one.*

*A ringing in his head, of voices past, of lives taken.*

His nerves vibrated. Immortals waited below. Takers of heads, or friends?

Before he had landed, his scimitar was drawn. He had no sense of having done so. In a small, dark square, he crouched and faced a crowd of people carrying torches and dressed in outlandish costumes: firelight flickered over sphinxes, goddesses, and monsters, *commedia* figures. They observed him with delight, clapping and smiling like children at a puppet show. A breeze off the lagoon riffled their feathers, silks, satins, and brocades. Eyes crinkled at him behind a dozen masks or more.

A demon cut an elaborate bow, furling his hand over his extended cloven hoof. He was dressed all in scarlet with horns and a forked tail such as Mr. Dante Alighieri had described a couple centuries back. (Or so Hugh Fitzcairn had claimed. It was blasphemous to insist that a man had invented the Devil, even if MacLeod was no longer sure there was one.)

Despite the kaleidoscope of costumes, it was another man who caught MacLeod's attention. Carrying no torch, he was clothed from head to toe in a jet-black robe, save for a flash of white above the collar and a fuller expanse of sleeve below his elbows. Beneath his flat, black hat, his hair was white. An elegant black domino hid only his eyes, revealing an aquiline nose and small, tight lips and chin. His face was angular and sharp. He reminded MacLeod of a fox.

The man plucked off his mask, took a step forward, and acknowledged MacLeod with a haughty smile.

MacLeod shifted his body weight forward in a challenging stance. "I am Duncan MacLeod of the Clan MacLeod." Moonlight flashed on his sword as he angled it slightly.

To his astonishment, the man applauded. The group followed suit. Someone called softly, *"Bravo."*

"Put away your weapon, *signor*," the man urged in a friendly, deep voice. "You cannot fight us all. And we would much prefer a cup of good wine in the moonlight with you to drinking your blood in the street."

MacLeod did not move. The man walked toward him, pushing away his scimitar blade and extending his hand. "I am Machiavelli," he said. "Niccolo Machiavelli. Though of course, here in

Venice, I am my own descendant, proudly named in honor of an illustrious ancestor."

The others tittered. MacLeod narrowed his eyes as he scanned the throng.

"They are like us," the man assured him. "Immortals."

All? An Immortal regiment? MacLeod had not dreamed such a thing was possible.

"We have no quarrel with you, Duncan MacLeod of the Clan MacLeod. So please, disarm yourself. Join us in our revels."

MacLeod made no move to put up his weapon. "Ye are a clan, then."

"Like a clan. More like a family." Machiavelli clapped MacLeod on the shoulder. MacLeod stiffened. "Our horses wait to take us to the gondolas. We have been at the Doge's ball. Five hundred, there were! We dined like Frenchmen. We go home now, and we would be pleased to offer you our hospitality."

Another swirl of merrymakers entered the square, but he could detect no Immortals among them. The false sense of privacy he had enjoyed with Machiavelli and his Immortal clan evaporated. There seemed no way to break from them without causing suspicion.

Yet he must rescue Mustafa Ali as soon as possible. In the past two years he had spent in Algiers, Ali had become as close as family to him. His son, Hassan, regarded the strange, tall foreigner as a favorite uncle. Ali was a respected warrior and one of the richest men in Algiers, and being included in his household had made MacLeod's way easy.

Ali had been the one to rescue MacLeod when he was lost in the desert, half-mad with grief and remorse over the death of Hamza el Kahir, another Ottoman—and an Immortal—who had befriended him. Ali had no other reason for doing so than that Allah decreed that all men befriend the weak.

Thus, it had been an honor and a pleasure to accompany the revered Ottoman general on his journey to Venice. If it meant his life, MacLeod would rescue his friend and return him safely to Algiers. This he vowed upon his head—the most serious oath an Immortal could make.

"Whatever engagement you have," Machiavelli pressed, "can it not wait?"

*Not one bloody moment*, MacLeod thought. But he couldn't

hope to break into the prison tonight. Shrugging to hide his disappointment, he said, "Aye, so it can."

"Then let's be off." Machiavelli raised his hand like a king on procession and began to walk with MacLeod. "I think you'll like my home, Signor MacLeod. No expense has been spared, no luxury denied my company. I possess originals by Bernini no other men have seen." He said in a lower voice, "And Immortals who are beyond compare. Each clever, each beautiful. Each very . . . useful."

Machiavelli proudly glanced over his shoulder at his followers. "From near and far they have sought me out." He cocked one eyebrow. "That's why you're here, is it not? Because you seek to join us? The Court of Beauties of the legendary Machiavelli?"

Though MacLeod hadn't the slightest idea who the man was, it seemed the wisest course to flatter the peacock, who spoke of the others as if they were possessions. "Aye. I've heard of you all over Europe."

"Then I welcome you." Machiavelli's hand lingered on MacLeod's arm, then fell to his side. "My friend, if you stay with me, you shall have whatever your soul desires."

"*Grazie, signor,*" MacLeod replied. He couldn't help one last glance at the silhouette of the New Prisons as the troupe of Immortals capered from the tiled square into the dirt and mud of Venice.

Machiavelli watched him like a hungry lion. "You seem to have a fascination with that building."

"Och, 'tis no' a fascination," MacLeod asserted. "I thought I heard screaming, is all."

"I'm sure you did. You've heard of the dungeons beneath the Doge's palace?" Smiling pleasantly, he shivered. "Venetians are artists in all manner of things. Art, love, and torment."

"Are ye."

Machiavelli bowed. "I myself am originally from Florence, of course. I have been here but a year." Which explained why MacLeod had not met him when he had been in Venice before.

Now the Highlander did hear a scream, followed by a wail of despair. Ice water skittered up his spine. It had not the sound of Ali's voice, but when a man shrieked in pain, it was hard to tell.

"Poor devil," Machiavelli said, still smiling. "Come, let's be off to happier places." He put his hand on MacLeod's arm as if to guide him. "And I promise you, Murano is a much happier place."

They walked on, the screams chasing them. MacLeod's body thrummed with the urge to fight. Deep in his gut, he disliked this man. He had no clear reason as yet for his feeling, but he trusted his instinct, as Connor had taught him. He set his jaw, forcing himself to appear calm, and kept on his mask. He had the feeling that unless he stayed cloaked, Machiavelli would read every emotion on his face and every thought in his head.

And the dominant emotion was urgency, and the dominant thought was, *MacLeod, you're in grave danger. Kill him.*

*Now.*

# Chapter Three

"At this point one may note that men must be either pampered or annihilated."
—Niccolo Machiavelli, *The Prince*

Though Venice proudly proclaimed itself the pearl of democracies, it was a tight-lipped mussel of despotism. Gold more than merit bought a man a title, and the "election" of the Doge was nothing more than a pretty play to appease the common folk. Like everywhere else MacLeod had traveled, the real ruling was accomplished behind thick, locked doors by a handful of powerful and dangerous lairds.

Yet the government of Venice was as virtuous as a convent lass compared to the fiefdom Machiavelli had made of the islands of Murano. From the beautiful summer villas and pleasure gardens of the Venetian aristocracy to the white-hot fires of the glass blowers, Immortal and non-Immortal alike displayed a servile attitude Macleod knew all too well. Fear made folk bow and scrape, smiling while you bought their daughters for whoring and unmanned their sons for guarding 'em, as the Turks were wont to do. Or made them murmur, "Thank ye, milord," while you raped their country, deposed their king, and made their native tongue illegal.

Many Scots bowed and scraped, but in every Scots heart burned an equal measure of hatred for their English overlords. That was the way of it, and a natural way it was, too. His Scots heart burned. But he would be damned if ever he licked the boot of another man.

It was not so among Machiavelli's subjects. They worshiped the Immortal. To them, he was not a merciless aristocrat, but a saint. Though he was a hard taskmaster, and greedy of their wares to boot, he gave them meat, and presided over their petty quarrels. On feast days he and his "Beauties"—his Immortal clan—flung florins and ducats to the cheering crowds. He arranged better marriages for their sons and daughters than the simple farmers and tradesmen could have ever hoped for. He declared half the water wells on the islands that made up Murano public, not a small thing in the salt lagoon of Venice.

He cited law to his people that took from them the work of their hands and their fields, then graciously offered to set aside the law and give back half of it. Thus, while he stole from them, they thanked the sweet Mother Mary for his mercy.

That's where the danger of the man lay. The local inhabitants were too simple to see that to Machiavelli, kindness and cruelty were the same: means to achieve his ends. The Muranese, who had hearts and hopes and ills as all people do, were nothing more to him than pawns in his huge personal chess game, like the one in Marostica.

MacLeod accompanied Machiavelli and the other Beauties to that famous game, called the *Partita a Scacchi*. It had been played every two years since 1454 to commemorate a wedding feast. On an immense field of black and white, costumed individuals representing the pieces of a chess set stood in each square, waiting to be moved, captured, crowned.

"This is the grand metaphor of life," Machiavelli said, with a sweeping hand. "People are as easily moved as these players, friend Duncan. Sometimes it take a little shove. Sometimes, the mere crook of a finger. A promise is as good as a threat. Remember that."

"Aye, that I'll do." MacLeod wondered which technique the Immortal planned to use on him. For he would one day, of that MacLeod was certain.

For his part, Machiavelli moved the mighty Doge and his counselors with the ease of wooden bishops, knights, and kings. Armed with false rumors about the new Pope and the military buildup of the French, and reacting to rampant, inaccurate speculation about the spice trade now that the Portuguese had found a new trade route, special messengers whisked through the mazes of colonnades and Byzantine mosaics of Machiavelli's lavish palace.

He moved MacLeod as well, isolating him on the islands that sat a thirty-minute voyage from Venice. Though wild to be gone, MacLeod had not yet managed either to secure the services of an island gondolier or to steal a gondola himself. He assumed he would be recognized in the city. That would not bode well for a man intent upon engineering an escape from one of the most notorious prisons in Europe.

Despite his anxiety, he found it within himself to chuckle at the self-important courtiers, blue jays in their foppish petticoat breeches decorated with rows and bunches of ribbons, more ribbons heaped on their shortened doublets, their sleeves, and their gloves. Their curled wigs tumbled down their backs as their bootheels and red high-heeled shoes chattered on the black-and-white—chessboard—marble floors. Though he dressed with the times, he clothed himself simply, in doublet and riding coat, wearing his hair loose. It was more dignified.

And easier to fight in, should the need arise.

There were scribes and secretaries and dozens of functionaries ensconced in Machiavelli's *palazzo*. The government revolved around the Immortal rather than the Doge and the Signory—the ruling body of Venetian government—and Machiavelli received dignitaries from foreign countries with the air of a prince. Talk of war increased—war with the Ottomans, with France, with the Pope. Everyone in the world was waiting for Venice to fall, so they could rape her.

As nonchalantly as he could, he hid himself from the scores of visitors. But everyone seemed to have forgotten that a tall, dark-haired Highlander had attended court just two years before. The Venetians were too distracted by their worries and the high fever of their desperate merrymaking.

Perhaps he should just swim to Venice.

Because Machiavelli was not distracted by anything, and he made merry only when it pleased him. What pleased him was to dine with the other Immortals, and to play chess and discuss his philosophy of life with his new chess piece.

"My board is almost complete," he said to MacLeod one evening as he set up the board for another game. He held up the pieces as he put them on the board. "I have two bishops. Two castles. And now, a second knight." He smiled at MacLeod. "Knights travel fast, attack fast, withdraw. They make their way through the twisted paths of treachery to power."

MacLeod put his own pieces on the board as he digested what Machiavelli was telling him. He didn't know the other Immortals well enough to know which ones Machiavelli referred to—rooks, bishops, knights. But the implication was that most of them were only pawns.

"You're very skilled," Machiavelli said, then added, "at the game. Who would have thought it from a man still smelling of sheepskins?"

MacLeod picked up his queen and put her on her white square. He still had trouble comprehending the reality of the strange and menacing court Machiavelli had brought together on the island. It was with a purpose, and they were not random choices he'd made in his selection of "pieces." Did Connor know of the Immortal Court of Beauties? Surely it must be legendary.

For though the Immortals who had joined Machiavelli carried, for the most part, the air of the bored hangers-on of a wealthy aristocrat, in truth each had been carefully selected by the master because of a special talent or ability. Bernardo Caprio, a forger, could make exquisite copies of the paintings of the masters that graced the *palazzos* and churches of Venice, which Eugenia de la Croix then stole, replacing them with the copies. Sergei Aloysovitch, from Russia, was Machiavelli's eyes and ears for things Russian. What were they, castles and horses or pawns? Annette Rouens was Machiavelli's French spy. Cristofori—simply Cristofori—kept track of Greece for him, vital for a power-hungry man such as Machiavelli, as Greece was forever the thorn in Venice's aching side.

Paloma Alcina danced. Giuletta Fantini worked her way into the beds of the rich and returned with detailed maps of their treasuries, and scores of family secrets whispered during midnight escapades that the proud Venetian aristocracy would pay dearly to keep secret. Machiavelli had a penchant for using such information to fan the tempers of the families, playing one against the other. All over Venice he had caused blood feuds, the famous, vicious vendettas, of the hotheaded Venetians.

The entire world, it seemed, was nothing but a huge chessboard to be mastered for his pleasure.

All the Immortals could fight, and some well, but for the majority, their hearts were not in their swords. They only played at dueling. There was no blood to their practicing, and it soon became clear to MacLeod that they had no sense of training for any purpose save that they lived in a society based upon the defense of honor. MacLeod could not fathom it, having been trained by his kinsman, Connor, that danger in the form of another Immortal could strike you at any moment.

That danger came in three forms on the island of Murano: the first was Machiavelli, who seemed capable of turning upon his closest friend—if he had any—with the deadly suddenness of a serpent.

The second danger was the Court of Beauties, who would, MacLeod had no doubt, rip him to shreds with their bare hands should Machiavelli order it.

The third was Ruffio Mocenigo.

He was a tall man, very young when he had died the first death, very agile, and very cruel. A fashion plate, his ribbons and buckles only masked the savage brute that he was, fond of whipping peasants and forcing their women. He reveled in his special position as Machiavelli's right-hand man, and lorded it over the other Immortals, who were afraid of him. His special skill was his ability to execute fully the wishes and whims of his master, to whom he was utterly devoted. He made no secret of the fact that he viewed MacLeod as a potential usurper, and that he would be glad of the day the Scot was gone—in whatever form that leave-taking was made manifest.

To allay Machiavelli and to keep Ruffio at bay, MacLeod pretended that he counted himself among the angels to be a Beauty, and endured Ruffio's bad humor with feigned good grace. His soul suffered for it, and at night he stole into Machiavelli's fabulous gardens and trained his body and mind for the inevitable confrontation with Mocenigo.

After a few days that alternately flew and dragged, he befriended Antonio, a page in the employ of the Cardinal. He reminded MacLeod of himself as a boy, eager to learn how to become a man. 'Tonio must have sensed MacLeod's pleasure in his company, for he came to regard the tall foreigner as something of a mentor.

As a result, MacLeod received news regularly from the mainland, including the situation at the prisons. Granted, it came from the eyes and mouth of a child, but together with what he gleaned from the other visitors, he was able to piece together what was happening. He learned that both Burlingame and Ali had been condemned to die as spies, the sentence to be delayed until after Carnival. It was only early November, so there was some time to hatch an escape plan.

That would have comforted MacLeod more if he had not also learned the manner of their executions: beheading, the corpses to be burned immediately after. The heads would be preserved in wax and displayed in a macabre museum behind the Chapel of St. Ursula. Perhaps it was the Italian lust for relics that prompted the bizarre collection. MacLeod only knew that the very thought of the museum made him seethe.

"Signor Mackio." 'Tonio approached quietly. His youth was more fortunate than his childhood had been. Poor diet had left his legs bent from rickets, and he bore scars from beatings, and a crooked nose. His hunger for affection touched MacLeod. "It's a letter, sir." He shyly pushed his reddish brown hair away from his face as he held out a sealed envelope in MacLeod's direction, not quite daring to touch his hero.

There was a coat of arms, a shield with a crown above and diagonal stripes of blue and white, but he couldn't place it.

He opened the thick paper and scanned it, able to read sufficient Italian for that. It was an invitation to a banquet at the house of the Calegri. The Calegri were an influential family who counted Doges among their ancestors, a good family. Powerful. He cast back, realizing he had been introduced to one of them briefly the day before on the chessboard floor, and was surprised at this quick display of friendship to a man short on credentials. He could not remember having met them when he'd been in Venice before.

"*Va bene*," he said to 'Tonio. "I'll draft an answer later." He had no idea how to respond.

"Can we have a fencing lesson?" 'Tonio asked, his brows shooting up hopefully.

MacLeod hid his smile. "Aye, lad. I'll get me loose of these infernal ribbons and then we'll have some sport."

"Friend Duncan." Machiavelli came up behind him and clapped him on the back. "You've gotten a love note, perhaps?"

"Secret information from my spies," MacLeod retorted, just to needle him.

Machiavelli chuckled. "Your eyes miss nothing, Scotsman." He took up the page with a flourish. "May I? An invitation to the Calegri. You must know that the Doge hates them passionately."

"That's naught to do with me."

"Come with me. We'll walk together." He put his arm around MacLeod's shoulders. To their left, Ruffio lounged against a column, picking his fingernails with a jeweled stiletto. He was dressed fashionably in white and purple and long sausage curls of unnatural blue-black. Despite his fussy clothes, his bearing was sinister. His features were cast in darkness, but it was clear he was watching carefully.

"My *chevalier*, I have been a friend to you, have I not?"

*Chevalier* was French for knight. Feeling a change in the tide, MacLeod answered simply, "*Si, signor*. You've treated me well." He was aware that 'Tonio was silently trailing them, and gave his head a surreptitious shake to warn him off. But the boy appeared not to understand, and kept following.

"You know that I treasure your presence here. That I would be bereft without you. I hope this engenders within you in return an appreciation for my patronage."

"Oh, aye," MacLeod replied, sliding his glance toward Ruffio, who had detached himself from the column and glided along the perimeter of the room, keeping pace with them.

Machiavelli chuckled as if at the lack of conviction in MacLeod's tone. "I have chosen you well. You have leadership potential beyond anyone here. Save myself. You are a true warrior. For you, a sword stroke rights things."

"Not always," MacLeod answered honestly, a lesson hard-won.

Machiavelli tapped the invitation. "As I have mentioned, this family is not fond of the Doge. And the Doge is a great friend to the house of Machiavelli. And as you are now of my house, well . . ." He inclined his head. "A certain young man, one Giovanni Calegri, tried to assassinate our beloved prince. He has gone unpunished only because no evidence has convicted him. We're practically at war. Our previous Doge lasted only a year. We cannot withstand the turmoil such petty and shortsighted politics would deal us."

MacLeod only looked at him. Machiavelli huffed as if irritated at the necessity to state the obvious. "The Doge would favor highly the man who dealt with this Calegri for him. He would give to him a boon."

MacLeod narrowed his eyes. "I'm no' an errand boy to do your dirty business."

Machiavelli looked taken aback. It was clear he wasn't used to being refused. "It's not dirty business, man. It's necessary business. And it is my belief you could make use of a favor."

Such as a pardon for Ali? MacLeod kept his face from showing his apprehension. He said, "I'm no' a man who kills to advance himself."

"No?" Machiavelli shrugged. "I think otherwise. You're too good at chess for that to be true. You know you can't move forward without clearing the board of the pieces that are in your way. In our game, you are a knight. I'm the king. Advancing me advances you. We can't allow me to lose."

MacLeod said flatly, "No."

Machiavelli flared. "Think twice on that answer, *signor*."

He snapped his fingers and moved away from MacLeod. As MacLeod watched, the Immortal was approached by a reedy, unsmiling man in a cast-off coat and worn bucket-top boots. Machiavelli walked apart with the man, taking with him MacLeod's invitation from the Calegri.

Ruffio turned, stared at MacLeod, and joined them.

'Tonio crept to the right, hurrying to catch up with Machiavelli and the others.

"No," MacLeod whispered fiercely, but the boy moved forward. The men's heads lowered together as they murmured at each other. 'Tonio tiptoed closer, straining to hear.

MacLeod shook his head sharply, catching the boy's eye. Reluctantly, the boy returned to MacLeod's side.

"Is it true you will murder someone tonight?" he asked excitedly.

MacLeod was alarmed. "Did you hear about that, then?"

"Aye," the little boy replied, imitating him. "And the man gave Signor some sticks of metal and told him something about the well with the unicorn on it."

"Pay no mind. Get out of here." He walked the boy the length of the hall. "I'll take you to the gondola *traghetto* and—"

"Can't we fence?" 'Tonio asked in a small voice.

"Next time. Now come, lad. I wouldn't have anything happen to ye."

'Tonio's face shone. It was a wonderful thing, MacLeod mused, to know that someone cared about you. "But what will happen to me?"

"Say nothing about what you heard to anyone. I will not be

killing anyone, do you understand? But it's best that you don't know of any of this. Don't tell your master the Cardinal."

"*Si, signor.*" He bobbed his head. "Signor approaches."

MacLeod gritted his teeth as Machiavelli and the man in the bucket-top boots came toward them. He put his hand on the hilt of his sword.

"I will run all the way to the gondola," 'Tonio said, and before MacLeod realized what was happening, the boy had scampered away.

"Wait," MacLeod called.

"Duncan."

Machiavelli rejoined MacLeod. The man in the boots broke from him, touching his hat in a respectful salute.

"We dine now," Machiavelli said, putting an arm around MacLeod's shoulders. "This beehive will buzz along without us."

MacLeod darted a glance in the direction 'Tonio had left. There was no sign of the boy. Troubled, he nevertheless allowed himself to be shepherded by Machiavelli through the cavernous room, past Grecian statues and Roman busts that might or might not be forgeries. Ancient crossbows and sabers formed a huge cross on one wall. Machiavelli claimed to be a thousand years old. Perhaps he had merely secured the loyalty of an Immortal who was that ancient.

"You're a very tense man," Machiavelli observed, his grip on MacLeod's shoulder tightening. "Is someone following you?"

"Is not someone always following the likes of us?" MacLeod replied. He didn't add that he disliked being touched so much.

Machiavelli laughed. "Touché! You have me there, *caro* Highlander. Come, let us feast in case we are challenged within the hour. Or," he added, patting MacLeod's cheek, "we challenge one another."

MacLeod's smile faded. "Is that your intention?"

"No, no. We play the same game. We are friends."

"According to you, there's no such thing." MacLeod watched him carefully. "There's only commerce in men's souls."

Machiavelli looked pleased. "I have said that, haven't I."

They came to a row of ornately carved doors shaped like portcullises, which were set in the middle of a fresco of the Virgin with the Holy Child. Machiavelli opened them with a flourish and stood back to let MacLeod enter first.

At once a claustrophobic frisson shot up MacLeod's spine, his fighter's reflexes shackled. The hall was so dark he couldn't see his own hand, the walls too narrow to draw his sword. He was acutely aware that Machiavelli glided quietly behind him. The hair on the back of MacLeod's neck rose as he listened for Machiavelli's every movement.

"Relax, *bello signor*, for the love of God," Machiavelli said, sighing. "Donna Maria, you're more suspicious than I. Tell me truly, you did come to me to join me and not to betray me?"

"I've said so." MacLeod relaxed slightly as light streamed into the tunnel and the sound of laughter and music filtered through the gloom.

"Then it must be true." Machiavelli was obviously amused.

MacLeod walked into the oblong banquet hall, where the Immortals were gathering for a sumptuous feast. Feeling the approaching presence, a few looked in his direction, acknowledged him and Machiavelli. Most, however, continued their conversations and drank their wine.

Ruffio had managed to beat them there. There must be another entrance to the hall. His eyes were an icy blue as he approached and made obeisance to Machiavelli. MacLeod he ignored. His charming yet calculating smile was reserved for Machiavelli alone. "May I sit with you?"

"Of course, Ruffio. And Duncan will sit at my left hand."

The young man glared daggers in MacLeod's direction. He would be a more likely candidate to murder one of Machiavelli's enemies.

"A *centesimo* for your ponderings," Machiavelli said to him.

"They're not worth that much," MacLeod countered.

"I'm not so sure." Machiavelli guided them toward the head of the table. They took their places. The rest of the company stopped speaking and waited until Machiavelli sat with elaborate dignity. The man on MacLeod's left was an unbelievable bird of paradise dressed in riotous colors. On Ruffio's right sat the lovely Giuletta, whose bodice plunged almost to her navel.

Machiavelli raised his glass. "To all my Beauties," he said. "My lovely women and my handsome young men. To a life eternal of pleasure and joy. To you all!"

"Here, here," they chorused, and all drank.

MacLeod sipped and put down his cup. The others avidly

watched the procession of dishes as the servers, dressed in silver and black, marched from the kitchen to display the meal. The scents of rosemary, thyme, basil, and tomatoes filled the hall. He was filled with a sense of doom and waste; these Immortals were not well served by their service to Machiavelli, if he did not prepare them for the Game.

He turned to Machiavelli and said, "There is more to our lives than eternal pleasure, is there not?"

Machiavelli half-looked at him. "What more could one require?"

"What of the Gathering?"

Machiavelli laughed. "That old wives' tale? Surely you don't believe it."

"What is the Gathering?" The bird of paradise piped in a shrill voice. He glanced shyly at MacLeod. "What are you speaking of?"

"Jean-Pierre, it's nothing." Machiavelli waved his hand. "A child's fairy story."

Jean-Pierre opened his mouth to speak. Ruffio glared at him, and he closed it abruptly and picked up his fork.

In that moment, the first of the dishes reached the head of the table. The server removed the gilt cover, displaying a succulent boar's head. Machiavelli inclined his head and breathed in the fragrance of cooked meat and spice. "Superb."

"We fight one another in the Gathering," MacLeod said to Jean-Pierre. "One-on-one, dueling with our swords. We kill one another."

"What?" Jean-Pierre was astonished. "Why?"

"It's a terrible Game we must play." MacLeod put his wine glass to his lips.

"A game?"

"*Signor*," Machiavelli said warningly.

"One of us must win. One must be the last." MacLeod drank deeply.

Machiavelli gestured for a servant to refill Jean-Pierre's wine goblet. "An absurd notion, is it not?"

MacLeod gazed levelly at Jean-Pierre. "An honorable man told me of it."

"And many honorable men have believed many absurd things," Machiavelli finished, admiring a towering confection of pastry crust shaped into a medieval castle. "Excellent," he said to the server, who inclined his head. "Enough of this chatter. It's dull and uninspired. I will not have tedious conversation before such exquisite food."

MacLeod surveyed the Immortals, who were applauding the presentation of the banquet dishes and toasting one another. There were a number of very beautiful Immortal women flirting outrageously with the men. Perhaps the members of this band would meet each other in battle. Did they not know it?

"Does no one here know of the Game?" he pressed.

"No one here needs to, since it is not true, *signor*." Machiavelli narrowed his foxlike eyes at him. Perhaps another man would be cowed by their angry darkness. MacLeod met his gaze and held it. "How different you are of late, Sir Chameleon. Not at all respectful." He set his mouth. "Not at all obedient."

"My apologies," MacLeod said flatly. "My understanding was that you and I had spoken of challenges. I assumed you spoke of the challenge one Immortal makes to another."

"Men duel." He waved a hand. "There is nothing mystical about that."

MacLeod picked up his wine. Machiavelli said, "And now, of that other matter. Of the house of Calegri. They have bothered us long enough, have they not, Ruffio?"

Ruffio turned his head and spat on the floor. "Bastards," he grumbled. "I'd like to see them all dead."

Machiavelli turned to MacLeod. "Do *you* see, *signor*? A man of your experience has killed, surely."

MacLeod remained silent.

"And you are from a nation that comprehends the necessity of lords and subjects."

Still he said nothing.

Machiavelli turned to Ruffio. "My dear friend, if I asked you to kill someone, what would you do?"

Ruffio laughed. "Have I ever hesitated before, *maestro?*"

"Never. You've always proven your loyalty." Machiavelli peered at MacLeod. "There is a price for the life you're leading here, young Immortal."

MacLeod set down his wine. " 'Tis time I left you, sir. I canna kill for you. I'm no use to you." He rose. Jean-Pierre was so stunned he dropped his fork. The other Beauties stopped talking and stared at him in silence. Protocol demanded that everyone stay until the lord and master left.

"Insult," Ruffio whispered.

The blood drained from Machiavelli's face. "Go to your room," he said dismissively to MacLeod. "You may not leave Murano. No gondolier will transport you until I say you may, and I'm not finished with you."

The room crackled. Hands went to sword hilts. MacLeod knew in that moment that were Machiavelli to command anyone else to take him on, they would.

His back stiff, he left.

In the palace gardens, he sat on a stone bench and watched the windows of the *palazzo* blaze with torchlight and candlelight. Many inside would be awake when the tallows guttered in the rosy glow of a new day.

The moon rose over the garden, and still he sat with clenched fists. It was too dangerous to remain here any longer. He would get a conveyance however he had to, get Ali, and quit this decadent place.

"Signor MacLeod?" It was Jean-Pierre, white as a statue in the moonlight. He wore a gentleman's sword, a thin, useless thing no Arab nor Scot would be caught dead with. He approached hesitantly, glancing left and right as if he feared being discovered. "If I may?" He pointed to the place beside MacLeod on the bench.

MacLeod nodded. Jean-Pierre exhaled as if in relief and primly held the flared skirt of his doublet as he sat. He crossed his legs and ankles, uncrossed them, and blurted, "I am as good as unarmed."

"I'm not here for your head."

Jean-Pierre flushed. He was very, very young. Practically a boy. "This Game . . ."

"Your master doesna believe such a thing exists."

"I, ah, I have heard of it before. I simply didn't believe it."

MacLeod said coldly, "That's your choice." He cocked his head. "Why are you here?" To rid Machiavelli of him? If so, it was a poor and dishonorable act on Machiavelli's part. This one could not defend himself from a starving dog.

"I love him as I love my life. Ah, but well . . ." He cleared his throat. "Some of us have gone missing. I had a close friend from my village, Brother Andre. Master Machiavelli sent him on a mission to Lombardy and he hasn't come back. He hasn't written.

When I ask about him, *il maestro* says all is well. But if another Immortal found him, and as you say . . ."

He took a breath and let it out slowly. "Maestro tells us we can never die. I have never seen a dead Immortal."

MacLeod shook his head. "He's lying to you. To all of you. The purpose of having a teacher should be to defend yourself. Sooner or later, others will come to take your head."

"Teacher?" Jean-Pierre echoed, clearly confused. "He's my master."

"Good masters teach their subjects," MacLeod ventured, not sure how to even start explaining the Rules to this ignorant Immortal. Not sure he should even attempt it, for he had no desire to take on the role of teacher himself.

Jean-Pierre ran his hands through his monstrous curls. "I died only a few months ago. Andre and I were at a monastery in Rome. Yes, I was a monk. Brother Jean." He smiled as if embarrassed. "*Signor* was visiting His Holiness the Pope, and I . . . I . . ." He hesitated. "You see, he told us he could make miracles. That he could bring us back from the dead."

"God's blood, man, you let him kill you?" MacLeod's earlier premonition of danger swept through him again, doubled, tripled in intensity. This was madness.

"He called us his bishops. Andre went first." His face took on an expression of adoration. "We lived again, as my master promised."

Did the man refer to Jesus Christ or Machiavelli? Or were they to him the same?

"We're born this way," MacLeod said flatly. "No one makes us so."

Jean-Pierre blinked at him. "How can that be?"

"You say some of you go missing."

Jean-Pierre tapped nervously at a ribbon on his doublet. "*Si.* Often his favorites. Andre was a favorite. He calls us his 'pieces' and he sends us on errands. I have lost several friends in this way."

"What does Machiavelli say?"

"That he has released them to go on their eternal adventures." He looked hopeful. "Perhaps he has." He raised his hand to his mouth and gnawed at his thumbnail. All his fingernails were chewed to the quick. He saw what he was doing and stopped, folding his hands like a proper brother of the cloth.

"Why are you here, Signor MacLeod? Did you come to warn us? To make some Immortals of your own?"

"I just told you . . . och." MacLeod moved his shoulders. Sleeping in a feather bed was making his body ache. The rich food at Machiavelli's table disagreed with him. He wanted to go home and found, to his surprise, that he thought instantly of Algiers.

"To warn us, or to murder us?" Jean-Pierre jumped up and drew his silly little foil. His hand shook. "If that is the case, *en garde, monsieur.*"

"Lad, put that away." MacLeod made a dismissive gesture. "I'll no' fight you. 'Twould be unfair."

"But that shouldn't matter, if your only goal is the killing of us." Jean-Pierre took one step forward. "If you're a man, fight me."

"Jean-Pierre," MacLeod began, and before the young man could react, MacLeod drew his scimitar, disarmed him, and held the evil half-moon of his weapon at his throat. "Do you see how it is? You must be prepared."

"Oh, help me," Jean-Pierre whispered. He fell to his knees. "I beg you, let me confess the sins of a poor monk to God before you kill me."

MacLeod resheathed the scimitar. "Your master told you you nae can die. Why believe me?"

"I don't know." He hung his head. "But I know he's lying, and you're telling the truth." He held out his hands. "Save me, *signor.* Save us all."

"I'll save ye with some advice: get out of here. Find yourself a teacher with some honor, who follows the rules and won't get you killed." MacLeod turned on his heel.

Jean-Pierre called, "*Per favore! Signor*, be that teacher! Be him! We need your help!"

"Aye, you do," MacLeod answered softly, knowing the boy couldn't hear him.

*Trapped.*

*Racing along the thicket walls, twisting, turning, fumbling for the way out.*

*Flailing and sobbing and darting this way and that like a rabbit. The thorns slicing his hands; he felt nothing. The thorns pricking his cheeks and temples, dangerously close to his eyes.*

*He felt nothing.*

Spinning in circles and fighting the panic. Dizzy and lost and panicked out of the ability to reason. The way out. The way out. Madonna mia, *the way out.*

The other, his footfalls heavy and closer, the smell of him pungent and evil. He hacked the barriers with his sword and charged into corridors; he thrust his sword through the foliage as he charged, several times missing his prey by centimeters.

Feeling his way, knowing no way. Drowning in the scent of the tamarind trees as he panted fire into his lungs. Still the other shuddered the earth, still he cut through the maze, charging like a giant in seven-league boots.

Then, by the grace of God, out! The prey tumbled to the exit and fell to the ground. Dirt covered his face. He struggled to rise. Failing that, he crawled to the copse of tamarind trees and pulled himself up on a thick trunk.

The prey trembled on legs of water, struggling to stay standing, his lungs bursting, his heart thundering one long shriek of terror. There was nowhere else to run, no other hiding place. His next dash would be across an expanse of lawn. The moon was out and full, a torch illuminating the gardens of the Palazzo Machiavelli.

Inside the palace, people supped and laughed. He could not comprehend how they could be so happy while murder flew at him like a mad dog. He held out a hand toward the yellow glowing windows, a drowning man struggling in the frigid sea beside a fine, gay ship. Tears streamed down his face at his futile effort, and he dropped his hand to his side.

If he could have a moment to rest; if he could only get some air, he knew he could save himself. But his pursuer was relentless. Even now he emerged from the maze and bellowed, "It does no good to hide! You know that, don't you?"

The quarry whispered, "Mama," and tried to run. He fell, rustling the branches.

The assassin swiveled his head in his direction. Madly the prey tried to still the movement. "Mama, Mama," he whispered. Sweat poured down his forehead, salt water in his drowning eyes. "I love you."

He heard the footfalls, so close now, whimpered, dragged himself behind the nearest trunk. Held on to it, pressed his forehead to the ground, and closed his eyes.

"There you are," said Death as the shadow of a man. The

*quarry sensed the rush of air as the other heaved his weapon above his head. There would be blood, gouting into the air like the fountains of Rome. There would be evidence.*

*"Pray," said Death.*

*He braced himself and begged for Heaven, begged for Heaven, begged for—*

*Who was it died?*

*Someone inconvenient. Someone who had heard too much and could say too much, and who had made friends with the wrong person. Someone who could cause problems. Nothing less, and nothing more.*

# Chapter Four

---

*"It is truly a natural and ordinary thing to desire gain; and when those who can succeed attempt it, they will always be praised and not blamed."*
—Niccolo Machiavelli, *The Prince*

Was it a Quickening?

MacLeod stopped at the lightning sound and turned around. There, on the other side of the *palazzo* walls. Did he see the flashes and crackling that signaled the death of one of his kind?

"It matters not," he muttered, turning back around. He was more determined than ever to quit this place. It was naught to him who had just lost his head. If anyone.

He took two more steps, and thought of Jean-Pierre. "God's blood," he muttered angrily, and went back in the direction of the *palazzo*.

As he crossed the garden, a figure stood shadowed against the night torches in their sconces. It was Machiavelli.

"Good evening," he said. MacLeod made no reply. "Tsk tsk. In a foul humor, are we?"

"What happened?" he asked bluntly.

"Happened?" Machiavelli cocked his head. "What are you speaking of?" He swept his arm in a gesture of welcome. "I believe we have something to discuss."

MacLeod put his hand to his sword. At that moment, Ruffio stepped from the shadows. Two other male Beauties as well. He was sorely tempted to take them on, but Ali was depending on him. Better to bide his time.

Seething, he followed Machiavelli inside. Ruffio followed.

They climbed the stairs to Machiavelli's apartments. He opened the door, ushered MacLeod inside, and then blocked the way of the others. "I must speak alone with Duncan," he said. Ruffio jerked as if slapped. He took a deep breath, glaring past Machiavelli to MacLeod, promising him with a look that they would settle this score later. With a curt nod, he withdrew.

Machiavelli shut the door. "Now we can talk about your unhappiness," he said pleasantly.

"I weary of the life here," MacLeod said.

"I can end it." Machiavelli chuckled and sat in a large chair on the opposite side of his great bed. "But I'm sure that's not what you meant."

He gestured for MacLeod to sit. MacLeod remained standing.

"The fault lies with you." Machiavelli sighed. "Do you not regard how I comport myself with the great and near-great? All this I will share with you, if you but bend a little." He rose and walked to the other side of the bed. Turning his back to MacLeod, he concealed his movements; a panel to his left slid open, but MacLeod was too far away to see what it contained.

He saw MacLeod's interest, and said, "I keep my most treasured possessions near me." He reached inside and retrieved a large wine bottle and two gold goblets. Filling them, he offered one to MacLeod. When MacLeod did not move, he shrugged and drank from the other as he sat back in his chair.

"Why do you do it?" MacLeod asked. "This island. This Court. You're Immortal. What is the purpose to all this?"

Machiavelli raised his shoulders, lowered them. "Must I have one? Why do you play chess?"

"It does not dominate my life."

"No, of course not. But what does?" Machiavelli slung one leg over the arm of his chair. "The need to survive. That is at core what motivates us all, don't you think?"

"Not you."

"Ah, there you are wrong. Thicker walls, better weapons, smarter followers. What puzzles you is how much I enjoy it all. For you, life is a deadly business. For me, it's the most exalted of games."

"Then you are in the Game," MacLeod said. "You know what I spoke of is true."

Machiavelli inclined his head. "We all have our religious beliefs. It would be much easier for me if you would leave off trying to convert my people."

"They have a right to survive as well."

Machiavelli flared. "I protect them."

"You use them." MacLeod glared at him. "They're nothing to you but cannon fodder. You'd sacrifice them all if it got you what you wanted."

"And what do I want? That's what you want to know."

"You just told me. To win the Game."

"Oh, but I know I'll do that. There's no sport there. It's simply a matter of time."

"Then why—"

"Because I *can*." His narrow face glowed as if from within. His eyes flashed. "Power, Signor Mackio. What is the point of this so-very-long life, if not to dominate and control? To snap my fingers"—he did so—"and shape my surroundings to my pleasure? From the top of a battlement, you can see your enemies coming. Down in the mud, you must slash blindly."

An alarm went off in MacLeod's head. The only person to call him Signor Mackio was Antonio.

"As I was saying to the Cardinal the other day," Machiavelli added, grinning, "God created a world, so why can't I?"

"And he said?" MacLeod asked, as he was certain he was supposed to. Was Machiavelli threatening him with 'Tonio's safety?

"He laughed and repeated the words of St. Theresa to me: 'God favors the bold.' And you know, God does."

He sipped his wine. "The Cardinal is off to Rome to quiz the Pope about his intentions toward us. His Holiness and the French love to attack us when we appear weak and friendless. I remember in Florence, when Cesare Borgia—"

He closed his eyes and shook his head. "That's over. Alas, poor Cesare. I knew him, Horatio." He waited for a reaction from MacLeod. "Ah, you don't know Shakespeare. Pity. Duncan, I wish you to sit."

Against his better judgment, MacLeod obeyed. Now that his concern for 'Tonio had been piqued—as he was certain had been Machiavelli's intention—he would listen carefully and well to what the Immortal had to say.

"This country is terrified, Duncan. High and low, the Venetians are drowning and gasping for air. And I am the only boat."

"Are you."

"Does it matter? They believe I am. What's the difference?"

In that moment, MacLeod saw him as he truly was, a grasping

conniver expertly painting himself as a genius, a strategist, a master collector of intelligence, that an entire nation could look to for rescue. Poor, foolish Venice. The political situation must be worse than MacLeod had realized. The government had poured its hopes into a man who didn't care what happened to the people and to their nation. He was reaping the spoils of their fear, and no doubt would continue to do so if Venice fell.

"You look troubled," Machiavelli observed. "Do you worry for the Republic?"

MacLeod shook his head. "These are not my people. Nor my cause."

"Your cause. A strange term, but not the strangest word I have heard you speak. I rather like 'Sassenach.' It refers to the English, does it not?"

Warily, MacLeod said, "Aye. It's our name for them."

Machiavelli laughed. "You bear them such a grudge. I thought we in the Mediterranean were the only ones to hold vendettas. Perhaps you shall be the next king." He sat forward. "Think of that, MacLeod. Who better to reign than one of us? I can help you. I have been a popemaker and a dogemaker and a kingmaker. Surely I can make you king of Scotland."

"You know nothing of my people. Our kings die."

"I know about people. And people are the same everywhere. What did I write in *The Prince*? 'For the mob is always impressed by appearances and by results; and the world is composed of the mob.' As for dying, why, you're Immortal!"

Machiavelli's dark eyes flashed. "This we must do. It would be glorious. First you must reread *The Prince*. It will be your handbook to greatness."

MacLeod had never read *The Prince*, nor any of Machiavelli's other books or plays.

"But for now, let's play chess," Machiavelli said, reaching toward the chessboard on a trestle table next to his chair. "All great men should know chess."

He picked up two pawns, put his hands behind his back, and held out his fists. MacLeod pointed to Machiavelli's left hand, who, with a flourish, revealed the white pawn.

"You move first, my friend," Machiavelli drawled, and sat in the curved chair behind the chessboard.

As MacLeod took the other chair, Machiavelli went on.

"Those two spies are in trouble. The Signory is talking about executing them sooner than planned. Burlingame had long wanted to trade with Venice. As you know, we have a rule that all such commerce must be conducted in vessels of our own construction. Our ambassador took Burlingame a letter from the Doge granting him safe passage through Venetian waters."

"But that Doge died. The affairs of state altered." MacLeod moved P-K4, pawn to king's four.

"Ah, you *are* learning something. The classical defense. By Señor Ruy López." Machiavelli mirrored the move on the chessboard. "Watch your bishops, young Scot. Your holy men. Your prelates. I delight in clearing them. It's so much easier to play without them zigzagging all over the country." He raised his brows. "I mean, all over the chessboard."

"His English ship was given to a pirate," MacLeod persisted, imagining the course of events.

"I think he would call himself a freebooter. His was the first Venetian foot on the deck of *The Protector*. According to our laws, he therefore lays claim to salvage rights."

"Which he claimed on open sea with the rightful owners in their beds."

Machiavelli made a theatrical display of pondering MacLeod's statement. "Top marks, my young student. At least, it sounds plausible."

A frisson of caution crept up MacLeod's spine. Was Machiavelli toying with him, telling him in so many words that he did know he'd been on the *Protector?* He must tread carefully. He couldn't afford to jeopardize Ali's rescue. "The Doge denied the safe-passage letter."

"As well as all knowledge of the envoy," Machiavelli added. "His predecessor agreed to the peace talks, not he."

"A misstep. Now their countrymen will be angry."

Machiavelli scratched his cheek. "Burlingame's an aristocrat with gambling debts and a pregnant Spanish mistress. The Turk is only a merchant. No one will miss him."

MacLeod moved his pawn to king's bishop four. "On the contrary. I've heard he's a respected general."

For an instant, Machiavelli looked startled. Then his easy expression returned. "Of course. That's common knowledge. How did you know?" He captured the pawn.

MacLeod shrugged. Had it been known that Ali was a person of rank and importance, someone better ransomed than executed? When the Ottomans heard that he'd been killed, they might be moved to war.

Which could be exactly what Machiavelli wanted.

Distracted, MacLeod moved another pawn, a stupid, useless action.

Machiavelli deftly captured the pawn. "You'd never deny a safe passage, would you. Not even to a man who had murdered your best friend." MacLeod said nothing and studied the board.

Machiavelli laughed. "You're as constant as the sun, MacLeod. In language, you'd be a noun. A thing that is what it is. Unchanging. That is why you'll never beat me at chess. Or any other Game," he added significantly.

They each moved swiftly, aggressively, the Ruy López opening abandoned.

MacLeod was losing. He said, "You just said people never change."

Machiavelli looked mildly insulted. "The mind of the mob changes with the times. What is heresy one day is science the next."

"Principles don't change. I have you in check, *signor*."

Machiavelli unfolded his arms and waved his hands dismissively. "Perhaps you aren't ruler material after all. A prince must be like a weather vane. But of course he should never appear to be one." He scrutinized the board and announced, "Duncan, you fool. You're in check yourself."

"A prince should be a compass." MacLeod saw that the game was lost and dawdled over his last move as he mentally sketched various routes from the *traghetti* to the New Prisons. If he asked Machiavelli any more questions about the prisoners, the Immortal would be alerted.

"Now, this matter of the Calegri."

Aye, of that matter. He could be away from the islands and on his way to the prison if he agreed. Once again, he wondered if Machiavelli knew more than he had let on. Was his intelligence about Ali's possible execution his baited hook? There was no way to know. MacLeod made a show of considering and nodded in defeat. "All right."

"Good." Machiavelli said. "You'll need new clothes, of course. We must dazzle them."

Machiavelli had MacLeod outfitted in cloth of gold, scarlet, and black, clothes splendid enough for a banquet at the Calegri *palazzo*, which was more appropriately called a *canalazzo*, since it hung over one of Venice's waterways. He pressed money into his hand—the coin of a murderer—and described to him exactly what Giovanni Calegri looked like.

The gondola was waiting; MacLeod left as if in state, like a titled knight, except that he traveled alone. The fewer who knew of a crime like murder, the better.

Except, of course, that he had no intention of murdering anyone. He had no intention of going to the Calegri at all. He must watch his back; he must watch all quarters. He must do all he could to take advantage of this shaky opportunity to rescue Ali.

But now, by God's bones, he was lost.

MacLeod reined in the sleek white mare he had hired near the *traghetti*, or gondola docks, and raised himself high in the saddle for a better view. At the entrance to yet another *calle*, a constricted, dank alley, he studied the maze of side streets, passages, and the camel-humped bridges that had no railings to keep one from sliding into the canals. Sagging balconies jutted from hovels, while the next two or three buildings over glittered with jeweled Byzantine shutters. Tattered laundry dried on lines secured to the edge of a neighboring wall sheeted in real gold. A messy confusion, fascinating in its way, but too alien and ornate for a man who was Highland-born and -bred.

With a grunt, he shook his head and wished himself someplace where this fine young skitterhooves could gallop at full tilt with no thought in her wee brain but going faster. The Nefud Desert was a place like that. So were the Highlands, of course. All of a green magic, with the mist rising off the heather, and you could run for a year and not have to stop.

But Venice was a floating, tight maze, the vendettas and the intrigues as labyrinthian and twisted as the city. On his way to the hiring yard, two gangs of youths in the colors of their houses had descended upon one another, screaming vengeance and blood. One young boy's stomach was ripped open, and MacLeod had stared down the swaggering bully who threatened to stop him with his foil from saving the lad's life. Giuliano, the young one's name had been, Zulian in Venetian dialect. Stomping humiliated from the scene, the nameless bully had promised retribution while MacLeod stanched the torrent of blood and ordered the boy not to die.

Zulian's mother had thrown herself down beside him, screaming and wailing. Assured by the condition of his wounds that the lad would live, MacLeod had refused her money but had accepted her offer to pray for his soul and to kiss his forehead as a blessing. He was eager to be away. Already he had drawn too much attention to himself.

"One day, I shall repay you, life for life," she vowed, nigh toothless though she could not be very old. Her breasts hung to her knees, the result, he surmised, of nursing many children, most of whom had probably died in infancy. Or in skirmishes such as this.

"Mother, do nae speak like that," he told her, remembering the last man to make such a promise to him, back on *The Protector.* "Only God can trade lives."

God, and Immortals.

"Damn it all." He swore now, frustrated, chilly and wet from the weather and the high canal water that pooled in the mud, and, aye, lost. How the devil could such a grand pile as the Doge's palace hide itself like this?

From a distance wafted a hint of smoke. The smell was not uncommon in Venice, for the homes of the poor were so tiny they did most of their cooking and dining out of doors.

His horse nickered. Absently he patted it as he clicked his heels easily against its sides. It took a few steps forward, then whinnied and violently reared.

Though surprised, MacLeod held on. The smell of smoke was stronger; curious, he urged the horse in its direction.

Then he heard the screams. The stink of burning flesh hit his nostrils. He broke into a gallop.

By the coat of arms over the entrance, it was the Calegri *palazzo.* Flames erupted from six stories of arched windows. Stained glass exploded and cascaded to the ground like razor-sharp raindrops. From the capitals of the ground-floor arcade and the pilasters and facades, statuary—lovely nymphs, saints, the lion of St.

Mark—plummeted to the ground, ancient and astonishing suicides.

Leaping off his horse, MacLeod tied the horse to the handle of a wellhead and ran toward a forming bucket brigade. There were perhaps a dozen men and women armed with but three buckets, one end stationed at the well where his horse panicked and reared; one in the middle; and the third so far from the building that the water it contained, when thrown, didn't even touch it.

"*Auito!* Ah! God bless you." A chubby, pockmarked priest slung a full bucket into MacLeod's arms. They couldn't hope to stop the blaze, even though more people came running to help.

But they could save the lives of those trapped inside.

"No, my son!" the priest protested, as MacLeod hefted the bucket over his head and doused himself. He threw the bucket down and wrapped himself like one of the primitive Highland dead in his sopping cloak. Bobbing his head at the priest, who made the sign of the cross over him, he covered his mouth and nose with the edge of the cloak.

"Follow me, Father!" he shouted. "What we're doing here is useless." The priest hesitated. "Come, if you truly are shepherd to your flock!"

They raced toward the *palazzo*. The priest kept pace as MacLeod dashed up the sizzling grand staircase made of stone. The front of the *palazzo*, ribboned with stained glass, shimmered and blazed like the very gates of Hell.

The heat was unbelievable. Blisters rose on MacLeod's face and hands before he was halfway to the wooden doors. The planks cracked and collapsed inward, leaving a gaping maw that belched smoke and rippling tongues of fire.

The other man fell back, crying, "No! Stop! It's no use!"

MacLeod leaped over the burning debris and balanced on a tiny portion of mosaic floor. Flames shot all around him. His cloak caught fire and he stamped on it, then unhooked it and dropped it to the ground. In a matter of seconds, it was ash.

The screams were terrible, but he saw at once that it truly was too late; he could see nothing but fire in all directions. For a moment he hesitated, hoping for a break in the inferno. The ceiling above bowed ominously. There was nothing he could do, save be burned to death for the sake of heroism.

He could not die publicly here. He still had to save Ali.

*Fool*, he cursed himself, for allowing this distraction. Had it been engineered by Machiavelli? He had no idea. He only knew he should be at the prison by now.

Then, despite the danger, he froze. In this room. Yes, somewhere near. To the left.

*An Immortal.*

His body prickled, all senses on alert. All he saw were row upon row of fiery eruptions, shooting up like fountains. All he smelled was fire and death. All he heard was dying.

He waited, scanning. His eyes watered. The other was nearing. Close now, very close.

He heard a whoosh, looked up.

A black-cloaked figure on a rope swooped down on him, blade extended. Easily, MacLeod ducked, then sprang with his scimitar extended in an attempt to inflict some damage. The tip of the scimitar caught the hem of the cloak; he pulled hard. The hood yanked back and slipped off the head. The figure was masked; MacLeod pulled harder.

If all he had seen was the hatred in the eyes, he would have known it to be Ruffio.

More flames roared between them, shielding them from each other. MacLeod realized the futility of a battle here, now, but his blood was pumping and his warrior's instincts engaged. He waited on the chance that Ruffio found a way to come to him, panting, readying to spring. When he didn't show, MacLeod turned and crashed back through the entrance.

He didn't realize that his clothes were on fire until the onlookers shouted and pointed at him. His doublet and sleeves were like an armor of flame; as soon as he realized the extent of the damage, the pain began to attack him.

He collapsed at the top of the stone steps. Over and over he tumbled, a wheel of fire, until he landed in a heap.

Instantly water spilled over him. Steam sizzled. He couldn't move, couldn't breathe. He knew what it was to die from burns such as these. It would be a hard going, and a hard coming back.

"*Signor*, have courage." It was a woman's voice. A shape knelt over him. More water poured down on him, the pressure ripping at his wounds. He groaned. The woman said, very far away, "Gather him up."

*I canna die in a public place,* he struggled to say. Nothing came out.

"Hush."

He was lifted by hands he couldn't see. The pain of being moved was excruciating. Unwilling or unable to cry out, he clenched his teeth, which began to chatter. He was going into shock; he was going to die. Again.

Memories of a life ebbing, or dreams that sustain life:

*The Highland battle raged from dawn to dawn. In the meadow, Iain, Duncan's great father and clan leader, fearlessly charged the bastards and they came screaming with their weapons raised. Dying and dealing death would be glorious today.*

*"Dhonnchaidh?" shouted the MacLeoid, his sword piercing the sun. What a giant! What a father! Rain showered down on the great head, the blue war tartan wrapped around his large body, "Dhonnchaidh, do you come?"*

*Duncan's heart soared and he made a fist as he raced after him. "Aye, I'm coming! 'Tis Dhonnchaidh indeed, your son!"*

*"MacLeoid forever!" his father bellowed, brilliant with joy and vitality. "Dhonnchaidh, my son! My only child! My son!"*

"Hurry." It was a voice accustomed to command. Then, more gently, barely a whisper, "It's all right. I know what you are. I'll take you to Machiavelli."

Machiavelli. No. Not a good refuge, not a good harbor.

No.

He slid away again and floated back to the sweet Highlands.

*Och, there she was! On the cliff, her bonnie red hair streaming free, her face turned to him. Calling for him.*

*Debra had been the first love of his first life, the only love of it, and the one he could not have. She was betrothed to Robert, his kinsman, and not for such as he. Then not for anyone, she'd proclaimed, not for this life. His honor be damned; she had begged, Run away, come away with me.*

*He could not, for the sake of honor. And then, almost as if God had willed it, she had fallen to her death, saving them both from disgrace.*

*My heart, my life, 'tis so lonely I have been. 'Tis a loneliness ye canna ken, for an angel would never know such Hell. If it's only death now that keeps ye from me, death and no my honor, which is stronger than death, then I come willingly, aye, I run to my end. Eternity without ye is unbearable. My heart canna stand it any longer; nor my soul.*

*Bonnie angel of death, my bonnie Debra. In life, lost to me. In death, can ye be my wife at last?*

*If so, to dying . . .*

"Signor?"

MacLeod bolted upright. He blinked and looked around. He had been laid in a gondola. Beneath stars and falling ash, a woman bent over him with a cool cloth between her fingers. She was exquisite, a delicate beauty with enormous amber eyes and tendrils of reddish blond hair—"Italian blond"—that spilled from beneath a simple black hood. Her cheeks were high and flushed; she smiled triumphantly, and whispered, with an eye on the gondolier, "Ah, you're awake."

Not simply awake. Back from the dead. For a confused moment he was filled with a longing so deep and powerful he thought he might weep. What had he dreamed? He didn't remember.

A woman's silk cloak was pooled in his lap. He looked down and saw that beneath it he was naked. He pulled the cloak around himself not so much for the sake of modesty but to hide his healed condition from the woman, who was mortal.

"Don't concern yourself," she whispered, daubing his forehead with the cloth. "I know."

He was alarmed. She was not Immortal. She had no business knowing what he was.

"I am Maria Angelina." She reached to her side and handed him a small flask. He pulled off the jeweled cap and drank. It was a spirit, cool and sweet.

"Duncan MacLeod," he began in an undervoice, realizing she already knew far more about him than he did of her. All he had was her Christian name. She had his deepest secret. "Did anyone else survive?" He thought of Ruffio.

She took the flask from him and sipped. It was an intimate act, her drinking after him. Her breasts were full and ripe, her throat long and white as she swallowed. The ghost of longing lingered, and beneath the cloak he stirred.

She murmured, "I don't know. But the family itself is wiped out. Lord, lady, sons, nephews. Even the females."

"A tragedy," he replied, thinking that if he ever died, his own line—whatever line that was—would end as well.

She paused. "Some would say that."

He took the flask from her and drank. Their fingers brushed against one another and she took a short breath as though startled. His desire grew. He swallowed deeply and wiped his mouth with the back of his hand, unmannerly perhaps, but he was having trouble thinking of manners and the other niceties of civilized men. "And others would say?"

"That they had it coming. At any rate, now they are cradled by the Blessed Mother."

She tilted her head. In the moonlight, she bore a resemblance to the statue of the Virgin Mary in the Veronese church where MacLeod had once courted a shy milliner's assistant. She glowed like marble; she was luminescent. She was beautiful.

As the gondola plied the water and the moon traveled with it, she seemed to change, becoming many women, all desirable. After a time he could no longer tell if he was staring at a changeling or a human lass. Mesmerized, he wondered if he was delirious, or if she had drugged the flask.

He cleared his throat. "How do you know the likes of us?"

"I live on the islands," she answered simply. "One of the littler islands of Murano. I have a villa. I live there alone." She touched his forehead. "No matter how often I see the transformation, I am awed."

"Transformation," he repeated.

"From death to life. I was horrified the first time. I thought Machiavelli was a witch. I was going to report him to the Inquisition." She dimpled. "I'm afraid I left him no choice but to reveal his secret." Then she grew serious, and MacLeod fell into her dark eyes. "Except that he could have killed me to keep me silent. He did not."

She was one of Machiavelli's chess pieces, then. He was disappointed.

She studied him. "You must be tired."

"Perhaps a wee bit. Life here has proved very strenuous."

"Life anywhere for those like you is strenuous," she rejoined.

"My scimitar," he said suddenly.

She lifted the edge of the cloak. The scimitar lay beside his naked thigh. He touched the razor-sharp blade, allowing blood droplets to pool on his skin. Then, assured that the weapon had not been damaged, he wrapped the cloak around his waist and inclined his head. "I thank you for what you've done. Had another found me . . ."

"You would have been taken to the graveyard. There will be talk. Many saw how injured you were. Some saw you dead."

"Bloody hell."

"But perhaps if you stay on the islands for a time, we can claim that you revived from a deep stupor, which is true. And that your burns were limited to your body, not your face, and that they are now hidden by your clothes."

He groaned. More time lost, and he was back in Machiavelli's web. She touched his hand, then quickly pulled away, blushing. "*Mi dispiace, signor.* I didn't mean to be so bold."

"I warrant you've touched the whole of me," he replied ruefully, and they both laughed.

The main Muranese island rose from the water like a castle in a moat. An occasional pennant or spire of the *palazzo* could be seen from this distance, but nothing more. MacLeod had explored much of the island, and hadn't realized any mortals there, perhaps excluding a few servants, had known the secret of the Immortals.

"We'll go straight to Machiavelli," she told him. "I'm sure he's very concerned about you."

"Oh, aye," he answered wryly, but she didn't seem to catch his sarcasm. Perhaps she was truly innocent, a bystander who had done good for the sake of it.

The gondolier steered the craft to a stone landing at the water's edge. He jumped out and secured it with a line, then helped the lady out. MacLeod disembarked, barefoot, sword in hand, feeling rather like a Roman in a toga.

"He knows about Immortals, too. He's one of Niccolo's oldest servants," Maria Angelina assured him, as if reading his mind. "He can be trusted. But he needn't know our business tonight, *si*?"

As if to assure MacLeod that this was so, the man, standing at a distance, pulled off his cap and bobbed his head.

"*Grazie*," MacLeod said. His hand went to where his pocket should be.

She handed him a few pitiful coins. "These are yours, I believe."

Machiavelli's money. He paid the gondolier with the Immortal's metal and offered his arm again to Maria Angelina. She laid her cool palm over the back of his hand. Beneath the scent of smoke lay a perfume sweet and clean, and it made his head near spin.

"You look at me so oddly," she reproved him, though she smiled.

He shook himself but said nothing. There was nothing to say.


"Good," Machiavelli said, clearly pleased as MacLeod finished his story. "Giovanni surely died in the fire." He smiled brilliantly. "And you are spared the trouble."

"So this was done on my behalf?" MacLeod asked with deadly quiet.

"Perhaps," Machiavelli answered, his eyes glittering as if with a private joke. "As I have previously stated, what advances me advances us. The Doge will be thrilled by this turn of events."

"Thrilled that hundreds of innocents perished as well as one man suspected of trying to assassinate him."

Machiavelli laughed. "*Caro* Duncan, no one in Venice is an innocent."

MacLeod adjusted the slashings of his clothing. This outfit was closer in style to MacLeod's own time, and simpler and easier to move in. That was good; if what he suspected was true—that Machiavelli had sent him to the banquet not to murder Giovanni Calegri, but to be beheaded himself by Ruffio—he would have need of agile movements very, very soon.

"Oh, Signor MacLeod!" a voice shrilled from the doorway. It was Jean-Pierre, wild-eyed and jittery. "*Grace à Dieu,* you're safe!"

He waited, then pranced into the room as Machiavelli indicated his permission. "News of the fire has spread like a, well, a fire!" He clapped his hands together. "What a tragedy!"

"You're clearly distraught," Machiavelli observed dryly.

Jean-Pierre appeared not to have heard him. "It was to have been a fabulous event. They were going to have real Turkish harem girls dancing on pieces of ice in the pools. Can you imagine? I hear they are always quite naked. They rip the hair off their sexual parts with melted wax. It's so painful they must be tied down. With velvet ropes," he added softly. "Black eunuchs pull on their nipples for hours to make them big and red and juicy for the sultan. Most of them are lesbians, you know. They are desperate for sexual pleasure. Their cucumbers are sent to them all cut up so they won't *use* them."

MacLeod almost laughed aloud. He had never heard such outlandish stories told of the Ottomans, and yet clearly Jean-Pierre believed them.

"I should like to have seen the *palazzo* burn up like a paper lantern with all those harridans prancing on their icebergs." Jean-Pierre snapped his fingers. "All gone into smoke and steam. The fleeting nature of true beauty. A moment to treasure, do you not think so?"

"What a strange creature you are," Machiavelli said. "It's hard to believe you were once a religious."

MacLeod observed them for a moment. Beneath the silly smile, MacLeod detected high tension in Jean-Pierre's manner. His utter faith in Machiavelli had been undermined.

MacLeod said to Machiavelli, "Tell me about the woman who rescued me."

The Immortal glanced at Jean-Pierre. "Maria Angelina? Your secret is safe." He cocked his head. "She is most ravishing, is she not? Not a harem tart, that's for certain, eh, Jean-Pierre?"

"Oh, *monsieur,*" Jean-Pierre said in dismay, and Machiavelli chuckled.

"All the men are in love with her," Machiavelli said. "Even Jean-Pierre."

MacLeod made no answer. She was a new piece to the puzzle of this place. And though the pieces did not yet fit, it would be to his peril not to solve this puzzle as soon as possible.

"What of Ruffio?" he asked bluntly.

"Ruffio? What of him?" Machiavelli sounded confused. *A master dissembler,* MacLeod thought. He had never met a better liar.

There was a clatter in the corridor. The door smashed open. Giuletta and Annette burst into the room.

"*Maestro!*" Giuletta cried. "His Excellency the Cardinal is dead. He died in Rome this morning."

Jean-Pierre blanched and crossed himself.

"How dreadful." Machiavelli did the same. "How did it happen?"

Annette said, "It was his bowels. Something he ate. It was quite slow and painful, his passing. There is to be a splendid requiem mass!"

"New clothes shall be the order of the day," Machiavelli decreed. To MacLeod's amazement, Annette and Giuletta let out happy cries. "Now, go, my cherubs." Machiavelli folded his hands and bowed his head. "Duncan, Jean-Pierre, and I must meditate on this tragic news."

The women departed. Machiavelli looked at MacLeod and smiled faintly. "What a relief the Papal Father did not eat the same thing. Or the king of France, who is this moment in Rome stirring up feeling against us. I hear they're both fond of wild mushrooms." He shrugged. "*Va bene.* Fortune smiled on him."

God's head, the man was poisoning popes and kings. What had the previous Doge died of? The bastard would pay if 'Tonio was dead with his master. If Ali died.

"I feel so sick," Jean-Pierre whispered. "Oh, poor *monsieur* the cardinal!"

"You look peaked," Machiavelli said. "You should lie down."

"Signor MacLeod, would you help me?" Jean-Pierre whimpered.

MacLeod understood that he wished to be alone with him, and wondered if Machiavelli understood it, too. He nodded.

"With your permission," he said to Machiavelli.

"Of course." He looked at him from over his shoulder. "Stay close to home," he said. "Maria Angelina was quite correct when she told you to take time to 'heal.' If anyone sees you now, they'd burn you for a witch."

MacLeod walked out of the room, Jean-Pierre tagging after. He shut the door and hurried to catch up as MacLeod strode down the corridor. MacLeod's fury was ungovernable. 'Tonio. If he had harmed that child, he would die for that alone.

"He murdered him," Jean-Pierre whispered. "I have wanted to see you, *signor.* There is much to tell you. I have learned of terrible things!"

"What?" On his guard, MacLeod held himself tautly and drew his weapon. From any quarter, there might be another attempt on his life. It was unnaturally dark; he had marveled earlier at the luxurious waste of candles and torches illuminating the interior of the immense palace. But now it was as cold and dark as the grave.

Many deaths lay on his conscience. If he lived as long as Connor had once told him he would, there would be more. It was a painful thought.

Almost as painful as the sword that sliced through his right forearm as he rounded a corner. With a shout of surprise, he changed his weapon to his left hand and lunged in the direction of the thrust.

"No!" someone cried. "Please!"

MacLeod sliced a piece of fabric in two, a hanging or curtain. Jean-Pierre screamed in terror as he swung the scimitar over his head, preparing to bring it down on his attacker.

"Duncan MacLeod," came the soft voice. It was Maria Angelina.

"What the devil are you doing, woman?" MacLeod shouted at her, lowering his weapon at once.

"Forgive me. I thought you were my husband."

Two fine-boned hands gripped his arm, and his adversary sank to the floor.

# Chapter Five

---

*"Men are so simple and so much inclined to obey
immediate needs that a deceiver will never lack
victims for his deception."*
                    —Niccolo Machiavelli, *The Prince*

In the pitch-dark, MacLeod knelt on one knee beside the still
form as Jean-Pierre held his breath and mumbled prayers.

"Maria Angelina?" MacLeod searched the darkness and found
the sleek fabric of her dress. His hand brushed her breast, the softness a shock against the stiff lace of her decolletage. Blood rushed
to his fingertips; he quickly moved his hand upward, across the
bared clavicle and the velvet of her skin, the hollow at her throat,
lifting heavy, satiny curls away from the side of her neck. Hearing
only the sounds his fingers made, sensing and hearing no other
presence, he pressed his hand against her throat to check her pulse.
It was beating like the heart of a hummingbird, shallow and rapid.

"Is she dead? Is she dead?" Jean-Pierre demanded. "I should
perform the last rites."

The blood from the cut in his sword arm dripped onto the marble floor. Had she been a true opponent, he would have been in
trouble: she had separated the tendons from the bones. Even now
it was incredibly painful; a swordsman of mediocre ability could
have taken his head while he suffered from the pain.

He realized that Jean-Pierre had just proved his loyalty. Or his
cowardice.

Maria Angelina stirred, sighing. Silky fingers touched his chin,
found his lips. Her hand smelled of rainwater and lilacs. His body
roused, and he felt dizzy; he caught her hand and held it.

"Ah," she murmured, "Duncan."

"Yes, milady. It's Duncan." He chafed her wrist to help bring her
around. "Did I hurt you?"

"No." She sighed again. "*Mi scusi.* I had thought . . . there was a message. I thought you were my husband." Holding on to his forearm, she sat up. The lilacs were stronger in her hair.

"And you hoped to attack him?" Jean-Pierre asked in a high, startled voice.

MacLeod was crestfallen. Married, she was. He had not thought of that.

She said, "He's a terrible man, Duncan. Please forgive me for lying to you."

"You nae told me you were unmarried. I nae asked."

Her hand cupped the side of his face. He took a deep breath, unwillingly remembering the sensation of his hand on her breast. Even now, in the darkness, he could recall each angle, each plane, of her face and the womanly curves of her body. Her scent was intoxicating him.

He edged discreetly away from her. In a moment, he promised himself, he would get to his feet.

"Maria Angelina, explain it to me, please," he said huskily. "Tell me of this husband."

"He's an Immortal. That's why I knew of your kind. Not from Niccolo." She took a breath. "They were once great friends."

He waited. He could feel her body heat. A tendril of her hair grazed the back of his hand and he focused on that, straining to ignore his other, more urgent reaction.

"He had no patience with me. He hated that I aged. I was but fourteen when we married. And now . . ." She trailed off. "I'm older."

"Madness," he blurted, seeing in his mind's eye the incandescence of her skin, the deep, unending amber of her eyes.

Jean-Pierre tugged at MacLeod's sleeve. "We must go. I need to tell you—"

"Every time he saw a wrinkle. Every time I displeased him. I wasn't educated enough. I wasn't pretty enough." She choked back a sob. "I wouldn't live long enough."

"He beat you." MacLeod's fists clenched. If the man had been here, now, he would have torn his head off with his bare hands.

"It got worse and worse. Niccolo implored him to stop. Finally he took me away, and I've been hiding here ever since. Two years, it has been. But now Niccolo talks of reports that indicate he knows I'm here. When I heard you in the hall, I panicked."

She put her hand over his. "My husband told me once he had eternity to find me if I ran away from him. He said he'd kill me the way the Turks kill unfaithful women." She shuddered. "He would torture me, Duncan." She paused. "As the Turks torture their women."

"Heaven help us," Jean-Pierre whispered.

"Och, no," MacLeod said, though he didn't have the slightest idea what she was talking about. The Venetians regarded all Ottomans as sadistic butchers, but it was the sultans who did the deeds that shamed the entire empire. One such had drowned all the women in his harem because someone had hinted that one, just one, of them had slept with a eunuch. MacLeod knew many Christians far crueler than almost any Turk he could name. As well as many Christian kings who, if there was a God, would rot in Hell for the things they had done to their subjects.

Most of the kings being English, and most of the subjects being Scots.

He covered her hand with his, knowing it was wrong to touch her. She was married, and though he fully believed in love at first sight—all reasonable people did—he also knew it was wrong to love her.

"No harm will come to you while I live." Not able to help himself, he slid his arm around her waist. His stomach contracted, and he wanted her, he wanted her, couldn't help the way his pelvis moved against hers as he lifted her up. He heard her sharp intake of breath and clenched his fists behind her back as her breasts pressed against his chest. He inhaled the sweet scent in her hair and closed his eyes. His heartbeat roared in his ears. "He'll not touch you again."

She whispered in his ear, her breath hot and moist. "Niccolo has been my only protector."

"I need to say . . ." Jean-Pierre pressed.

*If only you knew what Machiavelli really is,* he wanted to tell her. "This Immortal," he ventured. "Your . . . husband. What is your husband's name?"

She hesitated as if afraid even to utter his name. "He is called Xavier St. Cloud."

"Oh, *mon Dieu!*" Jean-Pierre shrieked. "Signor MacLeod, I must tell you something *now!*"

MacLeod reeled. St. Cloud was the murderer of his friend,

Hamza el Kahir. Hamza had been the Immortal who had saved him from slavery when he had left Venice on a galley with a Venetian family en route to a marriage in Spain. Attacked and boarded by corsairs, the company had been taken to Algiers. MacLeod was sold at auction as a slave. To rescue him—an Immortal he did not even know—Hamza had bought him and offered him refuge within his household. He had even helped him try to rescue the daughter of the house, although that proved to be a fool's errand—she had engineered the entire episode in order to marry the corsair who had attacked them.

Then Xavier St. Cloud had ridden in with the heat of the noon-day desert sun and challenged Hamza. Rather than accept the challenge and fight—the honorable thing to do—Hamza had tried to flee. MacLeod, shocked by his cowardice, had tried to take his place. At the last moment, Hamza had stepped in, and he had lost his head, as he had known he would.

For the sake of honor, MacLeod had pushed Hamza into combat. He felt as responsible for his death as he held St. Cloud.

For a moment he was so off-balance he thought the floor had shifted and sent him sliding the length of the corridor. "It canna be," he whispered. And then he thought, *No, it canna be. Something is amiss here.* "That is his name? You're sure of it?"

"What are you saying? Of course I know my husband's name."

What treachery was this? Was it too much of a coincidence that of all people, she should marry an Immortal he had claimed as a blood enemy? Was this some lie, some scheme of Machiavelli's? St. Cloud had surely known MacLeod had remained in Algiers after the death of Hamza. Had he followed him here? Had he been the one to tell Machiavelli about Ali's mission to Venice, in order to throw the death of another friend in MacLeod's face?

"Do you know him?" Her voice rose and she pushed away from him. "Is he a friend to you, too? Are you all like that, all brothers who follow a code of loyalty among yourselves, and betray us mortals?"

"A *friend*?" He shook his head as he grabbed her once more into his arms. Even now St. Cloud's face hung before him like a ghostly image: the pale chocolate skin, the almond eyes, the infuriating, taunting smile that had tricked him into insisting that Hamza sacrifice himself for honor's sake. His confusion notwithstanding, fresh rage and guilt hit him with the force of a blow across the face.

"No, not a friend." He seethed inside, his awakened passion translating into blind hatred. Connor had often warned him of the ferocity of his emotions. Survival required the ability to direct your emotion into the next move. Yet now he shook with thunder, urging her aside and grabbing up his sword. He fought everything within himself not to slash at something—the hanging, a chair, a statue.

"*Monsieur, signor,*" Jean-Pierre said excitedly, batting at him, unknowingly hitting his wounded arm. "It is of that very man I must speak!"

"What?" MacLeod whipped his head toward the direction of Jean-Pierre's voice.

"That person, that St. Cloud. He was with Ruffio at the Calegri's *canalazzo*. Together they started the fire. They were waiting for you! I heard them—"

"You were there?" MacLeod cut in. "You were at the banquet?"

"Yes, I was. Machiavelli sent me to meet up with you. He said you might not come, and that if I didn't see you, I was to tell Ruffio and St. Cloud. He said there were others waiting at another location should you decide on another course of action. What course of action? What was he speaking of? Is St. Cloud an old enemy of yours?"

"We must leave," MacLeod said, taking Maria Angelina's hand. He couldn't sort this out here, now. He had no idea if he could trust her, no time to decide. "Tonight we leave Venice, and no one will know where we've gone."

"Oh, where will I be safe?" she cried.

"I'll protect you." Every instinct within him told him that she must be innocent of this, that he must shelter her, care for her.

Every instinct told him that she must be, but not that she *was*.

"I'll protect you as well. I'll come with you," Jean-Pierre pleaded.

MacLeod grunted. There was little he could do save fight him to prevent him from accompanying them. But he wasn't welcome company.

And although his heart was warming for the lady on his arm, it would be better if he could trust her a little more as well. Her face resting against his chest, his heart begged her to be true. Murder crept these halls, and he would not prove a sacrificial pawn in anyone's gambit. No matter her scent, the lips, her touch.

"Duncan," she whispered.

No matter.

In the Doge's splendid private quarters, there was a fire in the richly carved fireplace, music by Pavel Vejavanovsky, the Moravian trumpeter, fine wine compliments of the duke of Burgundy, and twin blond page boys serving sweets and pomegranates. A lovely finale to a long, yet productive day.

Machiavelli had only just arrived. His cloak was still damp with canal water, and the brandy warmed him through.

Now, as the august and aging Doge, Carlo Contarini, studied the reports of Machiavelli's spies and examined the most recent of the couriers' pouches, Machiavelli remembered the thrill of his first life when dining with popes and kings. He chuckled with the fondness one has for childish pleasures gone by. Yet the excitement that coursed through his veins now was equal. A hundred years ago, his efforts were to keep Florence out of war. Now, he exerted his considerable acumen and influence to thrust Venice into one.

And to the victor he would go.

"You see, Excellency?" he insisted. "Attack is imminent. Our Greek subjects on Mythenos have led an uprising and are on their way."

Contarini shrugged his shoulders and waved a hand at an exquisite painting of Christ walking on the water as the frightened apostles were tossed by the waves. Such was Venice, he seemed to imply. And he had the right: Every year he married the sea in an ancient ritual endorsed by Holy Mother Church. It was the pope himself who sent him the wedding ring each season that he would cast into the lagoon. "What can they have, two or three leaky ships? That is nothing against the Venetian fleet. We have nothing to worry about, Machiavelli."

The gilt door to the private salon opened and a little old man in a black robe peered in. Several other pale, wrinkled creatures joined him. The Doge had many counselors, many elite groups of three or four who gave him advice, sought favors, and funded ventures such as civic building projects and, more importantly for Niccolo, wars. It drove them to distraction when the Doge favored Machiavelli with exclusive audiences.

"You disturb us," the Doge bellowed, adjusting the sleeves of his purple damask robe. The old fools drew themselves up; combined, they were richer than the State and deserved respect.

Machiavelli smiled apologetically at the unhappy group as if to say, "What can I do? I can't help it if he demands my company." The old men pursed their lips, bowed, and shut the door.

He would kill them with the same poison he had used on the Cardinal. But first he would find out why the king of France and His Holiness the Pope had survived it.

"Tradesmen," the Doge sniffed.

"They want only the best for you. Who am I, they wonder, that I should merit your attention? Just some strange old Florentine with a famous ancestor."

"You are too modest, Niccolo." The Doge smiled at him. "You've inherited the Machiavelli mind from your famous ancestor. I'm most pleased with the progress we have made." That being the fact that Contarini had been very obliquely hinting that he would like very much to be made Doge for life, something unheard of in the Republic for centuries. Doges past who had quested after the power of monarchs had ended up banished, deposed, or assassinated. That Machiavelli had destroyed the Doge's most hated enemies, the Calegri, had not yet been directly spoken of. But this audience, the fine wine, the delicacies—all spoke of gratitude, and of riches to come.

"And I am also pleased, my lord." Machiavelli smiled at him over a goblet of wine. "If we could contain Crete . . ."

"Ah, Crete." Contarini shook his head. "I wish by Christ that damn island would sink." He crossed himself. "God forgive my blasphemy."

"It won't sink. We'll have to control it, just as we need to rein in these upstart colonies. The Mythenians are just the ringleaders." He held out a report carefully written by the little friar, Andre, shortly before he'd beheaded him. The Quickening had been brief but satisfying. He was in need of another bishop for his board now, and as soon as Jean-Pierre was dead, he would need a second one. MacLeod's fate was still undecided. Shackled, he must be. Killed, perhaps.

His agile mind ticked back to the matter at hand. "Four hundred men from neighboring islands are reported to have joined them. And they have purchased the arms of German *condotierri*."

The Doge was silent, then grunted. This news clearly worried him. He made a steeple of his fingers and peered through it as if at an approaching armada. "Donna Maria, they're finally coming. In all the days of the Republic, no foreign invader has touched our city."

It was very difficult not to burst out into delighted laughter. The old fool was going exactly where Machiavelli directed. Playing along, Machiavelli clouded his face with worry and inclined his head.

"So it would appear."

Maria Angelina most sensibly pointed out that they would need money to get off the island, but she and Jean-Pierre both cried poor. MacLeod had the money Machiavelli had given him, but they would need much, much more for bribes and passage back to Algiers.

"I'll take you to the dungeon," Jean-Pierre said. "That's where he keeps his treasure chests."

"Yes," Maria Angelina agreed. "He's shown them to me. You can't believe how much money he has, Duncan."

MacLeod thought a moment. "No," he said slowly. "We'll go to his rooms."

"Are you mad?" Jean-Pierre said, agitated. "What if he's in there?"

MacLeod said nothing.

"Oh, let's go to the dungeon," Maria Angelina said. "If he sees us together, he'll . . ."

"He'll what?" MacLeod asked. "He will think nothing. Why should he?"

She said, "We must assume that the Beauties are against us. St. Cloud has tried to kill you. He has probably bribed everyone here to kill me. We're like pieces on one of those damn boards."

"Aye," Duncan said grimly, and led the way down the corridor toward a sconce. A candle burned softly there; he lifted it out and carried it. "You're right in that, milady. But I won't go deeper in this house than I have to. I'll not go to any dungeons today."

Machiavelli's doors were shut and locked. With his shoulder, MacLeod easily forced them. Maria Angelina covered her mouth at the loud crack of broken wood, then hesitated on the threshold until MacLeod urged her inside.

"There's a panel," he said, trying for a moment to remember how Machiavelli had opened it.

He looked around, retracing the Immortal's steps. He had sat in that chair. He had risen and walked past his bed. He had turned his back.

A lone chess piece sat on a mosaic table. MacLeod touched it, tapped it, tried to pick it up. It was stuck fast. Then he turned it.

The panel opened.

"Ah," Jean-Pierre murmured, as rows of gilt boxes glittered in the candlelight. Eagerly he approached. MacLeod indicated that he should pull back the lid of the nearest box, and the man did so.

"What is this?" Jean-Pierre asked in dismay as he rummaged through the contents.

"More of his lies," MacLeod grumbled. "I should have listened to Antonio more carefully."

MacLeod surveyed the vast array of counterfeit seals and wrinkled pages of practiced forgeries of the signatures of the most powerful families in Venice—Sforza, Calegri, Vedramin, Sarpi. " 'Tonio is the Cardinal's page. He heard Machiavelli talking about sticks of metal to some peasant but I didn't make the connection."

"Who knows what mischief he's been into?" Jean-Pierre riffled through the stacks of papers. "Oh, no, these look just like the letters Andre was supposed to have written us on his travels."

"He's dead, then," MacLeod said bluntly. "Machiavelli took his head."

Jean-Pierre went white and touched his throat. Maria Angelina crossed herself and held on to MacLeod's arm.

"And here's your supper invitation to the Calegri, or an exact duplicate," Maria Angelina said. She held out the paper to MacLeod, who recognized the paper and the seal. "He was trying to get you to the Calegri *palazzo* so my husband and Ruffio could kill you."

MacLeod forced himself to stay calm. "And these scarves?"

"Drop them anywhere, and another is blamed for whatever you've done." Maria Angelina picked up a blue, gold, and red scarf and draped it over her arm. "Now I am a Vedramin." She put it back. "Now I am not."

"To think I ever doubted you," Jean-Pierre said to MacLeod. He shook his head. "There *is* a Game, is there not?"

MacLeod only looked at him.

"What are you speaking of?" Maria Angelina asked in a tremulous voice.

MacLeod sighed. If he could believe her, Machiavelli and St. Cloud had not told her of the Game. He would have to reveal everything if they were to be together. It was only fair. "When we have more time, I'll explain. But now, we've got to go, with coin or not."

Jean-Pierre tried to open the next strongbox, found it locked, and started to reach for MacLeod's sword. MacLeod jerked violently, staring at the man.

"Have you no sense at all?" he demanded.

"I'm your student," Jean-Pierre said in a small voice.

"I have no time for a student." MacLeod hacked at the strongbox and Maria Angelina opened it. It was filled with coins and jewels. "Look, Duncan," she said. She gathered treasure in both hands and stuffed it into the purse at her waist.

MacLeod nodded, but kept his attention on Jean-Pierre. "Get out of Venice and head for another country. I cannot take you on."

Jean-Pierre hung his head. He stood dejectedly as MacLeod swept Maria Angelina out of the room and back into the darkness, candle in hand.

"Perhaps you should kill him," Maria Angelina whispered, grimacing as though the words cost her.

"Perhaps I should," he replied.

"I would be true to you," Jean-Pierre called brokenly. "Always."

MacLeod shook his head. "Go now. Find your own way."

"They may be waiting for me!"

"Then hurry." He walked Maria Angelina away. "Is there another way out of here?"

She nodded and took his hand. Together they moved slowly through the *palazzo*. That they had not been discovered worried him more than the prospect of being discovered. Something was not right.

"We'll go to the docks," he informed her. "I'll find someplace to hide you when we reach the mainland."

"Yes, Duncan." She took his hand and squeezed it hard. They moved silently down a blackened passageway lined with rusting Roman armor.

"I must confess my love for you," she whispered. "It cannot be wrong to declare myself a free woman." She touched his chest.

"Does love beat in your heart for me?" He remained silent. "I know it does. I shall make you happy for as long as I live." She sighed. "If you will have me."

His answer was to take her hand to his lips. There could be no other answer, not now.

"Ah." She sighed, then added, "We're there." She felt along the wall and found a doorway. Pushing on it, MacLeod found himself outside.

The moon was brilliant, illuminating the garden. He swore in Gaelic that their flight would be so brightly lit.

"Hurry," he told her, and they began to cross the lawn. A small object cast a shadow on the grass. He walked toward it, picked it up. A frisson skittered up his spine.

It was a small, red, high-heeled court shoe with the Cardinal's crest emblazoned on the buckle. A shoe the size a boy would wear. A page.

Such as 'Tonio might wear, and it was badly scuffed and dirty. There was dried blood on the instep and heel.

"Antonio? Lad?"

"What is it?" she asked, clearly not understanding.

There was no reply. He ran across the vast lawn, keeping his gaze sharp. There, to the left! A crouching boy.

No. It was a well, the cover removed and lying on the ground. MacLeod noted the ornate metal design of a unicorn with its head in a maiden's lap. 'Tonio had said something about such a thing, had he not? He reconstructed the conversation. The metal things had been in this very well. It was a drop-off point, perhaps, for stolen seals to copy and letters to forge and God knew what else. And the reedy man with Machiavelli must have been his go-between.

MacLeod unsheathed his scimitar. The stench of death hit his nostrils and he reared back; among his people, such a smell was an offense to God and a curse on all who came too close.

"We must go." Maria Angelina urged him away.

"Wait," he said, straining to see. He lifted the candle.

Peering in, he was sickened at what he saw: the remains of 'Tonio's corpse pushed against the side of the well.

"Oh, heavenly Mother," Maria Angelina said, falling to her knees. She covered her mouth. "Oh, help us. Death is on his way to us all."

* * *

The moon hung over the well, now covered, as MacLeod bowed his head. Tears wanted to fall, but he held them in check as Maria Angelina paced, frantic.

It was stupid to pause like this, to risk their lives to mark a death. But an Immortal's life seemed to be about little more than death. Dealing death, escaping it, watching it overtake lovers, friends, and little boys.

But it was the way of it, of the Game, and of the Rules of the Game.

He turned to her. "How do we hire a gondola at this time of night?"

"The gondoliers live quite close to the docks," she said. "We'll have to walk there."

It was a chilly night, and he had no cloak to offer her. They moved swiftly, she shivering now and then, turning her head slightly as if to bid good-bye to the life she had known on the island. He knew that feeling of loss. He had already said good-byes to many lives.

An owl hooted. She jumped and put her hand around his arm. "You have warrior's limbs," she said. "Oh, Duncan, shall we live? Shall we have a life together?"

She stopped him, faced him, put her arms around his neck. He found her lips. He put down his sword and swept her into his arms, bending her backward as he rained kisses on her forehead, her closed eyes, her temples, the curling satin of her hair.

"I cannot help it. If you are untrue, then I am undone. I love thee, bonnie Maire," he said, in a language fast dying, of a people who might die, too, save for those like him and Connor. *A son, I must fill her with a son,* he thought irrationally for a moment forgetting what he was. Then he heard his thoughts and shook his head. They were running for their lives.

"We must stop this," he said hoarsely, in Italian.

"Oh, I don't want to." She stood on tiptoe and kissed the line of his jaw.

"To live, we must." Firmly he pulled himself away and, taking her hand, walked on.

They reached a small cluster of houses, almost a tiny village. He said, "Machiavelli has forbidden me to leave. He said no gondolier would take me."

"I may come and go as I please." She held up her hand. "Stay here in the shadows."

He watched as she negotiated their passage at one house and then another. There was much shaking of heads, and MacLeod began to make plans to steal a craft if necessary.

"They're afraid," Maria Angelina told him. "They don't want him to find out they've put out to sea tonight. He left orders that no one is to leave the island, not even me. It will cost all the money we brought."

"Bloody hell," he swore, but was relieved they were to be off.

He watched her hand their booty to a man wearing a half-mask and a hood. The man gestured for them to follow him to the dock.

Once there, they found a luxurious craft larger than a gondola festooned with feathers and ribbons.

"What on earth?" MacLeod asked, amazed. "We canna take that!"

"It's a Carnival boat," Maria Angelina told him. "Machiavelli won't think of it. He would miss a gondola, though."

"We'll be as obvious as a peacock."

"There's no other choice."

"Och." He shook his head and led her to the edge of the dock.

The masked man got on deck first, helped Maria Angelina next, and slid the cabin lid back. MacLeod stared at him, at the eyes, and frowned.

"Who is this?" he whispered to her.

"I don't know," she answered nervously. "A hired man."

"Why is he masked?"

"No one would come if either of us would be able to identify him," she explained.

"We've no reason to trust him."

"I promised more money when we reached the mainland. His greed is our only guarantee. Come inside, where no one will see us."

She urged him down the companionway. Most of the cabin was taken up by an immense bed covered in satin, and there Maria Angelina lay down and stretched out her arms invitingly.

"It isn't safe belowdecks," he said unsteadily, half his attention on the boatman. "You stay here. I'll be topside."

The vessel rocked as the man cast off. She pulled on his hand. "Please, stay but a moment."

He put one knee on the bed. More than that he did not dare. She was beautiful, and the bed conjured images he should not entertain: she, naked and writhing beneath him, they together doing all the things men and women do to pleasure one another. He averted his gaze and cleared his throat. "Not here. Not now."

"Oh." The surprise in her voice made him look at her. "You don't want me, either. Not Xavier and not you. No one wants Maria Angelina. Old, used . . . mortal."

He touched her face. His fingertips unwillingly traced her lips. He knew that love could strike a heart as quickly and unsuspectingly as a sword could take a head, but the strength and suddenness of his feeling for her, at the same time allied with his unsureness of her, was almost too much for him to take in.

"After tonight, we will be free," she said huskily, her tongue stroking his thumb. "Love me, Duncan. If we must part tonight, I want the memory of you to carry me through my life."

She cupped his knee. Every nerve in his body crackled.

"No," he said.

"Yes, oh, please. *Per favore.*"

He turned from her. "We're in great danger. We must be on alert."

"You don't want me." Her voice was small and hurt.

"Of course I do. You're beautiful. You're . . ." He paused. "I have no poetry in me. I'm a warrior."

"Please, don't make me shame myself by begging." She reached for him again. This time he caught her hand.

"Woman," he whispered, "don't tempt me. I'll not have more blood on my hands. I'm a man, am I not? If you knew how hard I'm fighting not to throw you down and lift your skirt, you'd not say such things to me. I want you as I've wanted little else in this long life I've had, but more than that I want you to live. I'm going topside."

He cupped the back of her neck and raised her face to meet his. His kiss was soul-deep, his desire blood-deep. His body sizzled, on fire as she responded to him, reaching for him again, parting her lips with a moan. It was as if her secret voice whispered to his body: *Take me, do this to me, now this and this and this. Fill me. Claim me.*

Aye, a hundred times, a thousand, if he could.

"Maria," he said against her neck.

"I love you," she urged. "I want you, *amore mio*."

"I have no pretty words, in your language or any other." He wanted to plunge into every centimeter of her, every sigh of her soul.

She put her hands around his neck. "My *sigisbeo*, you must never leave me. Promise me. Promise."

He ringed her throat with kisses, her jawline, the smooth place behind her ear. "Maria."

"Promise, on your honor."

The hollow of her cheek, the tumult of her hair. "I shall try."

"On your honor." She began to recline. He caught her, held her, wanted her as he wanted nothing else.

He rasped, "On my honor."

In a rush, he kissed her again, grabbing at her blindly, thinking of nothing but the deep, throbbing pleasure that shuddered through him, seeking release, and the sound of a name as it penetrated his heart and the pain that was there: *Debra, my Debra, lost forever. My Debra.*

"Alone," he whispered against Maria Angelina's temple.

"Ssh, hush," she whispered. "You are no longer alone."

For the briefest of moments, for a single heartbeat, he allowed himself to believe that. He allowed himself to melt against her softness. But then his hand sought, and found, his sword. He straightened. His heart was racing. "Later, we'll have all the time in the world."

"All the time God gives us," she replied.

"No man knows his fate. I may die tonight." *Before you die,* he wanted to add, marveling at the strange comfort, almost hope, it gave mortals to know that they might one day stand over his grave and weep for him. Surely, if they had ever known the Hell of that pain, they could not wish it on anyone.

Yet they did.

On themselves.

"I pray God that you do not die tonight," she said.

"I, as well." Now he did smile, brightening, for this moment was theirs, and the adventure of Ali's rescue stood in the offing. "Topside," he said.

"Ah." She sighed. "I'll count the minutes until we're together again."

He looked at her with curiosity. Did she love him truly? 'Twas true he had loved other women, but not wisely. Could this be the woman who would bring him the joy that other men and women knew? Connor had known such a love.

And Connor still mourned its loss.

Would this lady kneel by a sword plunged deep into the ground to mark his grave, a sword only, and no cross, no angels praying for his soul? Would she give him peace, if God did not so favor His strange, outcast sons?

Or would she forget that they had ever loved?

As men like him could not?

"*Signor!*" the pilot shouted. "Please, it's an attack!"

Maria Angelina gasped and covered her mouth with her hands. "No. No, it cannot be!"

"Stay here," MacLeod said.

"What if it's Xavier?"

"I'll fight him. I'll take his head."

The hatch burst open as he flew up the companionway in two leaps and landed on the deck. His scimitar was out as he scanned the black water.

"*Signor.*" The pilot pointed in the distance.

The velvet sky was gray with smoke. Sparks on the horizon illuminated ships at battle; the soft thunder of cannon was muffled by the slap of water against the hull of their vessel. At hand, tranquility; at sea, chaos.

"You see! An attack!" the man said.

"Aye," MacLeod replied, turning to him. "We must—"

His words were cut off by the sharp report of the pistol the man drew from his pocket. MacLeod fell to the deck; the other man drew another pistol, aimed squarely, and shot MacLeod in the chest.

"Vengeance, you filthy bastard," the man said.

All thought, all feeling, all life, shattered.

# Chapter Six

"All men will see what you seem to be; only a few will know what you are. . . ."
—Niccolo Machiavelli, *The Prince*

*Here we are.*
*Across land and sea, we come to crush you.*
*We come in galleys pulled by madmen, and brigs and xebecs blown by the gale force of our lust for revenge.*
*We come.*
*There can be only one power in this ocean.*
*And we are here.*

Venice shrieked in terror. Harlots and holy sisters and toothless grandmothers flew screaming through the streets while sailors and grandfathers rushed down to the docks for assignments to warships. Machinelike, the vessels of the Republic filled, cast off, filled, cast off. Swaggering twelve-year-olds commandeered the gondolas and swore to the Doge and St. Mark that they would consign every single Greek rebel to a watery grave.

"For the love of Our Savior, wake up, *monsieur.* Wake up," Jean-Pierre shouted in his ear.

MacLeod jerked, and lived again. He touched his chest. There was no wound, although dried blood crusted his shirt.

"What the hell happened?" he asked as he got to his feet. The day was bright, the sun full and golden. He was aboard a heavily armed galley. Around him the air crackled with the presence of Immortals. Machiavelli's Beauties huddled together on deck, not a handsome chess set but a raggle-taggle of frightened children.

"He has her," Jean-Pierre said. "St. Cloud has Signora Maria

Angelina." He pointed to a brigantine on the horizon. "He put her on a galley, but he's on that brig."

"She approaches! God help us!" shouted a mortal crewman. The brig was coming straight for them, sails bulging.

MacLeod squinted at it, then looked around. Men were racing over the deck like mice, to no apparent purpose. "What's wrong with the crew?"

Jean-Pierre looked away. "Sergei. Do you remember him? His head came off and . . . and lightning emerged. It's a cursed ship, they are thinking."

MacLeod pursed his lips in displeasure. "Who killed him in the presence of mortals? Don't any of you know anything?"

"It was an accident, *signor.*" He hesitated. "I did it. He wanted to throw you overboard, and I challenged him." He looked stricken, no longer a foolish, ignorant youth. "I never dreamed I would win. I just got so angry." He crossed himself. "A mortal sin," he whispered. "God forgive me."

"You got the Quickening."

His eyes were huge. "I thought I was dying. Everyone saw it."

"Where's the captain?"

"He abandoned ship."

MacLeod huffed. "None's taken his place?"

Jean-Pierre's face was red with misery. "They pushed off from shore too quickly. They were unready."

"And how did I come to be here?"

"I don't know. I never made it off the island. Machiavelli returned and said everyone was putting to sea to fight off an attack. We took the gondolas and boarded this vessel. Giuletta found you in the hold only moments ago. Dead."

"And Maria Angelina?" She had set him up. He should have known, should have realized. His desire for her had made him stupid. "The queen?" he added angrily. He stood and ripped off the blood-drenched lace of his sleeve.

"No, she was captured."

"Don't lie to me!" MacLeod thundered, then saw the blank look on Jean-Pierre's face. Perhaps he truly did not know the truth.

A sailor rushed past them. MacLeod grabbed him by the back of his shirt.

"Where's the officer in charge?"

The lad was young and chalky with terror. "Oh, sir, it's a haunted ship. Better to drown, sir. Please let me go!"

"The brig!" someone shrieked. "She's firing!"

There was a huge explosion, a whistling, another explosion as something hit the deck and a section of wood shot into the air.

"Get the cannon out," MacLeod yelled. He staggered to the left. He would never have sea legs, not even in a crisis.

"Oh, *mon Dieu*!" Jean-Pierre cried. He clasped his hands and began to pray.

The younger lad flailed at MacLeod. "Let me go, let me go!"

"Calm yourself," MacLeod ordered, and when it was clear the lad couldn't, MacLeod backhanded him. "Listen to me. Get the others and roll out the cannon. We'll live only if we take that vessel!"

The boy responded as best he could to the voice of command. *"Si, signor."*

Another cannonball hit the deck. There was a sharp scream, followed by another. In the clearing smoke, two men lay maimed and bleeding.

"No, we must abandon this evil vessel! The Devil holds the tiller!" cried an old man. He pointed at Jean-Pierre. "He's a witch!" He wore a sailor's knit cap and ragged pants. There was no Immortality about him.

MacLeod drew his scimitar and pointed it toward heaven. He would have to sort out later how he had gotten here. Foremost was the need for immediate self-preservation.

"It's nothing to do with curses. He's not a witch. Prepare yourselves to fight now or you will surely die today." To the Beauties, he said, "Have a mind for your head, and fire in your belly."

*"Si, signor,"* said Giuletta, coming forward.

"Tack," MacLeod ordered, standing with the wind as they came about and charged the other vessel. "Prepare the cannon!"

Some men wheeled out a large cannon, fed it, tamped it, and set it off. The deck reverberated. The sails swayed.

The enemy ship came within range. "Kill the bitch!" MacLeod bellowed. "Shoot her out of the water."

Then he saw her banner: She flew the colors of Mustafa Ali.

Onto the deck stepped Hassan, Ali's only son. He wore a white robe and kaffiyeh, and in his hand he held an enormous scimitar twice the size of MacLeod's.

"MacLeod, friend of my house! What are you doing?" he shouted in Arabic. "Tell them to stop!"

"Halt the attack!" MacLeod shouted, but no one heeded. "Halt!" he bellowed again. The men swarmed over him like locusts, knocking him to the deck. "It's a trick!"

He got to his knees, and then struggled to his feet. The crew was electrified, terrified of the Turks. He grabbed the nearest man, a mortal, and shouted in his face. "Do not attack!"

"You're mad, you're in league with them!" The man was sobbing. "They'll flay us alive."

"No, they're friends!"

The man stared at him. He pulled away and drew a pistol from his belt, aiming it straight at MacLeod. "Traitor."

"Forgive me," MacLeod murmured, and ran him through.

Then someone—an Immortal—severed his left Achilles tendon and stabbed him in the calf. With a shout, MacLeod lurched sideways as he wheeled to face his opponent. But the other grabbed him around the chest. Steel nicked his earlobe.

"My blade is at your neck," Ruffio yelled into his ear.

"You bleeding whoreson." MacLeod grunted with the pain. "Why?"

"We knew they were Turks. Seems their captain wants his papa back."

A father's son MacLeod was honor-bound to protect. He tensed, readying to spring.

Ruffio pricked the area beneath his jaw with the sharp point of his dagger. "Don't move." He put his hand over MacLeod's mouth.

The Venetian ship approached and rammed the Turkish vessel. Struggling, MacLeod watched helplessly as the Venetian crew boarded her. One after another, Algerian sailors were run through.

With all his strength, MacLeod slammed his elbow into Ruffio's midsection and hobbled forward. "No!"

Ruffio grabbed him around the waist and held him. "Raise your sword," Ruffio told him. "Or as my soul rests in the bosom of the Holy Virgin, I shall kill Maria Angelina."

"Whose bed is she in, his or yours?" MacLeod demanded. "Or both of yours?"

"Then for the sake of the boy. Raise your sword and I'll spare Ali's son. We know his father is your comrade. We've known everything about you since before you got here. My master has contacts and spies everywhere, including Algeria." He chuckled. "I told him to use the story about St. Cloud and Maria Angelina. He didn't like it at all. He said it would be too obvious. That it would tip you off. But he indulged me. And he gave you too much credit."

Ruffio ran the blade along MacLeod's flesh. "I also told Machiavelli you would never become one of us. And I was right. But if you had joined us, I would have killed you eventually. Either way, you would have died."

Ruffio nodded and two of the Venetians grabbed Hassan. They threw him to the deck and aimed one of their swords above his neck. Hassan spoke in quick Arabic; MacLeod caught his own name. The Arabic crew took it up, chanting, "Mac-Leod! Mac-Leod!"

MacLeod fought to free himself. Ruffio stabbed him deeply between the shoulder blades and said, "Your head is next."

"You'll risk another Quickening in public?" MacLeod panted through the pain.

"I care not. We'll be gone from Venice soon, and we'll never come back." He shouted, "Kill the boy!"

"Stop!" MacLeod shouted. He realized he must surrender. "On your honor, you'll not harm him."

"On my honor as an Italian and an Immortal."

MacLeod hung his head and raised his sword. The Turks saw him. "Mac-Leod!" they screamed in anger. "Mac-Leod! Mac-Leod!"

Above the chant, a high-pitched shriek rent the sky. Something catapulted high over the heads of the fighters and thudded to the deck of the Venetian vessel with a ripe thud.

It was the head of Hassan Ali.

MacLeod threw back his head and a Highland war cry erupted from his chest. He grabbed Ruffio's sword with his open hand. Blood gushed from his palm and all-but-severed fingers, but he was unaware of the wound as he threw himself onto Ruffio.

Instantly he was dragged off him by two other Immortals.

The Turkish vessel was heeling hard. It burst into flame. Blood and sweat mingled with the tears of frustration that streamed down MacLeod's cheeks as he watched the vessel collapse, her crew flailing helplessly in the water.

"Who was this set up for, me or the Doge? For it'll mean war," he said to Ruffio.

Ruffio doubled over in laughter. "Take him below. The Doge will want to thank him for smiting our enemies today."

All Venice rejoiced in the vanquishing of her ancient foe, the Turk, who had claimed to be on a peaceful mission to negotiate the return of the doomed spy, Ali. But they had not been peaceful at all! And no, it was not true that they had been few in number and but lightly armed. Sailors and landlubbers alike counted coup: there had been fifty ships, no a hundred, no three hundred, no, the full force of the Ottoman Empire!

At any rate, no matter; nearly all the heathens had been drowned, and the few survivors were flung into the prisons to await their sentences. Few Venetians doubted it would be an agonizing, slow death.

All the intact Venetian vessels returned to the lagoon to be strewn with roses, their crews rewarded with gold coins. Hundreds of thousands of roses filled the canals, as a thousand women lined the bridges dressed in the brilliant red of Venice and the Contarini. They dropped scented handkerchiefs and rosaries into the water as the ships sailed past. Marriages were arranged on the spot between gallant heroes and aristocrats' daughters.

Now, in the night, perfume masked the ordure and blood of battle. Dressed in white, the youngest daughters of all the illustrious houses, the novitiates of the convents, and a discreet distance away, the little orphan girls who depended upon the largess of Holy Mother Church, sang a *Te Deum* of jubilation composed scant hours before by the man of the hour, Niccolo Machiavelli. After all, it was he who not only learned of the insidious surprise attack, but had masterminded the city's defense.

Altar boys carried the statues of the saints through the city. Huge bonfires blazed in the squares. St. Mark's cathedral and the Doge's palace shimmered in the fires, while overhead the sky burned with hour-long volleys of brilliant fireworks.

Dagger tips indenting his sides, MacLeod sat at an immense banquet table between Ruffio and Jean-Pierre, who was all smiles now, all laughter. Before him, the bounty of the sea and land was heaped on golden platters. Huge golden bowls of fruit made entirely of sugar decorated long embroidered runners of silver and cloth of gold. Sculptures of ice—unicorns, griffins, and the lion of St. Mark—glistened and gleamed.

At the crowded high table sat various exalted persons, including the Doge in his ceremonial robes and his jeweled *corno,* his cap of office; the Dogaressa, in red-and-blue damask, filigreed lace of gold clutching her elderly sagging bosom; Machiavelli, splendid and imposing in his signature statesman black, and a stunning companion:

Maria Angelina.

She was dressed in mountains of silk and lace, in the Doge's purple and Machiavelli's ebony. When she saw MacLeod, a smile played over her lush, full mouth. She saluted him with her goblet and leaned forward on her elbows.

"Drink, sir?" asked a page.

MacLeod touched his arm. "What is that woman?" he asked.

The page was surprised. Cautiously he looked left and right. MacLeod dug his fingers into his arm.

"She . . . she is a great lady, *signor.*"

MacLeod dug into his purse and held up a gold coin. The page licked his lips and bent to his ear. "Some say she is the Doge's, ah, friend, *signor.* His friend. So it is said. But I know not. Her husband is very famous, very great. Ah, he's gone some time now, *signor.*"

He scurried away.

Ruffio and Jean-Pierre tittered. "Gods, you are arrogant, Scotsman. You really thought she wanted to play your bagpipes," Ruffio said. They burst into laughter.

MacLeod's face flamed. *"Strega,"* he whispered, the Italian word for witch.

"Have a care, Highlander. The same is being said of you," Ruffio observed, gesturing toward a table of clergy who were devouring chickens in thyme and rosemary. "They want to know, where are the scars from your accident?"

"You're fools. He'll kill you. He has no thought for your lives save how he can use them up before your heads are taken."

*"That* again." Ruffio rolled his eyes. "Don't listen, Jean-Pierre."

"Oh, *mais non,* of course not. I never did." He patted his lips with the edge of the tablecloth and pressed his finger into a piece of sugar pineapple. "But I am a very good actor, am I not?"

"To a man, he'll kill you," MacLeod pressed.

"You're a tiresome, dour creature," Jean-Pierre flung at him.

MacLeod glared at Ruffio. "The Frenchman's stupid, but you're not. You must know the truth."

"And my master has been training me most efficiently," he said beneath his breath so that only MacLeod could hear. "He and I shall go on, ridding ourselves of men like you. The others, they're dispensable."

"And so is your honor."

"Honor is an outmoded concept. I'm practical."

"Like your master," MacLeod said with contempt.

Ruffio inclined his head. "Even so."

"And his whore." He was ashamed of the tenderness she had raised in him. She must have laughed at him when he'd told her how alone he was. He had been so stupid to believe the lie about St. Cloud. He hadn't had time to think it through. He hadn't had enough evidence to convict her.

Och, he'd loved her, pure and simple. And that had been all they'd needed to trap him.

"Have a care, sir." He wagged his finger. "She is devoted to my master."

Machiavelli stood and clapped his hands. "My esteemed lord, my lady, all assembled here on this great and glorious day of victory. I give you the heroes in our midst." There was thunderous applause as his arms embraced the entire company. The wealth and power of all Venice overflowed the huge golden salon like a living, invincible behemoth. Gold and jewels glittered from gowns and throats. Firelight swept the renowned paintings and statuary. MacLeod wished upon himself the strength of Samson, so that he could bring down the colonnades on them and avenge the house of Ali and all the Turks who had died this day.

With great ceremony, Machiavelli unfurled a scroll and began to read from it. He proclaimed name after name, most of them titled and listed in the Golden Book. The men stood, receiving the accolades of the grand house.

MacLeod heard his own name, stayed seated, and felt Ruffio's blade in his side. Grimly, he stood.

"Welcome, good sir," the Doge said to MacLeod, hefting his goblet. "I'm sure your name is being cursed from one side of the

Ottoman Empire to the other." The throng laughed. He drank, his knowing gaze meeting MacLeod's over the rim.

*Can it be that he knows it all?* MacLeod wondered. *About our Immortality, and that Machiavelli has set Venice on an inevitable course with war? Is she really his mistress?*

"What now?" he asked Ruffio, inclining his head as the Doge watched him, his own gaze never wavering.

"I have no idea," Ruffio said. He and Jean-Pierre burst into more merry laughter.

"You bastard." MacLeod balled his fists.

"Careful, careful." Ruffio turned to Jean-Pierre. "Maybe he doesn't really care about the Turkish spy."

"But surely he cares about his own head," Jean-Pierre rejoined.

Fireworks and cheers punctuated the hours as the reveling continued late into the night. MacLeod ate sparingly and drank less. He looked for his moment as Ruffio and Jean-Pierre drank too much and began to grow tired and careless. As he had hoped, they did both.

Just as he prepared to make his move, a man flew into the center of the room with his sword drawn. His face was red with fury.

"Where is the accursed foreigner, Duncan MacLeod?" he shouted. "Where's the son of a Turk who cuckolded me?"

Gradually the merrymakers quieted. All eyes turned toward MacLeod.

"MacLeod?" The man's voice was high and shrill.

MacLeod stood. "I'm Duncan MacLeod of the Clan MacLeod."

"And I am the Duke d'Fabrizi, and I call you out." The man rushed at his table. Ruffio and Jean-Pierre made a great show of rising and coming to MacLeod's aid. "Whoreson! Fornicator!"

MacLeod held out his empty hands. "I have no quarrel with you, *signor.*" But the man looked vaguely familiar. MacLeod couldn't place him, but he went on alert.

On the dais, Machiavelli made a great show of looking concerned. Maria Angelina's hands covered her mouth. Her eyes were enormous, her face drained of color.

"I have been in Tuscany, on business. You took advantage of my absence and made love to my wife! I left her in the protection of Signor Machiavelli, but he, too, failed me." Spittle flew.

"Nay, not I. Never."

"This cannot be. Have you proof?" Machiavelli asked, rising.

"*Si, signor,* I do! This man wrote her a note to run away with him last night."

The man pulled a paper from his coat and shook it in MacLeod's face. MacLeod caught the words, "My darling," and his own signature. It was a forgery, and a good job of it, too.

"I will be satisfied."

The Doge frowned. "Dueling is not permitted. But neither is adultery."

"*Signor,*" MacLeod said. "On my honor, I don't know what this is about."

"Liar! I was there! I saw you touching her!"

MacLeod shook his head. "You're mistaken, sir."

"Let me see the note," Machiavelli said. "With your permission, sir." He waited for the Doge to indicate his consent.

The distraught man ran to the high table and handed Machiavelli the letter. Machiavelli scanned it and looked dismayed. "My liege, it is true. This is in MacLeod's hand." He handed the letter to the Doge.

The Doge's face went ashen. He said, "This is a private matter. We will discuss it later."

Maria Angelina swayed as if she were about to faint.

"Friend Duncan, as you are my friend, what do you say to this? This lady is in my care," Machiavelli said, ignoring the Doge.

MacLeod shook his head. "That it's a forgery, and I know nothing of it."

"I want satisfaction," the duke insisted.

"You've been drinking," MacLeod said.

"Insult on top of insult! I will have satisfaction now!" the man shrieked, and stabbed MacLeod in the leg.

"Stop!" the Doge commanded.

MacLeod grabbed at the wound and parried a second attempt. "Stop, man, you're no match for me," he growled beneath his breath. "I didna write that letter."

"You liar!" D'Fabrizi flew at him, holding his sword with both hands in front of himself like a battering ram.

"Stop! Stop it now!" the Doge ordered.

It would be an easy thing to deflect the attack; MacLeod was confident of the outcome and paid only mild attention to what he was doing. But the drunk man tripped and fell forward. Before

MacLeod could move, d'Fabrizi was impaled on his scimitar. MacLeod's mouth dropped open as the other fell to the floor in his own blood, gasping, the brutal weapon in his chest.

MacLeod dropped to his knees. "Sir, *signor,* are ye sore hurt?" He pulled open the man's coat to check the wound. It was bad; nay, worse, it was mortal.

"My . . . wife . . ." the man gritted out. "I saw it all. I was warned. I saw you."

"On my head, I nae touched her," MacLeod said. "I don't know her."

The man lifted a shaking hand and pointed it at Maria Angelina. A hushed murmur went through the hall. "My . . . wife . . ."

MacLeod stared at her, then at the man. He heard again his voice. "Gods," he whispered. In his arms lay the masked pilot who had shot him the night before.

The man stared at him, his accusation no longer denied. Scant satisfaction for him: he was dead.

"Take MacLeod," the Doge ordered. "We said there was to be no dueling, and we see the outcome of ignoring our wishes. There's danger in combat for the sake of honor." He looked coldly at MacLeod, then at Machiavelli. "And in the bedrooms of women who are by law and conscience denied to us."

Guards surrounded MacLeod.

"But, my lord," Machiavelli protested. "This man saved Venice today. Do you remember the funeral oration for Pericles? Thucydides wrote these words:

> *For even those who come short in other ways may justly plead the valor with which they have fought for their country; they have blotted out the evil with the good, and have benefited the state more by their public services than they have injured her by their private actions.*

"Duncan MacLeod did the state a great service today. Does he not deserve pardon?"

"No one who has done ill deserves pardon."

Maria Angelina touched her throat and reached for a goblet, then put her hands in her lap as if sensing that she was calling attention to herself. The faithless mistress of the Doge, the equally faithless wife of a man who had died because of her. She was disgraced forever. Machiavelli must have written the note, hoping that the jealous, wronged man would dispatch her when MacLeod had been killed and stowed aboard the galley.

Machiavelli had tired of this particular queen.

MacLeod cared not. She had used him. He hated her. At that moment, any tenderness left within him shriveled and died. He wanted to kill her.

"I would request custody of him," Machiavelli persisted. "I will stake my honor on his behavior, and I swear that he will remain in Venice until my lord finds it convenient to question him privately on this matter."

"If it please the Doge," said another voice. It was one of the priests who had been wolfing down the chicken. *"Signor,* is it not true you were in a terrible fire?"

MacLeod said firmly, "I thank Jesus Christ for protecting me," and crossed himself.

"And that while you were on the galley, *Cross of St. Ursula,* a man was beheaded and demons poured out of his body? And the crew tried to abandon the cursed ship, but you were unafraid? You told them it had nothing to do with curses?"

Machiavelli looked startled. He hadn't been there; he must not have known about Jean-Pierre and the Quickening.

Before he could answer, another priest said, "We have witnesses. Sailors who were aboard the vessel you commanded."

"Take him, then," the Doge said unhappily. "Take the Duchess d'Fabrizi as well. She will be questioned as to her hand in the murder of her husband."

Maria Angelina stumbled and held out her arms. "My lord," she pleaded. "I have done nothing."

The Doge turned his back on her and left the room.

MacLeod ticked his attention to where Machiavelli had been standing. He was nowhere to be seen.

# Chapter Seven

===

*". . . for men do harm either because of fear or because of hatred."*
**—Niccolo Machiavelli,** *The Prince*

The lash, soaked in salt water and studded with metal teeth, sliced his naked back and tore it open. Manacled between two pillars, MacLeod exhaled between his clenched teeth, arched, and slipped in his own blood and sweat. As the pain burned down his spine and into the backs of his legs, the surface wounds began to heal. They had stripped him completely, to make him feel vulnerable, he supposed.

It was working.

After a beat, the lash came down again.

"By the Virgin, why don't you confess?" his torturer, grunting. "I'm exhausted. Have pity on me, if not on yourself. We've been at this all night."

The dungeon door behind him squealed open. "Paolo," a man called. "You're off duty. Gi'anni will take over."

"Praise to the Virgin," the torturer said. "I have a cramp in my arm from all this lashing." There was rustling, some footsteps.

"Aren't you going to take him down?" the first speaker asked in surprise. "It's freezing in here."

"Him? Not on your life. He's a savage."

The door shut.

MacLeod was alone in the half-lit room with pots of boiling lead, braziers, the rack, the boot, an iron maiden, cobwebs, and rats.

He shook his throbbing arms, trying to bend his wrists to reach the fastenings on the manacles. A rat ran over his bare foot. He made a face and raised one leg, then the other. His tormentor had informed him that at daybreak, the priests would observe his questioning. He tried to remind himself that as long as they didn't behead him, nothing they did mattered. All physical pain, no matter how intense, was temporary.

There was a noise in the opposite corner. MacLeod turned to look. A small boy crept forward, dragging an old-fashioned broad sword behind himself. It was Zulian, the boy MacLeod had saved at the hiring yard.

"A friend sends his compliments, *signor,*" the boy said, grinning. He showed him a ring of keys.

He raised on tiptoe to unfasten MacLeod's manacles and raced for the door. "Come on!"

"A friend? What friend?" MacLeod took the sword and hefted it. "Who sent you?"

Zulian ignored him. He ran to the door and tried the first key, then the second, and opened it. It squealed as before, and MacLeod winced. Zulian gestured for MacLeod to follow.

"A great, rich man. He's paid off all the daytime guards," Zulian said impatiently. "Come."

"What did he look like, this great, rich man?" Had it been Machiavelli?

"He spoke only to my mother." Impatiently, he gestured for MacLeod to follow.

Silently, MacLeod took the sword and tapped Zulian on the shoulder. He laid odds the entire thing was a trap. Poor Zulian. He was sure to get the gallows—or the block—for this.

A man in ecclesiastic robes—perhaps one of the Inquisitors—hummed as he sauntered toward them. The two fugitives pressed themselves into the shadows and held their breath. As soon as he was near, MacLeod sprang on him, cuffed him, and knocked him out. Hurriedly he undressed the man and put on his robe. It was too short by half a meter. His shoes were also too small, and pinched.

As they dragged the unconscious man around the corner, Zulian pointed to the left and said, "We can leave that way."

"Are the Englishman and the Arab imprisoned here?" MacLeod picked up the broadsword. Its blade was nicked and the blood groove caked with grime. "The ones they mean to behead as spies?"

The boy blinked. "Spies," he echoed, bemused. Then he nodded. "I know who you mean. The Englishman was sent home, *signor.* In a fine ship with many presents. He's not a spy. He's a hero of the Republic."

Paid off, then? Or compromised in the first place? MacLeod narrowed his eyes. "And the other?"

"I don't know."

"Then he might still be here. I need to find him." Seeing the fear on the lad's face, he added, "Tell me how to get out and then hie yourself home. If I know your mother, she's worried sick about you." He tousled the boy's hair and thought with a pang of 'Tonio. "Have a good long life. Have many adventures and grow up to be an honorable man."

*"Si, signor."* The boy shyly ducked his head. "Good luck to you, *signor.*"

*"Grazie."* He figured he would need it.

It was Hell, the dungeon of the Republic of Venice. Men shrieked and begged; jailers laughed. Brands sizzled and whips cracked. Women, held down in moldy straw, screamed for help.

Down dank passages lined with thick jail doors, MacLeod floated like a ghost, growing suspicious of the fact that no alarm had been raised over his escape. Surely they had discovered he was missing by now.

Then he saw her.

In a barred but exposed cell, Maria Angelina sat on a pile of straw, her face a mottle of bruises, her gay party dress stained.

"Maria," he said.

She looked up at him, cried out, hid her face. "Don't look at me."

"Maria."

"He forced me. He told me he would kill me when I discovered he was an Immortal."

He said nothing. His heart was cold, where once it had hoped, so vainly, to love.

"I was the Doge's secret mistress for years. My husband never knew."

"But if his job was to kill me on the carnival craft, why did you inflame him by pleasuring me?"

She shook her head. "I didn't know it would be him! Machiavelli was never certain when you would try to leave the island, so we couldn't plan for everything. It made sense to me that the gondolier would hide his identity for fear of reprisal. I never dreamed it was my own husband, the duke. I saw him so rarely." She smiled bitterly. "I can only assume Machiavelli wished me dead, and sent my husband the letter. Using our plot to ensnare you to ensnare my husband and me as well. I'm sure he assumed d'Fabrizi would murder me after he took care of you."

"Why did you try to seduce me? What was the purpose of all of this? He could have tried a dozen simpler ways to rid himself of me."

"Rid himself?" She shook her head. "It was his hope that you would join him. He wanted you to become dependent upon him. He wanted to isolate you from anyone who called you friend. That was why they put you on the galley today. So that you could never return to Algiers."

"But why?"

"Don't you know? He wants you to be his right hand. To go through the centuries together, lording it over mortal and Immortal alike. Ruffio thinks he is to be the one, but since Machiavelli met you, Ruffio has paled in Machiavelli's sights. Though of course, the brute knows it not." She laughed bitterly. "My front teeth are loose. Soon I truly will be an ugly hag."

"No," he said softly, unable to harden his heart completely against her. He told himself that she was getting what she deserved, but she was paying a terrible price.

"Machiavelli's going to rescue you. I guess he already has." She knelt on her knees and crawled to the bars, stretching out her arms and arching her chest. "If you did love me, thrust that sword into my heart and end my life. I beg you."

He stared at her.

She held out her arms. "For the love of the Virgin, I beg you. They are going to kill me slowly. Carlo—the Doge—has promised me hours of agony for my faithlessness. You must know his wife is delighted at the prospect."

The hair rose on the back of his head. Should he do it? Uncertainly, he said, "I will not kill a woman."

"You hide behind that?" she screeched. "You want me to suffer. You want me to die."

"I canna," he said softly. He turned his back.

"Don't let them torture me!"

Clenching his fists, he walked away, into the stink, and filth and the screams.

"Check!" MacLeod heard the single word at the same moment that he felt the presence. Machiavelli's voice, Machiavelli's Immortality. He knew he had been detected as well, and hefted the broadsword. The old scimitar was a better weapon. He was sorry to have lost it.

To his left, a jail cell opened. Dressed in his black robe, Machiavelli leaned against the jamb and crossed his legs at the ankles. *"Buona sera,* young Duncan. I'm about to checkmate your friend. You can play next."

"Shut the door and fight me, you bastard," MacLeod challenged. He held the sword with both hands and bent his legs.

Machiavelli tilted his head. "Why would I rescue you if I wanted to fight you?"

MacLeod lunged just as Ali appeared in the doorway. He was dressed in fine European clothes, his gray hair loose and his beard trimmed. He smiled and cried, "Duncan!"

"Get back inside, Ali," MacLeod urged, though he was relieved to see him. "This is a private matter."

The general crossed his arms. "This man has been most civil to me."

"I'll kill him and then we'll escape." MacLeod made tiny circles with his sword point, a ploy to distract his opponent.

"I think not," Ali replied.

MacLeod's eyes widened and he glanced at his friend. Machiavelli feinted; MacLeod shifted his attention back to him.

"What are you saying?"

"There's going to be a war. Peace is hopeless. The food here is good, and they'll move me to Signor Machiavelli's farm if I'm not quickly ransomed. He's been hoping you would join us there."

MacLeod couldn't believe what he was hearing. "Whatever he told you, it's a lie. There's no war. There's no need for one. This country is finished. The sultan can get whatever he wants through trade."

Ali shrugged. "I've developed a liking for noodles. And Venetian virgins. It will do me no harm to wait and see."

"You'll be dead whenever he decides you should be."

"Like his son?" Machiavelli cut in, smiling evilly. "His only child?"

"What?" Ali came out of the cell. "Whose child?"

Machiavelli whirled around and crab-walked sideways, covering MacLeod and the general with his weapon.

"Ask MacLeod. Ask him what happened to Hassan."

"Duncan?" Ali's voice shook. He faced MacLeod and clenched his fists. "Duncan?"

MacLeod hung his head. "He's dead. It's my fault," he said softly. "I took a ship to sea, and I fought him."

The general was silent. Then with a wail of fury he ran to Machiavelli and grabbed his sword. Machiavelli allowed it, smiling at MacLeod. MacLeod lowered his sword and waited. For this, he was willing to die.

"Murdering infidel!" Ali shrieked. "Son of a thousand jackals!"

Like lightning, Ali spun and thrust his sword into Machiavelli's chest. The Italian's mouth dropped open; he was utterly astonished. He grabbed at the blood streaming from his body, fell backward, and died.

The general's sword clattered on the stone. "My son," he keened, constricting into a ball. "Tell me that it is a lie. Tell me he lives."

"I canna." MacLeod adjusted the back of his robe, exposing the back of his neck. "A life for a life. Is it not written in the Holy Book?"

Ali composed himself. "You would not kill him. This one would. The page is written. The book is shut. I know all that I need to know."

MacLeod opened his mouth to speak. Ali held up his hand to silence him.

"My mourning must wait. We must go quickly. He expected you. We were waiting for you. I feigned my cowardice to lull him into complacency. I'm concerned that it appeared to work so well." Ali savagely kicked Machiavelli. "There will be guards." He bent down. "We'll hold him as hostage."

"He's dead," MacLeod said quickly. He didn't want Ali to see Machiavelli's resurrection.

"They don't know that." The great warrior hefted the inert form over his shoulder. "Go behind and cover me."

"Hold!" shouted a voice. Down a narrow passageway to their

right, six armed men approached, soldiers of the dungeon. "Put him down."

"He breathes," Ali told them.

"I'll slit his throat," MacLeod announced. "I'll cut off his head in front of you."

The men hesitated. MacLeod took the advantage and gestured to the left. "This way."

"No," Ali said. "He told me the layout. We must go the same way they came."

MacLeod's smile was grim. "Are you ready, then?"

"The fury of heaven rides through me. I will avenge my son."

They rushed the men, MacLeod taking the first one by surprise. Ali held on to his burden, managing swordplay nevertheless, and cutting off the arm of the man who lunged at him.

Attack.

Parry. Riposte.

Parry. Counterparry.

Parry. Counterparry.

Lunge.

Another went down. Blood sprayed MacLeod's chest and face.

Another.

One slipped and scrabbled to his knees. Hands extended, he begged, "Mercy, in the name of God!"

MacLeod lowered his sword just as Ali darted forward and skewered the man. "In the name of God, no mercy. I would never pray to a God who could excuse a father's not avenging his son."

The fifth man proved more skilled than the others, or perhaps it was because MacLeod was tired. They fought for several minutes while Ali, dropping Machiavelli unceremoniously to the floor, battled the sixth.

"Why aren't more coming?" Ali asked MacLeod.

"I was to be rescued," he said dully, "so that I could be his prisoner."

Another Immortal loomed nearby. He felt the tremor, strong and close.

Perhaps more than one.

Reinforcements of a far more lethal kind.

"We have company," he said. MacLeod's adversary turned his head to see, and in that moment, MacLeod killed him.

Ali finished off the sixth.

MacLeod scrutinized the passageway. Though the presence of Immortals was unmistakable, he could see no one. Laying his sword against Machiavelli's neck, he bellowed, "If you let us go, you have my word I'll not take his head. I'll let him live. If you try to take us, I'll finish him first."

Ruffio stepped forward. Behind him, perhaps a dozen Beauties were grouped. Jean-Pierre was among them. Ruffio glanced anxiously at Machiavelli and glared at MacLeod. "We don't care what you do to him."

"He hasn't yet taught you to lie well," MacLeod said contemptuously. "Go. We'll let him live if you do."

Ruffio shook his head. "Doing that's too stupid even for you."

"On my honor, I won't take his head."

Jean-Pierre cleared his throat. "He is much concerned with his honor, Ruffio. MacLeod, do you swear here and now that for all time, you will never take his head?"

"That's foolish," Ali said to MacLeod. "You know they won't rest until you're dead."

"I swear it on my honor," MacLeod said darkly. It was the only way he could think of to save Ali.

He waited. Ruffio spit. "We go, then," he said. He motioned to the group.

*"Mais non!"* Jean-Pierre protested. "This is foolish!"

Murmurs of disapproval rose to shouts. Ruffio barked, "What else can we do?"

Uneasily they retreated. MacLeod carried Machiavelli as they followed the Beauties down the passage, Ali watching the rear. Any second now, the man would awaken. MacLeod was ready to kill him again.

"We'll need money. And a ship," Ali said.

MacLeod nodded at Ruffio. "See to it."

Ruffio's reply was a murderous stare.

# Chapter Eight

*"The wise boldly pick up a truth as soon as they hear it. Don't wait for a moment, or you'll lose your head."*

—Hsüeh-Dou

"Tonight, one last victory celebration," Ali said to MacLeod. "And then you must go before the sun rises, my friend. If anyone knew that the great traitor, Duncan MacLeod, rested here, the walls of my house would tumble and I would not be able to save you. I know what really happened to my beloved son on the Venetian ocean, but others do not. Many died unjustly that day. Your name is defamed throughout the empire, and you are hated beyond reason."

"I'll be sorry to go," MacLeod said. They had arrived in Algiers only two days before. "Sorry to leave the company of a friend."

"You will be missed, friend Duncan. Now that I have no son . . ." Ali sighed. "It would be good to have a young man in my household."

"If it is the will of Allah, one of your wives will conceive."

Ali brightened. "Yes, if that is His great will."

They lounged in Ali's pleasure garden, savoring the luxury only a very wealthy man could extend an honored guest. MacLeod wore a white robe that smelled of spice and soap. Dates and sweets at MacLeod's right hand, an ornate thimble of mud-thick coffee at his left; water, blessed water, trickling from a fountain copied from a Moorish palace in Spain.

"You're quiet. Where are your thoughts?"

He wondered if Maria Angelina was still alive. "It was so easy," he said. "They just let us take him."

"Perhaps he had outlived his usefulness." Ali rested on his elbow and regarded his friend. He looked at him differently now that MacLeod had told him about Immortals. More cautiously, more curiously. MacLeod was sorry for that. "I wish I had your immortality," Ali went on, as if he'd read his mind. "But I don't envy him his."

MacLeod held up a finger. "I promised not to kill him."

"And so it shall not be." Ali bowed his head low. "On my honor."

A flute and a tambour picked up a steady, pulsing rhythm as Ali's chief eunuch clapped his hands for the females to appear. Beneath the brilliant moon, the dancing girls fluttered past the two men. Unlike women in the streets and marketplaces, who modestly covered themselves as Allah decreed, these wore filmy gauze MacLeod could almost, but not quite, see through. Their graceful bodies glittered with jewels that rivaled the twinkling heavens above the canopy of palms.

Paradise, surely. A glimpse at the reward Allah promised all faithful Muslims. It was almost enough to make him convert, particularly as one lovely girl with hair to her knees gazed into his eyes and smiled through her veil.

"Take her if you want her," Ali said, popping a date into his mouth.

"Och, no. She's yours."

"Don't insult me, man. I have offered you a gift. I'm surprised your manhood hasn't shriveled up and fallen off by now. You never use it."

The girl continued to smile at him as she unfastened her veil.

"Well," MacLeod ventured, and smiled back.


Hands seized him. A hood came down over his head. He shouted, and was cuffed for his noisiness.

"Where are you taking me?" Machiavelli demanded.

Thrown into a cart. Hours, traveling, and the world sizzled like an oven.

Another day, a night.

He was given no water.

He died, revived.

Was beaten.

Died again.

The cart stopped. He was pushed out onto fiery sand that raised welts everywhere it touched. He screamed.

"Be a man," said the voice of Mustafa Ali. "You won't die, although were it up to me, I'd take your head, pledge of honor or no."

Machiavelli couldn't stop screaming.

"Even before MacLeod rescued me, the Doge had been enlightened about your schemes to draw Venice into war with us. Our local agents in the Republic had already assured me that your Doge would have released me on the morrow, and beheaded you in the square for your treachery. But MacLeod, who is a man of honor, came for me before the Doge could act. It proved useful, for I may serve my sultan again someday in some secret capacity if I am required."

Machiavelli's hands were tied behind him. His ankles were trussed together. Still he screamed.

"The sultan has sent another envoy, and we will trade in peace. Know this: Venice is dangerous for you. Do not return there in this lifetime."

Screaming as he was thrown in a pit.

"Your Court of Beauties has been disbanded, your people scattered. Word has reached us that two have been found beheaded. I presume they were discovered by more seasoned Immortals. Perhaps one of them will find you as well. Perhaps not."

Fiery sand rushed over him, clogging his mouth. And still he screamed.

*MacLeod, MacLeod, MacLeod, MacLeod.*
*For this, you shall lose your head in agony.*

# MIDDLEGAME:
## Queening the Pawn

# Chapter Nine

*"Let go over a cliff, die completely, and then come back to life—after that you cannot be deceived."*

—Zen saying

*P-K4.*

At home in his loft, MacLeod shook his head and put the letter aside, still debating with himself over what to do about it. *Act, don't react.* It was a lesson he had taught himself, hard learned, and one he often ignored to his own detriment. But what else was the bulk of an Immortal's life, but reacting? To danger, aggression, to challenges. Even to the Quickening, which seized you and electrified you and transformed you into something you hadn't been ten seconds before. Almost by definition, his existence was one defensive maneuver after another.

The phone rang. Fully expecting to hear Machiavelli's voice on the other end, MacLeod calmly put down his coffee and lifted the receiver.

"MacLeod," he said, *Duncan MacLeod of the Clan MacLeod.* How proud he had been of his name and his heritage, back in his time. After he had been cast out, he had alternately despised them for the lies they were and clung to them because he had no one else to be. But over the centuries, he had come to realize he *was* Duncan MacLeod. His clan *was* the Clan MacLeod. He had defined himself, rather than be defined.

*Act, don't react.*

"MacLeod," he said again, flashing with irritation. He hated games.

"Sorry, Mac. I got distracted. It's the puppy. You okay, boy? Mr. Ron? Oh, for God's sake!"

MacLeod grinned and put his feet up on the table edge, settling back in his chair. "Baby-sitting not going too well, Joe?"

"Who said that?" The man chuckled ruefully. "Listen, if a hot-looking bass player asked *you* to take care of her dog while she was on tour, you'd do it, too."

"Never."

"Mr. Ron, stop that! What kind of name is Mr. Ron for a dog, anyway, for God's sake. You would so, Mac, if you saw her. Well, she's coming back tomorrow. Thank God for small favors. Listen, I heard from Woodrich, and he's got your suite at the Capitol Hilton all set, but he wants you to know you're more than welcome to stay at his place with us."

"Naw, you two have got a lot of catching up to do." MacLeod was pleased to be invited. He and Joe Dawson had a strange relationship, a friendship laced with a bit of tension. As MacLeod's Watcher, Joe chronicled MacLeod's every move. For the most part, MacLeod had gotten used to it.

For the most part.

"Mac?"

"Yes?" He idly fingered the letter. What the hell did Machiavelli want?

"I was telling you Woodrich has set up a meeting with you and that curator. The one whose name I can never get straight."

"Meyer-Dinkmann. The German." MacLeod brightened. Andreas Meyer-Dinkmann knew more about pre-World War II Japanese weapons than any other man alive. MacLeod had corresponded with him for a few years, but they'd never met. He was looking forward to this trip.

*"How do you stand it?"* Dawson had once asked him. *"Decade after decade. How do you stay interested in things? Don't you get bored?"*

MacLeod had replied, with an indulgent smile, *"Only stupid people get bored, Dawson. Why do you ask? Do you get bored?"*

"Mr. Ron! Oh, man, not on the carpet! Mac, I gotta go. Flight's at twenty-one hundred hours. I mean, nine."

"Roger that." MacLeod grinned. Alan Woodrich was an old buddy of Joe's from the Vietnam days. Dawson was already regressing into military talk. MacLeod knew how that worked. Old warriors never die.

He himself was an old warrior.

"Mac? Everything okay?"

*Why do you ask? So you can put it in your Chronicle tonight?*

"Everything's fine. I just got a letter from an old friend." *Throw him a bone. Why not?*

"Oh?"

"Yeah. Maybe I'll tell you about him sometime." A bone, but not the whole carcass.

"Okay." Dawson was clearly intrigued. "See you tomorrow night."

"Right. Give your bass player my regards."

"Not on your life, buddy."

MacLeod chuckled as he hung up, put the letter in the envelope, and rose to shower and start his day.

On his way out of the room, he spied his exquisite sixteenth-century chessboard, ebony on ivory, set up for a game. The kings and queens stared expectantly ahead, eager for the massacre to begin.

He moved the white pawn from the second row to the fourth. P-K4. Then he mirrored the move for black: P-K4.

"Dawson, would you get bored if every morning, you knew someone might try to kill you today?" he asked softly. Joe Dawson had lived with that. Every person in the armies of the world lived with that.

The only difference was with the duration of the tour of duty. That was all.

*Act, don't react.*

"Your move, Machiavelli," he said softly. "And God help you if you move toward me."

# *Chapter Ten*

===

*"From the withered tree, a flower blooms."*
—Zen saying

Tokyo

They met in a re-creation of the Cavern Club, the bar in Germany where the Beatles had played their first gigs. In the strange cross between a British pub and an Osaka beer hall, four Japanese men with the signature rice-bowl haircuts sang an incomprehensible version of "Yesterday" while Samantha and Mari waited at a picnic table for the others.

"Is my Watcher here?" Samantha asked. Ever since Mari had explained who she was, Samantha had become both worried and irritated by the fact that someone followed her everywhere and recorded everything she did. What normal person wouldn't be?

Were Immortals normal people?

Mari replied stiffly, "I can't say."

Samantha frowned and crossed her legs. "You mean, you won't say. From what I can figure out, you've violated every goddamned rule of your goddamned organization. But you still won't tell me that?"

Mari pursed her lips. Samantha knew the Harvard-educated woman didn't appreciate swearing in any of the five languages she spoke. She was like Machiavelli that way, fluent and articulate, conversing easily with the many high-level people who passed through their world. She was very glamorous in her elegant black couture clothes. Her jet hair in a stylish chignon, she looked every inch the sister of Ken Iwasawa, the CEO of one of Japan's most powerful multinational corporations.

Mari said, "I have my own code of ethics."

"How convenient for you." Samantha pulled out a mirrored

compact, popped it open, and brushed her cheeks with blush while she scrutinized the crowd behind them for another foreigner, or *gaijin*. It was a trick Umeko had taught her. Of course, it made little sense that the Watchers would send someone who stuck out in a crowd, as she did, a five-nine, blue-eyed redhead in the land of dark hair and relatively short female stature.

That was why Mari, who was half-Japanese, had been avidly recruited to become a Watcher in Japan. She had been Umeko's Watcher for the last two weeks of Umeko's life, until Umeko had lost her head. They had transferred her to Samantha's lover the following day.

Now Mari was flirting with death, and she, Samantha, with losing her head. Mari had come to them, to Satoshi first, because she knew things she hadn't fully shared with them, things about Machiavelli and her half-brother. She wanted Machiavelli out of Ken's life. More to the point, she wanted Machiavelli dead.

So did Samantha.

So did others in his organization. To the Immortals, "Nicky Macchio," known to his intimates to be the Immortal, Niccolo Machiavelli, was a bad *sensei*, a bad teacher and master. He provided his people with inadequate training; he sent them out to be killed for no good reason than that it might advance him a step or two in some plan he never divulged to anyone else. At first Samantha had not believed that of him; couldn't believe it and stay in his bed.

But then, three years ago, Umeko had come into her life. Angular, whiplike, a ninja among Immortals, the 165-year-old Umeko had told her the truth, made her see.

Umeko Takahashi, her sole female friend, ever, in her existence, her confidante. Umeko, kind and fierce, a woman who loved women, not just in a sexual way but as a mother loves her children. A patron saint of women. Umeko had given her self-confidence and convinced her she could one day leave Machiavelli. She'd told Samantha about the Game, and the rules by which the honorable played.

"But your man is not honorable," she'd warned Samantha, as they stood sweating inside the dojo where Umeko and Samantha secretly trained. "He is not a shogun, not a leader of samurai, as he claims to be. He is a petty and vindictive monster."

The long hours of battle practice yielded fruit. Samantha saw that Umeko was right, and that she, Samantha, was better than the men in her life had treated her, better than Nicky had treated her. Umeko trained not only her mind and her body, but her spirit. Through Umeko's belief in her and love for her, she became a free woman. Umeko told her she would transcend even this level of self-confidence and self-love, until she had so much brimming over that she would be able to give it to another.

"I pray that someone might be me," Umeko had said, but Samantha couldn't love another woman in that way.

Nor could she love a man undeserving of that kind of love. And she saw now that Nicky Machiavelli was undeserving of that kind of love.

Umeko had also told Samantha only days before her death that although Samantha had a long way to go, she might one day take the heads of mighty Immortals. And though Samantha had yet to take a head, she knew she would help the others take Machiavelli's, whether in a one-on-one challenge or by other means.

Now, at the Cavern Club, Samantha tugged at the bodice of her red silk jumpsuit. There were diamonds and rubies in her ears and around her neck. Machiavelli liked color and flash. In the early days, she had liked them, too, thinking they made her look sophisticated and rich. But of late, working first with Umeko and now with Mari, she had come to prefer quiet elegance and polish. She knew every man in the club had mentally undressed her at least once. Machiavelli liked that. He liked possessing what everyone else wanted. That was how he came to own you. He figured out what you wanted, and gave it to you—with a seemingly unbreakable string attached.

"I feel like we're in a James Bond movie," she drawled to alleviate the tension. Machiavelli and Umeko had both found her sense of humor amusing.

Mari, however, was not amused. Impatiently, she tapped her beveled red nails on the little table between them. "This is serious business."

Samantha bit back a sharp retort. She wasn't sure she liked Mari. She certainly didn't completely trust her. Mari knew things she wasn't telling. In a situation like this, that was deadly.

"We need to get down to business. Tonight I'll file my report on Nick and tell them everything is fine." Once a week, Mari sent a report on Machiavelli to Watcher headquarters. She always played down his activities to keep interest in him from growing. "And I sent the letter to MacLeod," Mari added. "He should have gotten it by now."

Mari had concocted the idea of enticing MacLeod to Japan from reading Machiavelli's *Chronicle*. MacLeod and he had clashed in the 1600s, and Machiavelli still made overtures to him upon occasion. MacLeod ignored him. Few who had ever gone directly against Machiavelli emerged alive, and he had made alliances with most of the survivors. Some of the alliances had gone sour, and he had taken their heads—or had one of his Immortal followers do it for him. MacLeod stood alone as someone who had fought him and walked away. This unfinished business intrigued Mari, and she insisted that he be lured into helping them. He wouldn't come if they simply asked, she had emphasized, because he wanted to have nothing to do with Machiavelli. So they would have to resort to subterfuge—à la Machiavelli—to obtain his help.

Samantha took a swallow of her Scotch. She drank it as a token act of defiance; Machiavelli preferred she drink white wine or fruity mixed drinks, which he called "ladies' cocktails." He insisted upon calling her Sammi—and everyone followed his lead—because she had been poor, bedraggled Sammi Jo when they had met. Now she called him Machiavelli, though not to his face. He still assumed he was Nicky, the man she loved.

It was to Samantha's benefit that he held women in contempt. It made him less suspicious of her. Or so she hoped.

Once she had pointed out that the queen was the most powerful piece on the board, moving as she pleased, devouring all the other pieces.

*"Everything she does is to protect the king,"* he'd retorted. *"She has no other function. Without him, there's no game at all. Never forget that."*

"We can only hope we've sufficiently intrigued MacLeod," Mari said. "If he thinks that bastard is after him, maybe he'll come and . . ." She glanced up. "They're here." Her demeanor lightened. She smiled brilliantly and waved.

Samantha turned. Machiavelli, her tall, white-haired lover; Mari's brother Ken; and Machiavelli's lieutenant and betrayer, Satoshi Miyamoto, walked toward them. Pretending to cough into his fist, Satoshi flashed the two women a wide-eyed look of pure terror.

"Look at Sato. Something's wrong." Samantha grabbed her purse and half-rose from her chair.

"Sit down," Mari hissed, grabbing her hand. "What are you going to do? Run?"

Samantha couldn't breathe. Because Machiavelli didn't know she was training, she didn't carry a sword. She hadn't felt so vulnerable since Dale had left her. "We were stupid to listen to you. He always knows everything. I'm sure he knows you're his Watcher. He knows what we're up to."

"No. I've checked in with headquarters numerous times. No one's reported any other activity. I'm positive he has no idea." She kept smiling. "Samantha, sit up straight and look happy. He's not going to behead you in public."

"Why would anyone else report any activity? No one else is Watching him. *You're* his Watcher, for God's sake!"

"Activity of the other Immortals around him," Mari said as if she were speaking to an idiot. "Except, of course, for the meetings you and I have had with the others. Those have been reported. But he hasn't sent Ruffio or anyone else on any special errands."

The mention of Ruffio made Samantha's smile fade. She hated the Italian Immortal. Machiavelli's oldest "Beauty," as Machiavelli called his Immortals, Ruffio was a sadistic bully. He hated Samantha for no other reason than that she was in Machiavelli's bed, and that made her powerful, or so he believed. She knew he wanted nothing more in life than to take her head.

And replace her in Machiavelli's life.

"If he doesn't know who you are, why ally himself with your brother?" she asked Mari, forcing herself back to the present. "Why involve himself in your lives?" These were questions she had asked a dozen times, and she had yet to receive completely satisfactory answers.

Mari drew herself up. "Ken is a very powerful and influential man in his own right. He was doing fine before Machiavelli approached him."

Samantha was tired of the woman's pomposity and self-importance. "Now that your brother is in bed with my lover, he's doing even better."

Mari said nothing, only looked down at the table. "Look, as far as Watching goes, no one else has ever had access to the technology I have. Thanks to Ken. Even though he doesn't know he's helping us." Mari managed a genuine smile at her, but it was obvious she, too, had been unnerved by Satoshi's fearful expression. "I can call in the cavalry at any minute and get us all the hell out of here."

"Do it. Make up an excuse and go do it," Samantha said. "We're in trouble."

"My darling." Machiavelli reached their table first and swept Samantha to her feet and into his arms. He kissed her behind the ear, as he always did, and murmured, "I love you, Sammi. And you, beautiful lady." Machiavelli kissed Mari on the cheek. He gestured to her outfit. "What designer is that, Armani? Miyaki?"

Mari's face was white. She said evenly, "A new one. Kimura."

"Ah. Kimura." Ken Iwasawa, dressed in an impeccable, very stylish gray silk suit, took off his sunglasses and gave Mari a once-over. "I see it now. In the cut." He smiled at Machiavelli. "You were right."

Machiavelli winked at Samantha. "Kimura just went public. I told Ken to buy some stock. That man's going to go places."

"Men who understand women always do," Ken said pleasantly. "Well, are you two hungry? Mari-*chan? Tabetai-desuka?*"

"*Hai,*" Mari answered. "I'm starving."

"Good." Machiavelli pulled out his wallet and dropped a few thousand yen on the table. "Will that cover it, my angel?"

"With a generous tip," Samantha said, fighting to keep steady.

"The service was good?" he asked her. She nodded. "*Va bene.* Good works should be rewarded." He nibbled her earlobe. "*Ikimasho.* Let's go, Sammi. We're going to have a most remarkable dinner." He led her toward the exit. It took all her resources not to break into a run. "You're trembling."

"I'm cold. I should have brought a wrap."

"I'll warm you later. Would you like that?" He pulled her close. A wave of dizziness washed over her, and she nodded woodenly.

"Yes, my love," she croaked. "I'd love that."

San Francisco, 1968

*Her name was Sammi Jo Smith and her boyfriend, Dale, had called her an ignorant piece of trailer-park trash and dumped her out of the microbus at San Francisco's Fisherman's Wharf. Before she realized what was happening, he peeled out and zoomed off.*

She was sure he didn't mean it. They had had terrible fights all the way from Tampa Bay to San Francisco, but they always made up. Lordy, how they made up. He was twenty-three and she was sixteen, and he had been around and understood all the complicated stuff like how to get a job and rent apartments, while she had simply run away from home to be with him.

Not that it took much prodding: her mama—who was not her real mama, but she was all Sammi Jo had—was for sure a piece of trailer-park trash, wearing too much makeup and no bras and long hippie dresses you could see through, sleeping with guys she picked up in bars. Their trailer reeked of marijuana, vodka, and sweaty men.

Whenever her mama passed out, most of the men would stumble out of the bedroom and ask Sammi Jo if she wanted to be next. The others didn't ask.

They just took what they wanted.

Dale had promised her he would save her from all that if she would just come away with him. She had really wanted to graduate from high school, but Dale was set on leaving, and that was that. It wasn't until they had crossed two state lines that she found out he was dodging the draft so he wouldn't get sent to Vietnam. He laughed until he cried when she started watching the rearview mirror for the military police or the FBI to come for him.

"You are so ignorant," he'd drawl, and she'd lash out at him because it was true, and she hated that it was true. Then he would start talking psychology to her, telling her about her fixations and her self-esteem, until she knew that if Dale ever left her, she'd be a ripe candidate for suicide.

Now, as the hours dragged by and she stood with the bright blue San Francisco Bay at her back and scanned the crowds of tourists and hippies for sight of him, she had a feeling that made her sway like a reed in a hurricane. She had to hold on to a streetlight to keep from collapsing.

"Help," she whispered, to no one. Her body tingled. She was hungry and thirsty, but she didn't dare move. If she did, she would die.

He would come back for her, she willed. He would come, he would come. He would be so sorry for scaring her.

But why should he come back? She was nothing but white trash.

*She was nothing unless he said so, and he wasn't saying so, not at the moment.*

*He would come because he loved her. Love didn't make no sense; you loved people just because. Leastwise, that's what Dale said.*

*But the shadows lengthened and he didn't come. She was mortified to her soul, wounded to the quick. Angrily she thought,* I ain't no damn dog, *but she felt like one, waiting pathetically for her master. She had one dollar in her macramé purse, fifty cents in the pocket of her jeans. She had no idea where she was, other than it was San Francisco. They had had a plan to meet some people who would help them get to Canada.*

*The fragrance of boiled crabs and sourdough bread was almost more than she could stand. She was so hungry she was afraid she was going to throw up.*

I ain't no dog.

*She sank in a heap to the ground. No one paid her any mind. The shadows melted into night. She couldn't call her mama. They had no phone in the trailer. She could call the bars her mama went to, but she would use up her dollar.*

*And her mama would probably tell her not to come home, anyway. She would tell Sammi Jo she was a burden and no amount of extra welfare money was worth the hassle it was to take care of some other woman's kid.*

*It was true: Sammi Jo wasn't no dog.*

*She was dog shit.*

*She felt awful. She was dying; it was starting to happen. It was just like Dale said it would be. Dying, with a horrible dizziness that made her innards spin.*

*Then a man's hand extended in front of her face, and a deep, wonderful voice inquired gently, "Signorina? May I be of assistance?"*

The restaurant Machiavelli had selected in the Shibuya district was very traditional. It was so exclusive that there was no sign on the street or on its door to announce it. The waitresses wore kimonos dyed with natural indigo, a revered folk art in Japan, and moved with silent grace. So many young Japanese women were coarse and unappealing, Machiavelli often said. However, Samantha now knew he liked to sleep with women like that. He slept with other women all the time.

When she'd been in love with him, she had never noticed his infidelities.

The restaurant floor was straw tatami, the walls of their private room shoji, rice paper. As they sat on their knees on silk cushions around a low wooden table, a koto played discreetly in the background.

Samantha knew men in suits dined on their knees in other rooms, guns beneath their suit jackets, fingers missing. From shoulders to thighs they were covered in ornate and vivid tattoos. They were members of the *yakuza,* the Japanese Mafia, and they were very dangerous men.

Machiavelli was with the Italian mob, and allied with the *yakuza.* He had told Samantha once that if she ever left him, she would have to deal not only with his loyal Immortals, but the Immortals in the *yakuza,* the Italians, and the American Mafia as well.

He had told her only once. He had needed to tell her only once.

Then he had begun to notice the muscles she'd developed working with Umeko. ·

"I've been going to a health club," she'd told him, and joined the Roppongi Fun Health Spa that afternoon to cover her tracks. He had complimented her, seeming unconcerned.

Shortly after that, Umeko had died.

"Fugu," Machiavelli announced, as the waitress brought them a woven tray of warm towels to refresh them. "What do you all think?"

If possible, Satoshi looked more frightened and stared at his chopsticks. Mari made a face of distaste, and said airily, "Not for me, Nick-*san.* I've never understood the concept of culinary Russian roulette."

"But you like to live dangerously." Machiavelli winked at her. "Do you not?"

Mari shrugged. "On my terms. Dying from food is not one of them."

"Relax. The chef is one of the great masters of fugu." He waved his hand to indicate the rooms beyond the borders of the rice walls. "Do you think these samurai would eat here if they didn't trust him implicitly?"

Mari laughed. "That depends on how many of them are eating fugu tonight."

Samantha marveled at her performance. Mari was mortal, and if the blowfish was incorrectly prepared, one bite could kill her. People died in Japan every year from eating fugu.

The waitress appeared with several bottles of sake and glasses of Scotch, and a single Pepsi topped with a cherry and a purple paper umbrella perched on the rim of the glass. It was for Samantha. She bristled but said nothing.

Ken spoke to the waitress in rapid Japanese. Samantha didn't catch much but the words for fish, *sakana,* and fugu. He was ordering their dinner. Machiavelli could have done it—he spoke at least a dozen languages—but he was letting Ken act the big man. Or maybe Machiavelli was covering his tracks in some way. The chess king, sitting in his square while his pawns did the work.

Mari said, "Get me some sushi, Kenny. I want some *maguro.*"

"No. We're all having fugu," Machiavelli cut in, smiling. "No exceptions. I insist." He spoke to the waitress, who nodded.

"I don't want any." Mari raised her chin. "I won't eat any."

"What's the matter, Mari?" Machiavelli raised his brows. "Don't you trust me?"

"I've never eaten fugu, and I never will." There was a quaver in her voice.

"What about you, Satoshi?" Machiavelli asked, shifting his attention to the silent man. "Do you trust me?"

"Whatever you want me to eat, I shall eat," Satoshi said shakily. He swallowed and looked up through his lashes at Samantha.

Like Mari, he was mortal. One morsel of badly prepared fugu and he would die. He had cause to fear death; it was he who had brought Samantha into the group that wanted to kill Machiavelli. It had taken a long time to win her trust; for all Samantha had known, Sato was Machiavelli's plant. But he'd proved himself again and again.

"My good and loyal servant." Machiavelli patted him on the back.

Mari rose. "I'm going home."

"Sit down," Ken ordered.

A shadow moved along their rice-paper wall. Mari and Samantha both stared. The figure grew; it was a man. A large and forbidding man.

*I could take him,* Samantha thought, and realized that here and now, she could not because she must not.

It stopped moving, and loomed over Mari.

"Kenny?" she murmured to him. "Kenny, what's going on?"

"What do you mean?" He poured some sake into one of the thimble-sized cups on the table, handed it to her. "Nothing's going on, little sister."

"That man . . ." She exhaled and took the sake, shaking so badly she spilled the clear liquid on the table.

Machiavelli said, "What man?"

Samantha glanced at the rice wall.

There was no one there.

En route to Washington, D.C.

Joe sipped his bourbon and branch and stretched out his legs. The first-class cabin was nearly empty. Joe was glad. He hadn't sat down with Mac for a good conversation in a while.

"Mac, there's something I've been wondering about. There's a reference to you in Peter Hale's Chronicle for 1658. Right before he died."

The Immortal smiled faintly. There was something troubling him, and Joe wanted to know what it was. Sometimes it helped if he drew MacLeod out on another subject entirely. With enough patience, Mac might open up about his current situation. But Mac was distracted and preoccupied tonight.

"Filling in the blanks, Joe?" MacLeod said gently.

"Won't live long enough to do that," Joe replied. To his surprise, Mac actually laughed.

"All right. Peter Hale," he said, and launched into a great story.

The fugu was presented with elaborate display, the chef standing proudly by the large plate set in the middle of the table.

Everyone stared at it.

"Well," Ken said, clearly nervous. He reached forward with his chopsticks.

Machiavelli held up his hand. "It's my pleasure, as host," he announced, and selected a shiny, perfect square of the potentially lethal fish. He popped it into his mouth. The others watched him.

He spread out his hands. "Perfect." He bowed to the chef and thanked him in Japanese.

Satoshi and Mari visibly relaxed. Mari reached forward with her chopsticks. Satoshi took a gulp of Scotch and picked his up.

Samantha reached impolitely past Mari, grabbed a chunk, and began to chew. Satoshi, watching her, put a bite in his mouth as well.

A strange, hot tingling flashed through her.

Intensified.

Her body went numb.

"No, stop!" she shouted. "It's a trap!"

With a strangled cry, Satoshi fell backward, his head punching through the rice paper wall.

"No," she keened.

Then she died.

"Oh, my poor *bella* Sammi," Machiavelli murmured to his little American Immortal. "Poor sweet darling."

Samantha lay fully clothed across their bed in his palatial penthouse apartment in the Ginza district. He loved the busy boulevards and espresso houses of the district, the stores that rivaled Knightsbridge and Paris, Rodeo Drive and New York's Fifth Avenue.

The girl's hair was disheveled, very sexy. Her chest rose and fell. Those breasts would be firm and round until the day she died.

The tea the maid had brought her was untouched. He picked up the girl's hand and kissed it. After all this time, he still thought of her as "the girl," sometimes almost forgetting her name.

"I don't know why the fugu took so long to affect me. I was sure it was all right. You know I would never have let them eat it if I'd thought it would hurt them." And that was true. He had not ordered bad fugu. He had had the chef killed for his ineptitude.

But he had also managed to use the situation to his advantage.

Of course.

"If you'd thought it would kill them," she croaked. "Kill Satoshi." Mari and Ken had survived, although Mari was in the hospital. Ken had not had any fugu.

"*Sì.* Kill them." He cradled her head against his chest. "You believe me, don't you?"

"Yes. Of course I do."

He closed his eyes and laughed silently. Poor Sammi Jo. Always so innocent, so transparent.

So pliable.

"Good, my darling. *Bellissima donna.* It's a good thing Dr. Sunamoto was in the restaurant, yes? To announce that you were not dead, but only in a coma?" *To hear you shout that it was a trap?*

"You should get away for a while," he said, stroking her beautiful hair. "A change of scene will do you good." She'd been waiting for a chance to escape, hadn't she? "I know. It's been a while since we visited Alan Woodrich. You'll see him for me, won't you, *cara?* In Washington?"

The pulse in her neck pumped like a jackhammer. "Nicky, don't make me. Let me go to the compound instead." The compound was located miles out of Tokyo in the lovely, green countryside of this busy little island. Among cherry and plum trees and old caves filled with the bones of many of his enemies, sat his traditional-style villa. It was fully staffed at all times, and he went there whenever he could. Thanks to modems, faxes, and e-mail, he could run his empire as easily from there as here. But he spent most of his time in Tokyo, exploiting the fact that his physical presence intimidated those who worked for him.

His American Beauty was practically in tears. It was pathetic, the ease with which he manipulated these naive conspirators. Did they truly believe he didn't know they were sending chess moves to Duncan MacLeod, trying to pass them off as overtures to MacLeod by him?

Duncan MacLeod. Little did the girl know that the man she sought—MacLeod—was on his way to Washington as well. Time for them to meet, time for him to come to Japan and lose his damn Scots head. Time to rid himself of all of them, faithless Beauties and old nemesis. Thanks to this brave new world, he was amassing power he could heretofore only dream of. Better to shed nettlesome distractions and potential obstacles as efficiently—and as soon—as possible.

Meanwhile, there she lay, stiff and trembling, trying to decipher his expression. He stifled the urge to burst out laughing and instead ran his tongue along her neck. She stiffened; for that alone, he would one day kill her.

"I've explained it all to you, my darling. Woodrich's government is doing things that could harm us and all other Immortals. We need to know what they're doing. We need the same technology. Since he no longer shares with us freely, we have to persuade him."

She lay still in his arms.

"All right," she said finally. As if she had actually decided to obey him; as if she had a choice.

"Good girl." He began to unzip her dress. That she didn't want him but would yield excited him. It had always excited him.

He wondered idly if the stiletto she had stolen from him two years before and hidden under her pillow was within her grasp. If she knew it had belonged to the Prince himself, Lorenzo de' Medici. And if she would ever have the nerve to use it. That would be diverting indeed. Useless on her part, but amusing nonetheless.

Far more interesting than simply beheading her while she slept, which was his current plan.

"What have I been thinking?" he whispered to her. *What a horse's ass I am! I should take her head while we're coupling. The Marquis de Sade wrote about such a death. It would be far more interesting. An orgasmic Quickening!*

"What, Nicky?"

Ah, the hesitation, the tremor in her voice!

"We should get married. We would be married for all time."

"Oh, Nicky," she managed. "How . . . wonderful."

He slid his hand under the pillow. *Si,* the knife was there. Excellent. He wrapped his hand around it. Sharp darts pierced his fingertips. Blood trickled; the wounds began to heal at once. He reveled in his power. He had never stopped enjoying it, and he never would.

Never.

He knew he was the one, the last one. Who else had the cunning and intelligence? Expert swordsmanship was such a minor component of the Game. Only Immortals who didn't have his cunning need concern themselves with primitive notions of physical prowess.

Immortals like Duncan MacLeod.

*"Si, si,"* he said jubilantly. "Very wonderful. Very, very wonderful."

* * *

The next day, Samantha brought Mari flowers when she visited her in the hospital. The somber nurse bowed when she took them and whisked them away, presumably to find a vase.

Mari's face was slack and her eye ticked as she smiled at Samantha and held out one limp hand. She said, "Welcome back."

Samantha sank into the chair beside her bed. A monitor beeped continually, making her edgy. "You know I died."

"I figured as much. I don't know why I didn't." She leaned back against the pillows. "Maybe this is a stupid plan after all. I'm not sure we can successfully lure MacLeod here with our fake messages from the great Machiavelli, no matter how much they despise each other. Maybe only Machiavelli himself can do things like that." She smiled languidly at Samantha. "We should have sent him photos of you. It's difficult for him to say no to beautiful women."

Mari knew Samantha had become infatuated with MacLeod after reading his Watchers' Chronicles and seeing pictures of him. Before, he had been a simple legend to Samantha, as he was to most Immortals. Now he was a handsome man with an unforgettable face and a name that conjured romantic images. A hero of flesh and blood, and a desirable one at that.

"Maybe we should be more direct," Mari went on. "Just call him up and ask him for his help. He might do it."

"If he doesn't, whoever calls will have broken cover for nothing," Samantha countered. "We don't know that Machiavelli meant for the fugu to be bad. He did give you CPR, you know. He could have let you die."

"Oh, he knew. Of course he knew. This way, with me alive, it's grayer. He can confuse us. It's working, isn't it?"

Samantha touched the petals of Mari's flowers. They were already dying. Mortals died a little every day. How did they stand it?

"Let me think tonight about contacting the Highlander," Mari said. "Meanwhile, try to find out if the second letter went out today. I gave it to Taro before dinner."

"Taro?" He was one of their secret band, the newest Immortal in Machiavelli's camp.

"You're not the only one who gets turned on by men who're good with weapons." Mari's chuckle was deep and guttural.

"Ladies," Machiavelli said from the door. *"Buon giorno. Cara,* how sweet of you to visit our patient." Machiavelli swept into the room and gave Samantha a kiss on her cheek. "How are you feeling, Mari-*chan?*"

"Tired," she admitted. "I understand I have you to thank for my life."

He preened. "Your heart stopped. I started it again. I would do the same for anyone. Would I not, Sammi?" He looked at Samantha and grinned.

Samantha gave him a sad half-smile and remembered:

*Too many drugs, way too many, the scourge of the sixties, as the room whirled and she sank into the piles of cushions. The moving black lights played over the posters: Ship of Peace, Jim Morrison, War is Not Healthy for Children and Other Living Things.*

*Her nose was bleeding. Her heartbeat was irregular.*

*"I'm dyin'," she said, as he came into the master bedroom of his mansion. He had given her the drugs and promised her they would make her feel like she was in heaven. "I ain't worth nothin', and now I'm gonna die like a sick dog."*

*"You are going to die," he said, "but don't be afraid. I will make you live forever. Have no fear. Trust me. Look into my eyes, and you will live forever."*

*"Oh, Nicky, I don't wanna die."*

*"Hold on to me. I promise you, you will rise again."*

Mari's eye ticked. Samantha's heart was in her throat. She didn't know what to say, what to do.

"You look exhausted. We should go, Sammi." Machiavelli took her hand and gave it a shake. "We can visit again tomorrow."

"All right." Samantha pushed back her chair and stood. "Mari, I'm sorry." For doubting her, for disliking her.

Mari smiled bravely at her. "I'm going to be fine. See you tomorrow."

Samantha looked again at the flowers. "Yes." They clasped hands. Mari's flesh was icy. Samantha was alarmed, but it would do no good to ask how Mari was doing. Japanese physicians did not share the condition of their patients with anyone, even the patients themselves.

Machiavelli led Samantha away.

Outside in the hallway, her knees buckled and she pressed her forehead against the wall. Sato, her friend, dead forever. Mari, on the threshold, perhaps. Machiavelli had killed before, and she had known about it and done nothing to stop him. She had cowered and wept and twisted her hands. He would kill again, and she knew that, too.

And if she failed, each death would be her fault. Umeko had taught her that she had an obligation to stop him. Each head taken, each soul dispatched, lay on her head.

If she kept her head.

*"Cara, cara,* don't despair. She will be fine."

"Oh, Nicky," she whispered, remembering when he had been her hero.

*MacLeod, please. Please save us,* she thought, as Machiavelli gave her a hug and said, "I'll make everything fine, baby. Don't be afraid."

"Afraid?" she echoed, trying to sound calm.

"Death comes for them. They expect it. But I'm sure she'll live a good while longer."

"I hope so." She gazed at him earnestly. "I pray for it."

"Sweet girl." He patted her cheek. "You go home in the limo. I'll be home very late tonight. Will you be all right?"

"Of course."

"Not too bored?"

"No. I'll find something to do."

Mari's Watcher report. She hadn't been able to file it. How much of a time window did she have? Would they investigate if they didn't hear from her?

As the limo pulled away from the hospital, Samantha told the driver to stop at Mari's penthouse apartment. If he reported to Machiavelli that she'd gone there, she would tell him she'd gone to get some things Mari had requested.

A few months before, Samantha had inadvertently stolen the security key, thinking it belonged to Machiavelli's private office. Now this key let her into the building, past the doorman, and into the private elevator.

And into Mari's luxurious apartment.

She hesitated. She had never been here alone. She took off her shoes and shuffled across the yards of white velvet carpet soft and deep as powdered snow, into and through the sunken living room, and up a trio of stairs to Mari's office.

Mari's computer sat on her desk. Samantha flipped it on and went to the main menu. There was no password, which surprised her. Maybe Mari figured the house key was protection enough.

One of the files read, *Wfile. Watcher file?* Samantha took a chance and opened it.

*Subject took girlfriend and others to dinner.*

That was the only line. She must have planned to finish it when she returned from the restaurant.

The phone rang. Samantha jumped guiltily. The message machine came on. A familiar male voice spoke in rapid Japanese, too fast for Samantha to decipher. Nor could she quite place the voice. Mari had many friends, male and female. Samantha had met many of them.

The caller hung up and Samantha nervously typed in, *Dinner remarkedly uneventful.*

*Mari Iwasawa.*

The phone rang again. It was too much activity for her comfort level. What if Mari really had asked a friend to drop by and get some things?

"How long are these things supposed to be, anyway?" she muttered, and hit *send.*

This week's was real short.

# Chapter Eleven

===

*"A flower falls, even though we love it; and a weed grows, even though we do not love it."*

—Zen saying

There's no time for us.

*She was running to him, her mouth a scream, her eyes depthless pools of fear. Running and shouting his name, but the sound that shattered his heart was the report of a gun.*

"Tessa," MacLeod whispered, and woke himself up. He lay in a sweat in his hotel room, the sheets thrown off, the air chilly on his bare skin.

His cheeks were wet with tears.

He sat up and wiped his face with shaking hands. How many dawns before this nightmare left him?

He knew the answer he wanted: Never. As long as she came to him in his dreams, bad or good, she would never really be gone.

As long as she never left, he could go on.

Tessa, his mortal lover for thirteen years. Tessa, an artist, a generous, creative and lovely woman, who had been killed by a random act of violence: a junkie's bullet, when he had spent countless sleepless nights worrying that an Immortal would end her life to get at him.

"When I die," she had once said, very seriously, "you must love again."

He had believed then that he would.

There had been others.

But to love someone again as he had loved Tessa? He wasn't sure that was possible.

*There's no time for us, because time has lost its meaning. Time is a mortal concept.*

He looked in the window and saw a ghost. Perhaps the ghost of the man he once had been, facing one lifetime of passion, of despair, and of hope.

Ah, yes, hope.

He lay back down.

"Good night, bonnie Tess," he whispered, and closed his eyes.

*She ran toward him, her mouth a scream.*
Who dares to love forever?

*The man was kind to her.*

*He took Sammi Jo to his mansion above the bay and told a woman to give her something to eat and to put her in bed. There were all kind of people there, and it wasn't 'til much later that Sammi Jo learned that most of them would never die. Thanks to the man, whom she called Nicky, they were what you called Immortal.*

*And, thanks to him, she would be, too.*

*But in the beginning, she didn't know that. She only knew that Nicky had a lot of money, and friends in high places, as they said, and that speaking of high, they smoked a lot of grass in Nicky's fine, big house.*

*They dropped a lot of acid.*

*And in the swirling, happy visions of iridescent sounds and chiming colors, he fed her pills like grapes, his face the sun and the center of her universe. Held in arms both strong and gentle, her face showered with kisses, new clothes and shoes heaped around her bed.*

*He gave her books, fully expecting she was smart enough to understand them. He talked to her like she had a brain.*

*He did not treat her like a dog.*

*But she would have lain down at his feet like one if he'd ever snapped his fingers and told her to.*

*"That's the problem, bella mia," he said once, sighing and looking frustrated.*

*She hadn't gotten what he meant until it was too late.*

Mari was missing.

Samantha had called her that morning at the hospital to let her know she had filed her Watcher report. But Mari Iwasawa was no longer listed as a patient.

"He's killed her," she told her coconspirators.

In the thirty years Samantha had known Machiavelli, he had always gathered around himself a group of Immortals he called his Beauties. He also named them by chess pieces. She was the queen. Ruffio was the king's rook. No one found this questionable; indeed, it was a great honor to be one of the seven pieces of the inner sanctum. He called no one a pawn, but they all were pawns. Sometimes it took the Beauties a while to figure that out. In her case, almost twenty-seven years. Ruffio still hadn't figured it out.

But the ones who had were gathered with her under cover of darkness in an abandoned sake storage facility near the harbor. Seven Immortals and at least a dozen mortals sat in silence as Samantha described the fugu incident, her visit to the hospital, and now, the fact that Mari was no longer listed as a patient. Dead silence filled her pauses as she fought for control. She was terrified and grieving. Satoshi had been her best friend within the rebellious group. He had trusted her enough to tell her about the others and defend her when they'd refused to meet with her. It was a tremendous act of courage on Satoshi's part: she was Machiavelli's mistress, and she might have told him everything rather than align herself with the other side. For none of them wanted anything less than his head.

It was a risk each was willing to take. The alternative was worse: their existence precarious, their lives controlled and dominated for the rest of eternity by a man with an insatiable need to control and dominate. Their new God for the new millennium, and they, less than the dust beneath His feet.

Their unhappiness and fear had been brewing for a long time, but no one had known what to do about it. They had all been afraid to speak of it, not knowing who was loyal to him and who dreamed of being free of him forever.

Then Mari, whose brother had just consummated business ties with Machiavelli, took over as his Watcher when her first Japanese assignment was killed, and discovered things that had frightened her so badly she was willing to do anything to stop him. She had never revealed the details, but they had to do with controlling vast computer networks.

She had carefully approached first this one, then that one, bringing them together into a band who shared that common goal of taking his head. "If he's not stopped soon, he'll be the most powerful entity on earth," she had warned them. "The time to act has come."

But they were outnumbered, and outgunned. Machiavelli had vast resources in intelligence and loyal followers, mortal and Immortal, who would do anything, kill anyone, he told them to.

Now she was gone. They were leaderless.

"Did you actually see Satoshi-*san* die?" Aaron, a new Immortal from Israel, asked Samantha.

"I saw him fall. Then I died," she said.

"Could it have been a trick?" There was hope in Aaron's voice.

"Yes." After the initial shock, she had thought of that, too. Hoped that.

"Maybe he's holding him somewhere. If we could find him—"

"That could be what he wants us to think," Samantha interjected. "To distract us. We have to stay focused."

"I still don't think he knows about us. I really don't," Aaron insisted.

From the darkness came the deep, resonant voice of Ed, formerly an investment banker, and now one of Machiavelli's most trusted lieutenants. "I have never understood why we don't simply approach MacLeod and tell him what's going on."

There were murmurs of assent.

"Machiavelli's sending me to Washington," Samantha announced. "I'll get a layover on the West Coast and go to MacLeod. I'll talk to him."

"Yeah, I'll bet you will," Aaron teased. They all knew she was intrigued by Duncan MacLeod. They were, too, but in a different way.

"Don't book the layover in advance," Taro warned her. Taro was a very new Immortal. Many of Machiavelli's Beauties were. He was rarely joined by any of the older Immortals. Mari said it was because of his reputation for using young Immortals to achieve his ends, risking their heads unnecessarily. "Machiavelli-*sama* might find out." He paused. "Somehow." Machiavelli's vast knowledge of things he shouldn't know was puzzling and frightening to them all.

"Yes." She nodded. Butterflies danced in her stomach. She was going to meet Duncan MacLeod of the Clan MacLeod. She was going to talk to the Highlander himself, try to enlist him in their cause. What if he said no? What if Machiavelli found out what she had done?

MacLeod would protect her. Mari had told her all about him. He wouldn't turn his back on a woman in danger.

"Please excuse, let's go now," Hiroshi said. He was Machiavelli's relief driver. "We have to get Sammi-*san* back to the apartment." Machiavelli was "out with the boys," which could mean he was drinking in a hostess bar or murdering his enemies in slow and painful ways. He usually came home after two, but that was no guarantee that he might not decide to make it an early night. Samantha had taken a great risk staying this late. In that, he *did* treat her like a dog: she was to stay close to home, dutifully and eagerly waiting for him.

"*Domo sumimasen.* I have one request," Taro said, clearing his throat as if embarrassed to speak.

"*Hai?* Yes?" Samantha answered kindly.

"When you meet MacLeod-*san,* try to buy his sword. I've heard his *katana* is the finest ever made."

"You've got to be kidding," Samantha said. "He'd never part with it."

"Not even for my Corvette?" He had just purchased a shiny, candy-apple red, 1958 'Vette. In Japan, such a car cost more than a house. He'd told her that now that he was Immortal, he could indulge his appetite for fancy things, since he'd have centuries to pay off his credit cards.

"I doubt it. But I'll ask." Samantha resisted the temptation to laugh at him. He was young and untrained—he had no idea how ridiculous his request was. She held out her hand in the dark, found his shoulder, and kissed his cheek. He hissed, the Japanese reaction for shyness or surprise.

"We may never see each other again," she said somberly.

"We will," Taro insisted. "If MacLeod comes, I know we will."

Samantha prayed he was right.

And that MacLeod *would* come.

# Chapter Twelve

===

*"When you are going to attack nearby, make it look as if you are going to go a long way; when you are going to attack far away, make it look as if you are going just a short distance."*

—Sun Tzu, *The Art of War*

Washington, D.C.

Alan Woodrich had left a note and a house key for Dawson at the Department of Justice, explaining that he had been called away on unexpected business but hoped to be back in a couple of days. Dawson didn't mind; he had war buddies to see and a memorial to visit.

It was almost ten in the evening of the fourth day when MacLeod and Meyer-Dinkmann parted in the chill at the Metro station near the quaint seafood restaurant where they had dined. It was located in the historic section of Alexandria, Virginia, the posh Washington suburb where corporate attorneys and high-level bureaucrats lived.

MacLeod and the German curator had spent the last four days going over the swords in the Smithsonian's collection, and this was their farewell dinner. Dawson had called MacLeod that afternoon to tell him Woodrich was back and they'd meet MacLeod in the lobby bar of his hotel, the Capitol Hilton, for drinks after dinner.

Glad of his warm turtleneck sweater and duster, MacLeod caught the next subway train to Washington. He compared it to the Parisian métro and the ease of travel in large, historic cities. With his portable computer closed on his lap, he allowed his mind to wander, remembering Paris, the model city for Washington, as it had been when he had first visited it, and how it was now. It had fared better than its progeny.

The Capitol Hilton was in a good location for tourists and politicos, a short walk to the White House and an even shorter limo ride. The lobby was furnished like a men's club, which it essentially was: except for a scattering of female politicians and sexy young "aides," the bar was populated with older men in dark suits. Younger men hovered around them. Great whales and darting, voracious pelicans—or were they albatrosses?—in the uneasy and murky seas of government.

*Sassenachs,* he thought wryly, as he walked toward Dawson's chair. The aristocrats. The elite ruling class.

He caught sight of the salt-and-pepper crown of Joe's head above the back of a burgundy chair facing away from him in a secluded corner of the bar. As he walked toward him, a slender Japanese woman in a black crepe dress brushed past him, murmuring, "Looking for someone?"

For a second he was taken aback; then he realized she was plying the world's oldest profession and grinned to himself.

"Always, and not right now," he told her. *"Domo arigato gozaimasu."*

*"Domo sumimasen.* Please allow me to present my *meishi."* With an incline of her head, she handed him a demure white business card and glided away. *Umeko Takahashi, private escort to distinguished gentlemen.* Surprised, MacLeod pocketed it.

"Hey," he said as he reached Dawson's table, giving him a nod.

"Mac," Dawson replied in a soft voice. MacLeod cocked his head; Dawson tipped his head toward the chair facing his. A gaunt man of perhaps fifty sat hunched, staring at the cocktail table. He had short, gray hair, a suit a level or two above standard government issue, and enormous circles under his eyes. His skin was pasty and his lower lip trembled as if he might burst into tears. There were two empty tumblers in front of him.

Mac sat in a leather chair at Joe's right, sinking into the richness of it as he set his laptop carrier on the floor. A waitress arrived with a tray and put another tumbler before the man and gave something tall and clear to Dawson. Soda water, MacLeod guessed.

"Single malt whiskey," he told the waitress. Dawson's companion heard his voice and started, looking up. MacLeod extended his hand. "Duncan MacLeod," he said to the man.

"Joe's friend." His brief smile was genuine. "I'm Alan

Woodrich. Which you've probably figured out." The man shook MacLeod's hand as if he would have preferred to grab the tumbler.

"How'd it go today?" Dawson asked. It had become something of a joke between the two of them: even Immortals could get tired of discussing swords for four entire days. Maybe intelligent people could get bored after all.

"Meyer-Dinkmann certainly knows his weapons." MacLeod thought he might have recognized one or two from days and battles gone by, but even an Immortal's recollection dims upon occasion. He sipped his drink. "I'm glad you could get back to Washington," he said to Woodrich.

"Yes. Unexpected business. You know how it goes." This time, when Woodrich smiled, it appeared the effort would crack his face apart.

"Did I mention Al works for the National Security Administration? The spookiest of the spook departments in our great nation's branch of espionage?" Dawson supplied.

Woodrich shook his head. "Joey, enough with the jokes. How can I work for a department that doesn't exist?"

"Same way we fought in a war that wasn't a war," Dawson countered.

MacLeod thought, *That's one for you, my friend.* Vietnam had been wrong.

So many battles were.

Woodrich threw back his drink. MacLeod traded looks with Dawson, who shrugged uncomprehendingly.

Woodrich said, "So how do you like our poor, sad city?"

MacLeod thought of the men who had dreamed the capital into being. The hopes they had had for mankind; their high regard for the human spirit. They would be desolate to see what a wasteland the beautiful temple to democracy had become.

"It has many points in its favor," MacLeod allowed. "There are many national capitals far poorer and sadder."

"But we weren't supposed to be." Woodrich gazed into space, haunted, exhausted. "We were supposed to sow the fruits of freedom. Liberty." He laughed bitterly and threw back his drink. He slammed down his glass.

"They must have bar snacks in here, Mac," Dawson hinted. "What do you think?"

MacLeod was anything but hungry, but he understood that Dawson wanted to sober up his friend. He said, "Nothing as good as your buffalo wings, I'll bet."

Dawson waved regally. "You're probably right. But some wings and some coffee would do me."

Woodrich huffed, then bobbed his head. "I could use one more drink." He held up his finger. "One more for the boys who didn't come back, Joey."

"Al . . ."

"For the bright-eyed boys who never came back," he said. "You. Me. We didn't come back."

Dawson sighed. "All right, Al." He signaled the waitress.

"We're cabbing it," Woodrich told MacLeod, as if to apologize for his drinking. "My car . . . I had a little mishap while I was gone."

"Oh, you drove?" MacLeod asked easily, but his curiosity was piqued. This man left town when one of his best friends was on his way to see him; he was halfway to a nervous breakdown; and he had just been in a car accident.

"It's easier than the train. It only takes an hour." He seemed to realize he was giving away information. The fact that it mattered to him made MacLeod even more curious. "Or so."

The round of drinks came. MacLeod stuck to his first single malt, making it last while Woodrich sucked down his fourth whiskey. Maybe the man was getting a divorce. Maybe he'd gotten bad news from his doctor. Whatever the case, MacLeod was sorry for Joe that they'd come all this way to visit a man who was in no shape to entertain company.

"Did you hear Beauchard's speech last night?" Woodrich asked them. "I thought it was brilliant." His mood lightened. "He could really turn this country around."

Senator Anthony Beauchard of Virginia was stumping for the Republican presidential nomination. He was billing himself as someone who could "Take Back America."

"But do you think he'll get the votes?" Dawson asked. "Some of his positions aren't very popular."

MacLeod hid a smile. Dawson hated Beauchard. More than once he'd said he'd move to Australia if Beauchard became the next president.

"People have a knee-jerk dislike of him because they don't want to admit he's right. This was a good country. But it's been ruined by people who won't take responsibility for their lives. Welfare cheats and drug pushers. It's time to get tough."

"Al, you sound like a *Nazi*. What're you going to do, line all the poor people against a wall and shoot them?"

"I'm amazed at you, Joey. I can't believe you even said that. Listen, Tony has some great work programs to get people off welfare. He believes everyone has a chance. They just have to take it."

"A chance? If you're some black kid in Harlem?"

MacLeod crossed his legs, finished his drink, and listened quietly as the two men began to argue.

He tensed as a tingle spread through him: an Immortal loomed nearby.

On alert, he scanned the room, assessing each face, anticipating a subtle nod of acknowledgment.

The tingle vanished.

MacLeod cut into the discussion. "I'm still pretty wiped out from the time change. I think I'll make it an early night."

Dawson nodded. "Good night, Mac. I'll call you tomorrow morning. Say, nine? Alan's got a tour of the Pentagon set up. You're welcome to come."

"Yes," Woodrich said. He raised his hand as a waitress neared. She nodded and came toward them.

"That'd be interesting." MacLeod stood and held out his hand. "Nice to meet you."

"Until tomorrow." Woodrich shook with him. His hand was clammy. MacLeod could smell his fear. He wasn't sure he wanted Dawson going anywhere with him. Ah, well, Joe had always been able to take care of himself.

He pulled out a credit card; Woodrich waved his hand and said, "On me. I insist."

MacLeod thanked him, retrieved his laptop, and began to sweep the lobby. There was nothing suspicious, just the albatrosses, whales and occasional mermaids conversing at tables, bellhops steering luggage carts toward the reception, the concierge on the phone.

He put his hand on the hilt of his *katana* and headed for the elevator. A small group clustered in front of the doors, waiting. None was Immortal. He folded his hands and rocked back easily on his heels.

As soon as the elevator came, he made a sharp left and took the stairs.

His room was on the fifth floor, and he made quick time. The hall was deserted. Though he detected no Immortals, he eased the *katana* out and kept it at the ready. There were other dangers in the world, and his instincts told him to be cautious.

Ninjalike, he crept toward his room. His footsteps were soundless. When he reached his door, he put the laptop carrier on the floor, withdrew his key card, and inserted it into the lock. The green light blinked, and he threw the door open. His left hand found the light switch while the right pulled out his sword.

Nothing.

He inspected the rooms—the sitting room in green and white with the ubiquitous television; the luxurious bathroom; the bedroom with its large, empty bed. The closets were clear; so was the space under the bed. Nothing had been moved. No Immortal was near.

*How would you feel, Joe, if you woke up each morning of eternity knowing someone might kill you today?*

Woodrich looked like a man who felt like that.

MacLeod went back to the front door to get his computer. On the floor beside it was a folded note on an ornate silver tray:

*P-K4.*

No Immortal had left the note in the hallway. He would have sensed it.

He turned the paper over. There was an address handwritten at the bottom of the page: 4 Piazza Chondo, Tokyo, Japan, along with the postal code and a fax number. Did he remember Machiavelli's handwriting? Were the thin, Gothic letters his? He examined the tray, realizing it probably belonged to the hotel. It wasn't as fine as it appeared on first glance, just cheap plate.

MacLeod shut the door and put the note on the table in the sitting room. He pulled his laptop out of the case, plugged into the phone jack, and booted up. He brought up the main menu. There were three messages from someone named GRAND MASTER in his mail box:

*P-K4.*

*P-K4.*

*P-K4.*

It had to be Machiavelli. He read the forwarding addresses. The last address in the header was for a server in Tokyo. That Machiavelli was computer literate surprised him not in the least. He would expect the Immortal, a ferreter of intelligence and exploiter of information, to have tentacles in all the latest forms of technology.

He turned off the computer without answering and made a request for a wake-up call in the morning. Then he took a shower and was in bed with a book Meyer-Dinkmann had given him when his room phone rang.

He picked it up. "MacLeod."

"It's Alan Woodrich. Can you come right over? There's been trouble. Joe told me to call you."

"What kind of trouble? Where's Joe?"

"He's, um, injured."

MacLeod jumped to his feet. "He's hurt? What happened?" With his free hand he gathered up his clothes.

"He's . . . I think he'll be okay."

"Did you call an ambulance?"

There was a pause. "I can't. Please, just come."

"Give me directions."

Woodrich rattled them off. MacLeod slammed down the phone, dressed, and grabbed his sword.

Samantha flew into her hotel room down the street from the Capitol Hilton, threw her carpetbag on the floor, and fell backward onto the bed fully dressed and in her cowboy boots.

*Duncan MacLeod was in Washington.*

Incredible. Amazing.

And too much of a coincidence.

Per Machiavelli's orders, she had followed Woodrich after her meeting with him to his own meeting with the other mortal in the bar of the Hilton. Watching from afar, she was almost sorry for his distress.

Machiavelli had never explained the exact nature of the threat Woodrich posed, and at first, she had trusted his statement that the man needed to be controlled. Now she was not so sure. But she wasn't sure of anything, anymore.

As for example, when Duncan MacLeod had walked into the bar. *Duncan MacLeod.*

One look at him, dark and tall and intimidating, and she had fled. She knew he had sensed her; she knew he had tried to locate her.

She should have seized the chance and approached him.

But why was he there? More to the point, why was he there with Woodrich? What did he know?

Was he working with Machiavelli?

"Ask him," she said aloud, and pushed off the bed. She would go straight to MacLeod, right now. This time she wouldn't lose her nerve. Her head, maybe, but not her nerve.

The others were counting on her.

She picked up the phone and dialed Taro's home phone number in Japan. "C'mon, c'mon," she urged the connection, as a series of clicks and soft background noises in the earpiece made a counterpoint to her heartbeat. Finally the phone rang. His machine picked up. She couldn't leave a message. It was too dangerous.

She called a couple others. No one was home. That terrified her. *Someone* should be home.

She licked her lips and picked up the large bag that served both as purse and overnight case. And she picked up her sword, a short *Shinto o-dachi* that Umeko had given her. It had been forged in 1655 by a Shinto priest named Buso. Samantha knew Umeko had taken the sword from someone she had killed. Would MacLeod eventually take it from her?

She took a breath, put on her coat, and went out the door.

MacLeod ran to the parking garage, where his rental car had sat unused for the majority of the trip. He gunned the engine and sped away, his reflexes coming into play: within the hurricane of his fear for Joe lay a seed of deep calm and steadiness. Despite his urgency, his mind began to map out contingencies and strategies: what to do if an Immortal was there; if a common mortal criminal was there; if Joe was severely injured; if Joe was dead.

*No, not dead,* his mind insisted; he wouldn't let himself go there. He had to stay in control. His sword was ready. He must be, too.

It took him thirty minutes to reach Woodrich's apartment building, a Colonial of brick and green trim. He announced himself to the doorman, who had already received instructions to let him up, and this time took the elevator, only because it was quicker.

He rapped sharply on Woodrich's door. It opened immediately. Woodrich stood before him in a dim foyer, his white shirt streaked with blood. MacLeod pushed him out of the way.

"Joe!"

"Mac. In here."

Following Joe's voice, MacLeod strode into what looked to be a home office. The room was a shambles, filing cabinet drawers upside down on the floor, papers everywhere, a chair and a coffee table overturned.

On a black leather couch, Dawson reclined with an ice pack on his forehead. His face was mottled with cuts and bruises. He waved a hand at MacLeod and said, "I'm okay. Just a little shaken."

MacLeod crossed to him and lifted the ice pack. A bump the size of a plum bulged from Dawson's forehead. MacLeod checked his eyes. They were reassuringly clear.

"What happened?" he asked.

"The cab driver was having trouble making change. I took the key and came on up because I had to use the can. I surprised two guys. They were ransacking the place."

"Two guys," MacLeod repeated.

"One Asian. One had some kind of European accent. Maybe Italian."

MacLeod made himself breathe. Machiavelli wouldn't do his dirty work himself. If he had anything to do with this.

"Where else does it hurt?" MacLeod pressed on Dawson's rib cage.

"Damn!" he said, catching his breath, and waved MacLeod off. "Mac, I'm okay. Trust me. I know when I'm really hurt."

MacLeod stood and looked hard at Woodrich. "Who were they and what were they after?"

Woodrich shook his head. "I don't know."

MacLeod said, "If I don't get answers, I'm calling the cops."

"No," Woodrich blurted out. He didn't realize MacLeod was no more anxious to bring in the police than he was. More than one police investigator of more than one department had observed that a certain Mr. Duncan MacLeod had been present at a few too many crime scenes. "Please."

MacLeod waited. When Woodrich made no answer, MacLeod pulled his cell phone from his jeans pocket.

"All right," Woodrich said.

"Tell me all of it," MacLeod ordered sternly.

"I have access to . . . technology. I . . ." He looked toward the wall. "I'll be killed if I tell you this."

"You'll be killed if you don't."

"No. Because he doesn't have . . ." He sighed. "He doesn't have all of it yet."

"And that's why those men were here."

He shook his head. "My contact understands that we aren't finished with the project. There are some big bugs in the software."

"Who is he?"

"I don't know."

"You've been selling secrets to him and you don't know? NSA secrets?" MacLeod gestured for Woodrich to follow him out the door. Dawson started to get up. MacLeod growled at him, "Stay put," and ushered Woodrich out of the apartment and into the corridor.

"My place is clean. I have devices that sweep for bugs on a continual basis," Woodrich huffed, sounding insulted.

"You also thought it was safe enough for my friend to enter," MacLeod responded. "Or maybe Joe was your first line of defense."

"No, never." Woodrich stuffed his hands in his trouser pockets. "Look, please take Joey back to your place. I'll deal with this. It's not your business."

"Wrong." MacLeod waited.

"I've already said too much."

"And I'm telling you, if you don't tell me everything, you'll be dead before tomorrow."

Woodrich's eyes widened. "Are you threatening me?"

"I'm trying to help you," MacLeod said, exasperated.

"Why should you?"

"Why shouldn't I?"

"Joey said some things about you," Woodrich observed. "Things I'm beginning to believe."

MacLeod was on his guard. "What kind of things?"

"That you're one altruistic son of a bitch. Some kind of throwback knight in shining armor."

He relaxed, ashamed for having doubted Joe's discretion for even one second. "We all have our faults. What's yours?"

"Beauchard." He sighed. "I wanted him elected. I started ah, checking on things for him."

"Checking on things. What things?"

"I captured and copied e-mail that would help Tony. Classified stuff. Senate e-mail. Whatever his opponents sent out."

"That's what your contact is after? Political information?"

Woodrich shook his head. "That's small potatoes. What he wants is . . ." He trailed off.

"Go on."

Woodrich reddened. "Ever read William Gibson? The science-fiction writer?" he asked.

"Yes."

"You know in those books how he pictured the future? Electronic messages captured at the point of origin, saved or modified, rerouted?"

MacLeod narrowed his eyes. "Yes."

"Anyone can do a lot of the lower-level stuff. There are all kinds of products that capture your phone number and match it with census data, buying habits, your credit report. For sixty bucks you can buy a gizmo that'll alter your voice on your home phone. You can sound like a woman if you're a man, a child, whatever you want." He was warming to his subject.

"But we're talking about a serious, all-encompassing capture system. A global network where all the routers are programmed to send a specific user whatever he wants."

MacLeod said, "You can program the routers?"

Woodrich turned to him. "They're like satellites for computers. They usually look like little computers themselves. They're the devices that receive Internet messages, among other things, and route them to the next router, which sends them to the next one, and so on, until they're sent to your netserver and then to you."

MacLeod was stunned. His mind raced as the implications sank in: you could access military secrets, court records, hospital test results. Telephone calls were routed via computers now, and voices digitally processed. You could invent false messages. You could delete others.

"How can he implement it?" MacLeod asked. "Wouldn't you have to have direct access to the routers?"

"They're working on that part of the project with someone else. I don't know how." Woodrich cleared his throat. Confession might be good for the soul, but it was taking a toll on him. "Another NSA department is working on that end. There's a buffer between us.

We have no communication. To make it . . ." He trailed off and looked at his hands. "To make it impossible for people like me to give away the store."

MacLeod let that go for now. He needed Woodrich. There was no sense in making him less forthcoming with recriminations.

"He's pressuring you to find out about accessing the routers?"

"No," Woodrich murmured. "So he must have someone in our other department. Someone like me. A traitor."

"Can you access NSA files from here?" MacLeod asked, fishing in his pocket. "Can you identify this person?"

He handed Woodrich Umeko Takahashi's business card. Woodrich's brows raised a fraction, perhaps at the description of her occupation. "I can get into some parts of the system."

"Let's go," MacLeod said.

They reentered the apartment and went into the study. On the couch, Dawson raised his head and grunted from the effort. MacLeod looked at him anxiously.

"I'm all right, Mac."

"You're a lousy liar," MacLeod shot back, smiling at him. No matter what else happened tonight, the fact that Dawson was relatively unhurt was enough to steady him.

Woodrich picked up an overturned chair and cleared a space on the littered floor to set it down. The computer was already on. MacLeod wondered what sensitive secrets Joe's attackers had managed to mine before Joe had surprised them.

Woodrich punched in a few character strings and began answering protocol prompts. MacLeod observed, eyes narrowing as he tried to memorize each string as Woodrich typed it in. He made no effort to hide what he was doing, although Woodrich was clearly uneasy at the way he hovered over him.

"I'm not getting anything on Umeko Takahashi," he said.

"What about Niccolo Machiavelli?"

Woodrich guffawed. "You're not serious."

On the couch, Joe raised himself up on one elbow. "Mac," he said.

MacLeod gestured at him without looking at him. "Lie still, Joe."

"Mac."

MacLeod turned to Dawson. Dawson mouthed, "Watcher." Of course. Dawson could find out all kinds of things about Machiavelli from his Watcher's reports. If he was involved in the attack, there was no sense MacLeod's revealing his hand to him via a computer trail he might possibly be able to capture.

"Stop." MacLeod sat on the edge of Woodrich's desk. "Tell me. How do you communicate with your contact? Via e-mail?"

"Oh, no. In person."

MacLeod's eyes widened. "What?" Perhaps the presence in the lobby had been Machiavelli after all.

"Well, through a go-between. A woman."

"What does she look like?"

He blushed. "She's beautiful, actually. A redhead."

MacLeod decided to press for details later. "She tells you what he wants."

"She gives me letters."

MacLeod crossed his arms. "That was the nature of your unexpected business, wasn't it. You had to meet her."

Woodrich flushed again. "Yes."

"Where's the letter?"

Woodrich moaned softly. "Please, don't. I'm in so deep as it is."

The man had no idea. MacLeod held out his hand. "I want to see it."

"It won't make any sense. It didn't to me." He lifted the computer up and slid out an envelope. He handed it to MacLeod.

MacLeod extracted a note and unfolded it.

*P-K4.*

Why was he not surprised? But he was. Machiavelli knew he was in Washington. How? What did he want? He was making himself very difficult to ignore. "Where are the other letters?"

"In a safe deposit box. I'm not completely stupid. None of the others are like that, though they are usually coded. But in a different code. Warning me not to hold back. Threatening me with bodily harm if I don't hurry. That sort of thing."

"Pack," MacLeod said. "You're leaving town."

"What? I have to report to work tomorrow."

"Do and you're dead. You're coming back with us." He held up a hand to quell Woodrich's protests. "Your life here is over."

Woodrich stared at him. "Why the hell should I do what you say?" He looked to Dawson. "Who is this guy?"

"The good guy," Joe replied. "Come on, Al. I'll help you pack."

* * *

"Not in?" Samantha echoed as the Capitol Hilton desk clerk politely smiled.

"No, miss. I'm sorry. Mr. MacLeod doesn't answer. Would you like to leave him a message?"

"No. I'll wait for him."

"We have a nice lobby bar."

"Yes," she said faintly. Resolutely she made her way to one of two burgundy leather chairs grouped on either side of a low table. She sat and drummed her fingers, and wondered if Machiavelli had a spy in the lobby. If her Watcher was here, too.

"Coffee, please," she said to the waitress. "And keep it coming."

MacLeod drove to Alexandria and checked the three of them into the Embassy Suites by the station. "Tomorrow we'll retrieve the letters from the safe deposit box," he said. "And I'll check out of my hotel and get my luggage." He wondered if any more notes or other surprises would be waiting for him. He had to see.

The night clerk looked askance at Joe's bruises and cuts, but said nothing.

"Miss? Excuse me. We're closing the bar," the voice said.

Samantha jerked awake. The lobby of the Capitol Hilton was deserted. The carved wooden clock on the wall read three.

They were kicking her out.

"Thanks," she said, covering her yawn with her hand. She picked up her bag, glad she had brought it. "Do you have any rooms?"

A cold chill went down MacLeod's spine as he watched the single sheet of paper zip through the Embassy Suites fax machine. His answer to Machiavelli had been sent.

The Game had begun.

He went upstairs to shower. Droplets of water glittered in his hair. When he'd been born, a man seldom bathed; he supposed he'd had more baths and showers than all the men in his clan for their entire lives, combined.

He toweled off and put on his jeans, alert to the soft rap on his suite's entry door. He picked up the sword and checked the peep hole.

It was Joe; MacLeod pushed back the dead bolt and stood aside to let him in.

"I thought you'd be asleep by now," MacLeod said.

"Al is. But I'm on the rollout, and how the hell you going to sleep on that? I knew you'd still be up." Joe sat on the couch. "Listen, Mac. If you clue me in, I can help. You know I know Machiavelli is an Immortal." Dawson would have read about him in the Chronicles of MacLeod's seventeenth-century Watchers.

MacLeod considered. He had known Joe would offer to help, but he thought he'd have a few more hours to decide what to ask of him.

"I want the name of his current Watcher, and I want his Chronicle."

"Mmm." Dawson drummed his fingers on the armrest. "I know it's important or you wouldn't ask."

"And I know you aren't supposed to give it to me."

"As I recall, he's got a female Watcher. She's related to some big shot Japanese industrialist."

"Japanese?" That was interesting. He thought of the Japanese address, the Japanese woman with the escort service. She had to be part of Machiavelli's organization. To escort him, MacLeod, to Japan?

"I'll have to look it up."

MacLeod thought for a moment. "Don't use your computer or my laptop. Or a phone."

Dawson frowned. "Mac, what the hell are you on to?"

"You must have some kind of code you use," MacLeod continued, half-thinking to himself. "You've probably got secret names for all of us."

"Yeah. We call you Errol Flynn." Dawson laughed uncomfortably, which fueled MacLeod's suspicions that it might actually be true.

"Has the code list been compromised?"

"Compromised how?"

"Is it on a computer?" MacLeod asked.

"What's all this about computers? What's going on?"

MacLeod shook his head. "I'm not sure. But if any part of it is computerized, you're going to have to go to Watcher headquarters in person to retrieve the information physically. Don't tell the others about this, Dawson. Don't write it down in your Chronicle about me."

"Mac . . ."

"Don't do it," he insisted. "Later, maybe. But hold off."

"All right." Dawson scratched his cheek. "Looks like I'm going to Geneva. How about you?"

"I'll go home. See if he's sent me anything else. Woodrich will go with me."

"All right."

"Thanks." MacLeod shook hands with him.

"I want to know what this is about when I get back. That's my price."

"You'll know," MacLeod promised. "If I can figure it out."

Dawson clapped his hands on his thighs as he rose. "That's all I can ask. Thanks, buddy."

He left the room. MacLeod relocked the front door and began walking into the bedroom when Dawson shouted to him from outside, "Mac! He's gone!"

MacLeod slammed the door open and burst past Joe into Joe's suite. Sure enough, Woodrich was not there.

"That bastard." Dawson pounded the jamb. "Mac, I'm sorry. I should have stayed with him."

MacLeod shook his head. "I should have insisted they unlock that door." MacLeod had asked for adjoining rooms, but the clerk had explained that the door that would have created a larger suite for them was broken and had been secured for safety reasons, and the rest of the hotel was full.

"Stay here in case he comes back," MacLeod told him.

Then he took off. He searched the entire hotel, the grounds, the Metro station. A light snow fell, covering any footprints that might have led him to his quarry. A single observer, a drunk seeking shelter, stared at the half-naked man in trousers and bare feet, carrying a sword.

"Hey, man, yougottadime," he slurred. MacLeod ignored him, hoping tomorrow the man would remember nothing.

He returned to the hotel and gave Dawson the bad news. "Damn." Dawson again pounded the jamb. "Now what?"

"You get your flight to Geneva arranged. I'll search for him. Tell me all the places he might go."

"We haven't stayed in very close touch," Dawson said. "I don't know his routine anymore. Maybe he went to his office."

"Give me the address," MacLeod said.

"Or he might show up at his bank tomorrow to get the letters out of his safe deposit box," Dawson went on. They both shook their heads. "No, that's not likely."

"Does he have a favorite bar?"

"I think they're all on his list, from the way he drinks." Dawson snapped his fingers. "Maybe he went to the Memorial."

"I'll check," MacLeod said.

He finished dressing with chilled, stiff fingers, and went out into the night.

At the Memorial:

A man stood with a bowed head.

MacLeod walked gingerly toward him, put a hand on his shoulder. The man jumped and turned around.

It was not Woodrich. Tears streamed down the man's face.

"I'm sorry," MacLeod said, apologizing for startling the man.

"How many you lose, man?" the man asked. "Me, I lost my whole company. I was the only one left. You know how that feels, man?"

MacLeod felt the chill of the night, the thick dew like tears on the grass, on his face. He said, "Yes, I do."

The man burst into tears and turned back to the Memorial. He put his hands on the lists of names and leaned against it with his forehead. "I come every night and ask forgiveness," he whispered.

"They do forgive you," MacLeod said softly.

"I know." The man wept. "But I can't forgive myself."

His keening echoed through the trees as MacLeod left him.

In her room at the Capitol Hilton, Samantha grumped at the six-thirty wake-up call. It had been just three hours after she had secured her room. She asked to be put through to the room of hotel guest Duncan MacLeod.

"Hold, miss. I'm sorry. He's checked out," the operator informed her.

"*What?*" Samantha bolted out of bed. She threw on her clothes, splashed water on her face, combed her hair, and ran to the elevator.

At the front desk, she said to the sleepy-looking, blond clerk, "I missed my friend again. Mr. MacLeod? What time did he leave?"

"Let's see. Oh, yes. What a coincidence. Just minutes after you booked your room. You were very lucky. We have a convention coming in and we usually don't have any extra—here it is. Yes. There was some confusion."

The man typed rapidly into the computer. "He had indicated he wanted express checkout when he arrived, but then a gentleman came and paid his bill with cash. He had a note requesting Mr. MacLeod's things. We had to verify all that."

The clerk pointed to his screen, although Samantha couldn't see it. "I called a cab for the gentleman. For the airport."

"The *airport?*" She was on a classic wild-goose chase. "What airline?" she asked.

"I'm sorry, I don't recall. He did say something about Tokyo."

*"What?"*

"Ah, yes."

"Please check me out, too. And call me a cab. For the airport," she croaked. She would check out of her other hotel via her cell phone and ask to have her things sent on.

Sent on to where? Her own flight to Tokyo was in four hours. Had MacLeod gone to Tokyo? As she had discussed with the others, she had planned to approach him on his own turf during a layover on her way home. How was he involved with Woodrich?

What the hell was going on?

"Which airline will you be using, miss?" the desk clerk asked as he picked up the phone.

"I don't know," she muttered. "Just get me there, okay? I'll figure it out."

# Chapter Thirteen

---

> "Invincibility is in oneself, vulnerability is in the opponent."
>
> —Sun Tzu, *The Art of War*

*I am the God of kingdom come.*

*Soon I will change the past, the present, and the future:*

*I will alter wire service reports about Senate hearings, stock-market fluctuations, whatever I please.*

*I will send false reports to the air-traffic controllers at Dulles and slam Duncan MacLeod's return flight into the Potomac.*

*I will retrieve the specs on every military weapon built anywhere in the world, including launch codes. I will order spy satellites to announce that nuclear weapons are headed toward Washington, Beijing, Tokyo, and Toronto, and I will not permit the tracking systems to verify that information, nor will I permit retaliatory strikes to be launched. I will sit back and laugh and watch while the world cowers at the thought of destruction.*

*They will all be my toys.*

*I will track the movements of every Immortal on earth if they so much as charge a meal in a restaurant or pick up a telephone.*

*I will take their heads.*

*I will be the one.*

Sometimes it frightened Machiavelli that it was so easy. If he could do it, why hadn't someone else at least attempted it? Were they all truly so shortsighted?

Or did no one else wish to be as powerful as he wished to be? What was it that made Machiavelli . . . Machiavellian? He loved it that his name was in the dictionary now. He loved it that his cleverness and clearheaded quest for power was now legendary.

"Niccolo?" Ruffio said on the phone. He spoke in seventeenth-century Venetian dialect. "MacLeod was furious when he went back to the hotel and discovered that we had checked him out. We got all his luggage, including his computer. He went to Woodrich's apartment, but the man was not there. We couldn't find anything, either. Now they've scattered. The Watcher's going to Europe. I assume *that woman* is on her return flight to Tokyo."

*Debatable,* Machiavelli thought. "Good work, Ruffio."

"Friend Duncan would collapse into hysteria if he knew I was still around, don't you think?"

"*Si, caro mio.* He would be enraged." Machiavelli stifled a yawn. In this day and age, a person such as Ruffio was referred to as "high maintenance." He had enough to do besides constantly stroke this idiot's ego.

"One assumes MacLeod set Woodrich behind himself on his white charger." Machiavelli checked his Rolex. "I estimate they're riding into the sunset just about now." On their return flight home to the American West Coast, Woodrich on Dawson's ticket. He had known MacLeod was on his way to Washington in the first place because one of the routers had captured activity containing his name—his plane reservation—and sent it to Machiavelli's home machine. He chuckled.

"Shall we come home now?"

"No. Not yet."

"It's my fault that that Watcher surprised us. *Mi scusi, maestro?*"

"Of course I excuse you, Ruffio. After all these years together" *(and all the stupid mistakes you have made),* "do you doubt my affection for you? My heart remains yours." *Until I carve it out of your headless body and force MacLeod to eat it.*

"She was acting strange with Woodrich when she met him at the farmhouse."

"*Si,* it's all right." Ruffio never tired of undermining Machiavelli's faith in Sammi. Not that he had any left.

And it was not a farmhouse at all, but the code word for a Georgian apartment in Maryland rented under the name of Lorenzo de' Medici. The overdressed, bored wife of a local politician had not even blinked at his choice of false name. Ignorant barbarian.

"We wanted to follow her, but we went straight to Woodrich's apartment, as you told us to. Ah, you know the rest."

"*Si.*" How they'd been surprised by Joe Dawson, and had left without getting the updated software. Now it was gone. Woodrich had to have it on him.

"I must go now," Machiavelli said, grinding his teeth. A quick death was too good for this worthless man. He had not kept up with the times. Primitive brutishness was no match for cleverness, and he had far cleverer Immortals on his chessboard now. A duplicitous, treacherous knight, and any number of pawns . . .

"I have a business meeting. *Ciao.*"

"*Cia—*"

Machiavelli hung up. He made a steeple of his fingers and circled his chair until it pointed toward Ken Iwasawa, then barked, "Report."

Iwasawa deferentially inclined his head. "We've been able to make the software you provided compatible with our router configuration with 80 percent success."

Machiavelli frowned. "You promised me 85 percent by now."

Iwasawa bowed his head. "I am desolate. But as your contact told you, there are still many bugs in the software. We need the update."

That son of a bitch Woodrich; he had been dancing a jig last time he'd spoken to his friend, Tony Beauchard. Bragging about the new update and how much more it would help Beauchard with the election. Machiavelli had the whole thing on tape.

As soon as he found Woodrich, he was going to put the fear of God into him. The spineless little man would spill his guts to save himself. Machiavelli grimaced in distaste. Men like Woodrich, men easily bought, physically revolted him.

He circled his chair in the opposite direction and picked up a decanter of cognac. Iwasawa darted forward to do it for him, but Machiavelli waved him off. He poured Iwasawa a drink, who gracefully accepted the burden of such a courtesy from his feudal lord.

"Do you know why I allied myself with you, Ken?"

Iwasawa savored his cognac. "Because my *kaisha*, my company, makes most of the routers used in the computer communications systems in place today. If you compromise our routers so that you have access to any system you choose, you can override the few routers we did not manufacture. Essentially, you can make any network your own."

"Wrong." Machiavelli chuckled. "It was because you play good chess." He indicated the board and material to their right. He had made three moves, P-K4 for himself; P-K4, MacLeod's faxed answer; and P-KB4, his own next move.

Seeing Iwasawa's confusion, he smiled and leaned back in his chair. *"Va bene.* The fact that you were useful had its attractions."

"And the fact that my partners want Beauchard to be president made you attractive to me."

"Your *yakuza* friends. And why is that? How is he in their pocket? Has he promised favorable trade regulations? Offered to sell them nuclear weapons?"

Iwasawa shrugged, obviously enjoying his secret. Machiavelli truly didn't yet know why the mob of Japan was interested in the politician. But it was useful to know that Iwasawa's good fortune was tied to the election of Beauchard.

The phone rang. He picked up. It was his driver, sent to escort Samantha from the airport. *"Grazie,"* he said, and hung up.

"The *signorina* was not on the plane," he told Iwasawa.

Iwasawa stared at him. "She has openly defied you?"

"No matter. I'll kill her when I catch up to her. I've gotten what I wanted."

"I would like to know what that is," Iwasawa said. "What you wanted."

"Why do you fight for your company?" Machiavelli asked.

Without hesitation, Iwasawa replied, "I owe NKS my loyalty. It is my duty to do whatever I can to make the largest and strongest corporation in the world."

"I feel that way about myself," Machiavelli replied, pleased. "I owe myself that kind of loyalty. I fight to advance myself. I know that's contrary to your Japanese concept of the group." Iwasawa nodded. "But I'm a Westerner. We're individuals."

"It's a concept that eludes me, I agree," Iwasawa observed. "A Japanese would find your individualism isolating. It would make him feel lonely."

"I never do." Once more he pulled out the fax from MacLeod and admired it as one might a fine Tintoretto. *P-K4.* How easily he moved them all. He guessed that MacLeod would be on a plane to Japan within twenty-four hours. After he had made love to little Sammi Jo, the damsel in distress. MacLeod was weak for weak women. He thought of Maria Angelina and smiled cruelly. He had been told that she had lasted far longer than anyone had expected, despite the vigorous application of all the latest tortures. She had died begging to die. He was sorry he had missed seeing that.

Pawns were promoted to queens by the player; it was not a rank they attained simply because they thought they deserved it. When she neglected to make the signal that she and MacLeod were leaving the island—a white handkerchief hanging over the second-story balcony—he knew she had fallen in love with the Highlander and would do whatever she could to protect him. That was not acceptable.

Not then, and not now.

*The searing, white-hot sands baking him.*

*Screaming as the heat sizzled away his flesh.*

*Hating with everything in him. Hating, and vowing that he would take the Highlander's head. If not in this century, then in the next, or the next. At the perfect right moment, he would do it. This was his blood oath.*

*The only one he would never break.*

No, he had never begged to die in the burning sands. He had only dreamed of avenging himself. And of never being at anyone's mercy again.

"What move would you make at this point, Ken?" Machiavelli asked, gesturing to the board. He imagined MacLeod in his fine Venetian black velvet studying the pieces, that craggy face set in thought. He wondered how Duncan dressed now.

Machiavelli sighed. He missed the Scot. He was almost sorry that he was going to kill him.

"Ken?" he prompted.

"PxP. It's the King's Gambit."

"Even so." Machiavelli captured the sacrificed white pawn. *Finally, caro Duncan,* he thought. *Take that pawn, and we will play the game we were meant to play.*

On the plane home:

*"MacLeod."*

*MacLeod's old friend, Hamza el Kahir, floated headless in a shimmering cloud of energy. From his neck poured his life essence, the Quickening that Xavier St. Cloud had won from him in 1653. The culmination of final death, all that Hamza had known, and been, and suffered, and enjoyed. Futile and fragile dreams and hopes; what was he now? Dust, only, and memories.*

*"I died for the sake of your honor, not mine. You dared speak to me of honor, you infidel dog, I, who was ten times the man you can ever hope to be. You paraded your pride before me like a swaggering youth. You humiliated me before my blood enemy, Xavier St. Cloud. Know that I spit on you in the dust I have become. I deny your belief in honor. It is for you but a convenient thing, and you will forswear it as well someday, as you foreswore our friendship. . . ."*

"No," MacLeod said aloud, waking.

The flight attendant said, "Sir? Are you all right?"

"Yes," he lied. It was only a dream. His waking mind knew that Hamza was at peace; that his friend had forgiven him, even before he died.

Yet there was truth in the words of the Dream-Hamza, he feared. Was his honor a thing of convenience only?

MacLeod was bone-tired by the time the freight elevator descended to carry him home to his loft. He had not been able to locate that idiot, Woodrich, though he had looked all night. Someone had stolen MacLeod's things from his hotel room at the Capitol Hilton and checked him out. Had it been Woodrich? Was he even now handing MacLeod's computer over to Machiavelli? To what purpose?

There was a telegram taped to one of the slats. A dramatic, archaic gesture in this age of e-mail and answering machines.

He ripped open the envelope.

*PxP.*

An answer to his faxed chess opening to the number on "Umeko Takahashi's" business card. So she had been Machiavelli's way of giving him an address. The attack on Woodrich had been the way of finally capturing his attention. To what end?

He put down the telegram and opened his front door. With the thoroughness of a police detective, he inspected the premises. Everything appeared secure. No one had broken in. Or else they were so good at it, they had completely hidden their efforts.

He checked the phone messages; there were a dozen but none important for the moment. He put the kettle on and went to the desktop computer on the nice walnut rolltop desk he had purchased years ago in Paris.

There were some business messages. As he read them, his computer signaled that he had new mail. It was GRAND MASTER in Tokyo again, and it read:

*Buon giorno, caro Highlander.*
*Come to Tokyo, where we may play the Game in earnest.*
*I await you.*

*I'll take you on anytime,* he wrote back, but stopped himself from sending the message. In 1655 he had sworn never to take Machiavelli's head. Seething, he deleted the message and sat for a full minute. The tea kettle screamed.

Must he still honor his oath? Or did the circumstances warrant breaking it?

*And if oaths are broken by circumstances, then what good are oaths? Honor was not a transitory thing.*

*Honor was what a man was, Immortal or no.*

There must be plenty of ways to stop Machiavelli without killing him.

"Bloody hell." He turned off the computer.

The kettle shrieked for all it was worth. He walked into the kitchen, lifted the kettle off the burner with a hot pad, and slammed out of his apartment.

Outside, the world was a slab of slate miserable with the foreshadowing of a storm. His duster flapped around his shins as he bent his head into the wind. The stakes had been raised, the field of play expanded to include the whole world, and not a dying Republic in a century when the world was small. How Machiavelli must be reveling in the power of the modern age.

Feeling powerless, hating the feeling, MacLeod turned a corner and strode past an abandoned commercial bakery that was on his jogging route. The wind whipped up, slapping him. His eyes stung but he walked on, oblivious. He'd been far colder than this.

*He was not alone.*

The sense of an Immortal presence was thrown over him like a net. He pivoted in a slow circle, inspecting the handful of pedestrians who, like him, had braved the bitter weather.

Down the street on the other side, dressed in a long black coat and black cowboy boots, red hair flying, a figure faced him.

MacLeod put his hand meaningfully inside his coat, on the hilt of his *katana*, and approached. It was a tall woman, not a man as he had at first surmised. She was incredibly striking, with deep blue eyes and fragile features strengthened by full, wide lips.

Unsmiling, she watched him come closer. She, too, put her hand on the hilt of a sword, the outline of which made a jet silhouette inside her coat.

"Duncan MacLeod of the Clan MacLeod," she said. He made no answer, only waited. With a sharp movement, she defiantly raised her chin. She was afraid. "I'm not here to fight."

"Who are you?"

"I'm Samantha August," she told him. She took a deep breath. "I'm freezing to death."

"It's not a bad way to go," he replied evenly.

The wind flew at them, billowing out his duster and her coat. To a passerby, they might appear as two Western lawmen, or two temple guardians with large, obsidian wings. By their stances, their energy, they were set apart in some way, epic, heroic.

Immortal.

Her eyes dropped to the outline of his sword, back to his face. She said again, "I'm not here to fight."

"If we have no business to discuss, I'll be on my way." He waited, knowing full well they did have business.

Samantha didn't know what to do. Despite reading Mari's Watcher files on MacLeod, she hadn't expected him to be so gruff and imposing. Such was a warrior, she guessed. He'd been born in a time when men were like this.

The only reason she'd known he was coming here was pure luck. On the airport escalator, she had seen MacLeod heading for a gate. From her vantage point, neither she nor he had felt each other's presence. She had noted the gate number and estimated his departure time; then worked her way backward to figure out where he was going. Not to Japan after all, unless he was going home first. That had given her the courage to follow him.

Now she was here, and she had no idea what to say to him. Seeing him with Woodrich had changed everything. If MacLeod wasn't working with Machiavelli, he might be working with

Woodrich, or the NSA. Maybe they were after *her.* As far as she knew, Woodrich had no idea Machiavelli was the one who periodically sent her to meet with him. Whom could she trust? She had no idea.

She had managed to reach Aaron on the Sky Phone during her flight, and he had assured her that all was well. He couldn't account for the fact that so many calls to so many of the conspirators had gone unanswered during the previous night. Machiavelli had said nothing about her absence, he went on to report, although several people had asked after her.

Now, to MacLeod, she said truthfully, "I'm on the run." He was impassive, his face brooding, eyes hooded. "I'm, ah, I have a friend."

Still he waited.

"He's trying to track me down."

The strangest smile crossed his features. He asked softly, "Is he your husband?"

She knew he was getting at something, but she wasn't sure what it was. That made her even more nervous. Shaking her head, she said boldly, "Lover."

"Immortal?"

"I don't want to say."

He turned to go.

"Wait!" She lowered her head so he couldn't read the confusion on her face. *Just tell him,* she told herself, but she couldn't. Not until she knew more about his current dealings with Machiavelli. One misstep and she and the others could be dead. "Yes. Yes, he's an Immortal. You haven't heard of him. We're both pretty new."

He cocked his head. Was he buying it?

"We got together and now he wants to go off with this teacher. And I don't. I don't think the teacher's very good." She thought for a moment. "Someone named . . ." *Machiavelli. Say it.* "Um, Janine or something."

He frowned. "That's someone new to me. Where does she live?"

"I, ah, I don't know. I don't know who she is. I don't really want to be with him anymore. He's, ah, too out of control. He wants to challenge people. We aren't ready." Perhaps he would be more charitable toward her if he figured she was defenseless. Machiavelli used to tell her that women were the stronger sex because they could exercise their feminine wiles. Umeko had hated that.

She had insisted that there were several, if not many, newer Immortals whom Samantha could defeat in battle. Samantha's need to hide her increasing body strength from Machiavelli could work to her advantage with others, Umeko had pointed out.

"They will expect a cherry blossom," she had told Samantha one day on a stroll through the Empress's Iris Garden at the Meiji Shrine. Umeko claimed you could see the ghosts of emperors and empresses past in the garden, but Samantha never had. "Impermanent and fragile. But you are a willow. You appear to bend but cannot be broken."

However, MacLeod looked as if he could break her with one blow. Though he wore a heavy coat, she could delineate the muscles of his shoulders and chest, his thighs as the wind blew the fabric from around his legs. Umeko had bested strong men much larger than herself. But she had never faced Duncan MacLeod.

"What has this to do with me?" he asked crisply. Ah, yes, what indeed? Where was she going with this half-baked story? "Why don't you want to go to this Janine?"

"I told you. I don't want to be with, ah, Nathan anymore. I was kind of hoping you might take me on."

He kept staring at her. She smoothed her hair, caught herself fidgeting, and stood with her legs wide apart in a warrior's stance.

He said, "I'm not taking any students at the moment." There was a gentleness in his voice that hadn't been there before.

"Oh, but you're the best," she breathed. "So I've heard."

"So you've heard." His craggy jaw softened. God, he was handsome.

"You have an annoying habit of repeating things." She did smile at him, daring him to remain so distant.

His answering smile was brief, but it was a smile. It was the sun warming her frozen bones; it was a small flame of hope.

"So I've heard." He gestured with his head in the direction he had come. "I assume you know where I live." She nodded. He began to walk, then slowed to allow her to catch up with him.

He looked down at her, the smile still faint on his features. "Who gave you the *Shinto-o-dachi* you're carrying?"

"How did you see . . . ?" She closed her hand protectively over the hilt. "Someone else," she said. He raised his brows questioningly. She searched for a plausible answer. "A man who owned an antique store." Uh-oh, she'd unthinkingly lifted that out from

MacLeod's Chronicle. It was he who had owned an antique store, with his mortal lover, Tessa. According to his Watcher, Joe Dawson, Tessa had been the one true love of his life.

"This man had a name? I'm in the trade."

There had been an exhibition of swords in Washington. She remembered seeing a write-up of it in the paper at the farmhouse. Surely he'd seen it, too. What were some of the names of the people involved in it? A couple of men had been extensively quoted in the article.

"Mr. Meyer," she supplied, forcing herself not to wince, hoping she was even close. "At the museum?"

"Andreas Meyer-Dinkmann?" There was a tinge of surprise in his voice. "Does he know you're an Immortal?"

She shook her head. "Just a fan of old swords." Great. He knew the man. One or two casual questions directed at him and her story would go down in flames.

"He thinks the same of me."

"Ah." Her throat was dry.

They reached his building. He took her up in a freight elevator. Though it was large for an elevator, she was acutely aware they were in an enclosed space. She smelled spice and soap, wondered if he could smell the last traces of her perfume. He rolled his shoulders back and bent his head forward, stretching. She stared at the nape of his neck, considered in Japan to be a very erotic part of the body. And the headsman's target at an execution.

"I've been traveling," he offered. "But you probably knew that, too."

"Actually, I've been here for some time," she fabricated. "I was just about to give up and leave."

"And go where?"

She shrugged. "I wasn't sure."

"Will Nathan try to force you to go with him? Try to take your head?"

"I hope not."

The elevator stopped, and he bent down and rolled up the door. His movements were catlike, filled with grace, but laced with the alertness of a predator.

"I'll take your coat," he said, shedding his duster. He held out his hand. She wasn't sure what to do. She wasn't used to carrying a sword. She didn't know the etiquette among Immortals in a situation such as theirs.

And what was their situation?

Awkwardly she got out of her coat and handed over her sword, which he barely even glanced at. Maybe that was some form of politeness. She didn't know. Machiavelli didn't permit his Beauties to wear their swords around him. They armed themselves only when they went out alone. She bristled, thinking how often he had sent her to Washington defenseless. How could she ever have thought he really cared about her?

"What's wrong?" he asked her. His tone was brusque. He was back to business.

She shook herself. "Nothing."

He said, "I'll make tea."

*She looked like Tessa.*
*She looked like Debra.*

And yet, she didn't look a thing like either of them. Different features, different hair, different build. What was it then, her eyes?

MacLeod's hands were unsteady as he prepared Japanese green tea, swirling the boiling water over the loose leaves in a one-handed ceramic pot from Kyoto. *If you sent her, you selected well, Machiavelli,* he thought, as he inhaled the fragrant steam. *Promotion of a pawn to queen, that's what you're after, isn't it?*

She was curled up on his sofa, her boots removed. She was looking at his pages of calligraphy, staring at each one for perhaps fifteen seconds, laying it down carefully, staring at the next one.

She didn't hear him approach; he searched her profile for clues about her identity. She was pale, with the ivory complexion so flattering to redheads, but tinged with a pallor born of nervousness and exhaustion. Her lashes were full and long. Tessa's had been so. Her mouth was rich. Debra's had been so.

But was her reason for being here more like Maria Angelina's?

"It's *bokuseki,*" he said. "One of the seven traditional martial arts."

"Painting?" she asked in surprise.

"The stroke of a pen, the stroke of a sword," he answered lightly, although he was uncomfortable. He wished she had not seen the pages. To a practiced eye, they revealed far more about him than he wished. The teachings of *bokuseki* held that the brush brought forth the depths of the unconscious, teaching the painter of the ten thousand things of the universe, sending him from the present moment to beyond time. Since Tessa's death, he had struggled hard to rediscover the inner core of serenity vital to a warrior's survival.

"Here." He held out a Japanese teacup brimming with fresh green tea.

She put down his papers, accepted the hot liquid gratefully, holding her teacup in the correct Japanese way, and sipped.

He sat down at the other end of the couch. She moved her feet, sitting upright. The pulse at her throat jumped. Despite his caution, he found himself wishing to put her at ease.

Methos often chided him for his chivalrous attitude toward women. If she'd been a male Immortal, they'd be fighting by now unless the man had divulged who and what he really was. He knew that, and yet he could do nothing but allow this woman to lounge on his couch and drink his tea.

She smelled of an early morning on the heather. Her hair was wind-tossed as if by the wind dancing the craggy hills and meadows of a time long past.

He rose and returned to the kitchen to rinse the sink. Though to the casual observer he might have appeared engrossed in his task, he was acutely aware of each sound she made. She sat quietly. He asked without looking at her, "Where are you staying?"

She didn't answer. He walked to the couch and looked down at her.

The teacup, empty, lay on its side where she had dropped it onto the couch. In the growing shadows of the cloudy afternoon, the light played over her face, her closed eyes. Her shallow breathing indicated a respite from deep, overwhelming fatigue.

She must feel safe here. With him.

His heart tugged. *Watch it, watch it,* he told himself. *You fell for this before, in 1655.*

"I know what I'm doing," he muttered aloud, and went to the linen closet to get her a blanket.

Hours later, while he sat in the darkness and worked on the puzzle of Woodrich's revelations and Machiavelli's chess moves, his attention roamed repeatedly to the still figure on the couch. She scarcely moved. She was going to have a neck ache when she awoke. As his mind wandered, he caught himself imagining giving her a neck massage; then, his hands stroking downward along her taut spine, the knotted muscles at the small of her back. He became aware of his detailed fantasy and shook his head at himself. What he was doing smacked of voyeurism.

With a grunt he rose from his chair to make more tea.

"Oh," she whispered, raising her head. He stopped. "I'm . . . please, I'm sorry. What time is it? I should go."

"It's late. You can stay on the couch, or downstairs."

"Oh, no," she said quickly, but her tone was hopeful. She was afraid to go out. By her movements and the way she had carried herself on the street, he guessed she realized she couldn't protect herself very well.

She laughed shortly. "This is all so strange. This worrying about other Immortals." She ran her hand through her hair. "But most of our existence is strange, isn't it?" She looked to him for confirmation.

"You'll get used to it." He wasn't sure he had. "Perhaps you'd better stay here. I'll take the couch."

"How do you know," she said, smiling awkwardly, "that I won't get my sword and sneak over here and . . ."

"I don't." That bastard. What hold did he have on her to make her do this? "To bed," he said.

She flushed, nodded. "Yes."

He led her past the kitchen area, his thoughts on that empty bed and the sweet and terrible nightmares of lost love that awaited him on the couch. *Not alone, not tonight,* he thought.

She fidgeted while he got himself some bedclothes, a pillow, and a robe. When he brushed past her, she jumped.

"You should have everything," he said. "I keep extra toiletries in the bathroom. If there's anything you need—" he was given pause by her uneasiness, the way she almost touched his arm, as if for comfort—"let me know."

"Yes," she said. "Thank you."

He went into the bathroom, pulled off his sweater and stood bare-chested in the room; then, cursing himself for a fool, he opened the door and stepped out.

"Oh," she murmured, coloring. She had been in the midst of undressing. She wore a black camisole and tap pants edged with black lace; her feet were bare.

"I, do you have another pillow?" she asked. "I was going to look for your linen closet."

Or for something of interest to Machiavelli? He said, "There should be one on top of the extra folded blanket," and brushed past her. He walked into the living room area and got her sword. He handed it to her.

She smiled wanly and took it. "Great minds think alike," she said. "Well, good night." Her gaze ran up and down the length of his body, resting on his bare chest, his shoulders. His face. Evidently she was pleased with what she saw; her mouth curved and her cheeks turned pink.

"Good night." He crossed to the couch and made it up. Outside, the storm broke. Lightning shattered the shadows along the wall and thunder threw sonic booms against the panes. The rain torrented down in thick, mercury-colored buckets. He was glad he hadn't sent her out in it.

Had Machiavelli?

The fog wrapped around Tokyo Tower as Machiavelli stood on the observation deck. On a clear day you could see Tokyo Disneyland from here. On a day like today, when you could see nothing, you could pretend you stood in the Eiffel Tower in Paris.

His cell phone rang. With a rush of anticipation, he flicked it open, eager to hear MacLeod's voice.

"It's 'Umeko.' " She laughed.

*"Si, cara mia."*

"Sammi followed MacLeod home. She's in his house."

"Excellent. You did well, my darling."

She took a breath. "Will it be soon?"

"Yes, very soon. I promise you. I have promised you from the start, haven't I?"

"Yes. I've done everything you've asked—"

"And I will do what you have asked." He made kissing noises. "Come home. I'll send the boys out there to deal with him."

"All right. I'm counting the hours until I'm with you again."

"I, as well, beautiful lady."

He disconnected her.

Stupid cow.

# Chapter Fourteen

---

*"Draw them in with the prospect of gain, then take them by confusion."*
—Sun Tzu, *The Art of War*

Conscious of the presence of a woman in his house, MacLeod rose at dawn and went running instead of going through his forms. Dressing in navy blue sweats, he had been both eager and reluctant to leave the apartment: she was too near, too close, for comfort. He had tossed and turned all night, not dreaming of loss, but imagining pleasure.

For all of wanting her, he trusted her less in sunlight than the romantic close quarters of a stormy night. Who knew what she had been sent to retrieve? Perhaps at this very moment, she was bugging his apartment or modifying his computer to Machiavelli's precise specifications. Leaving her alone was tantamount to giving her permission to do whatever she wanted. Correction: what Machiavelli wanted.

What neither of them knew was that MacLeod never left anything to chance, nor was he sloppy with his privacy. He kept nothing in his loft that he would miss or that could be used against him, including everything on his computers. After all, a thief—or another Immortal—could break in at a most inopportune moment.

Still, to be on the safe side, he had left out for her a computer he no longer used. Last night while she slept, he had moved both his laptop and desktop into the dojo.

His instinct was to hop a plane to Japan. That would probably accomplish nothing, and if he knew Machiavelli, be very dangerous to boot. Fools rushed in, young fools; Immortals who had managed to live for four hundred years moved wisely and slow.

He ran steadily, his breath steaming as he wiped his face with the towel around his neck. After five miles, he headed for home.

Savory breakfast odors greeted his return: bacon, eggs, toast, and coffee. She had two plates warming in the oven, and poured two cups of coffee as he came into the apartment.

"Good morning," she said. She seemed happy as she handed him a cup. Then their fingers touched, and she jerked as if his skin had burned her.

"Thanks." He drank and indicated the plates. "That smells good." He daubed his face. "I'll take a shower. Don't wait for me."

She said, "I don't mind," and carried her cup to the window and peered out. "It's so dreary here."

"Outside it is," he said softly, and carried his coffee to the bathroom.

The computer in Senator Anthony Beauchard's home office was on. At Machiavelli's direction, operatives had installed surveillance equipment in Beauchard's computer months ago. Whenever it was on, Machiavelli could flip a few switches and listen to everything the man said. His next plan had been to install a camera. But it was probably too late for that.

*"You've got to hide me, Tony. They're after me. They're gonna kill me."*

*"Alan, are you crazy? Who? What have you done?"*

*"Tony, listen, um, I'm involved in something. I have some other people I helped."*

*"Helped? What are you talking about? Who'd you help? If you told that bastard Thurman anything—"*

Machiavelli smiled. Jeffrey Thurman was Beauchard's main rival in his bid for the nomination.

*"No, it was nothing like that. I, ah, I . . ."*

*"Get out of here. I don't want to know about anything you're messed up in."*

Machiavelli picked up his phone and dialed a number. After one ring, the connection was made.

*"Si, maestro?"* Ruffio answered.

*"Caro mio, come sta?* As I predicted, Woodrich went to the senator's home."

*"Bravo!* We're only one kilometer away."

"Grab Woodrich as soon as he leaves.

*"Si."*

"Don't let anyone see you. Get him to the plane."

Machiavelli hung up and listened. In Beauchard's office, the conversation was becoming more heated.

*"Did anyone see you come here? Were you followed?"*

*"I'd know if I was being trailed, wouldn't I? I work for the goddamn NSA. Tony, get me out of the country. Put me somewhere safe in Italy with your people."*

*"You promised never to bring that up. We're Beauchards now, not Boccarinos."* A fine old mob family. Machiavelli knew them well. Like the Japanese, the Italians had also appreciated the idea of Beauchard as president, though for more immediately apparent reasons. Such as the Boccarino mob syndicate, run by Beauchard's friends and relations.

*"I'm in trouble with the people you're involved with. They want to kill me."*

*"People?"*

*"The Japanese. Nick Macchio."*

*"Macchio? I'm not involved with him."*

*"Tony, yes, you are. He's ah, I sold him something. I . . ."*

*"You sold him some information about me?"*

*"No!"*

*"You sold a foreigner secrets? Do you know that's treason? How am I involved? Did you use my name? Use my computer account somehow?"*

Machiavelli shook his head. The senator was practically computer illiterate. But now he knew too much, or was on the verge of it. In his panic, Alan was not thinking very well.

*"Protect me. I'm begging you. I helped you—"*

There was the sound of a fist on a desk. *"I never asked for your help. Never. You compromised me, Alan. If anyone ever finds out about all that information you sent me, my career is over. And now you tell me there's more crap you've gotten me into?"*

Another noise like a pounding. *"You didn't ask, but you didn't complain! I believed in you. In what you wanted to do for our country. Take America back!"* There was a jerking sound. *"Tony, is your office rigged? Are we being taped?"*

*"Who do you think I am, Richard Nixon? How can you talk about America? You're just some two-bit spy."*

A click. *Madonna,* did someone have a gun?

"*Tony, what are you doing?*"

"*Get out.*"

"*Tony, no. We're friends.*"

"*We knew each other when we were boys. There's a difference.*"

"*I'll turn myself in,*" Woodrich threatened. "*I'll tell them everything. I'll tell about your family. I'll drag you down with me.*"

The sound of footsteps, of a scuffle. Furniture falling over.

Machiavelli redialed the cell phone number. "Go in now, Ruffio. Immediately. Someone has a gun. Get the pigeon out of there and then kill the eagle." Eagle stood for the senator. Pigeon for the mouthy little coward who would, unfortunately, live to see another dawn.

Maybe two.

"*Si, mi signor.*"

Machiavelli stayed on the line.

The splintering of a door.

The crack of a gun.

Shouts.

Another crack.

Ruffio, swearing in seventeenth-century Italian.

Ruffio's cell phone hitting the floor.

Another crack.

A thud.

Footsteps. Running.

Panting, Ruffio said, "I'm after the pigeon. We're covered downstairs. The eagle's dead."

"Call me later, Ruffio. Pay attention to what you're doing." Ruffio would be running after him now. His partner would be waiting downstairs with their car. It was imperative they get away from the scene with Woodrich intact.

He picked up the phone and said, "Get me Iwasawa-*san*. I'm afraid I have bad news for him."

MacLeod squinted his way through the sheet of microfiche, his gaze wandering longingly to the computer at his right. It contained the library database files of indexed newspaper articles, corporate book abstracts, and every *Who's Who* ever published. MacLeod had no way of knowing if Machiavelli could tell if he accessed computerized files. From what he understood, it would be possible for Machiavelli's altered network of routers to search for proper names, key words, addresses, phone numbers—whatever Machiavelli desired.

So he stuck to the manual means of researching, even though it took him ten times as long to do so.

Macchio Worldwide Enterprises was the name of Machiavelli's Venice-based multinational corporation. According to various accounts, it had been linked to many unsavory activities. A reactor built by MWE had melted down in India. His company had been accused of conducting disastrous illegal pharmaceutical trials in Thailand. MWE was linked to selling munitions to Bosnia.

In every case, MWE had not been found guilty of any crime, nor fined a single penny. No one had been able to touch him.

That had not surprised MacLeod. But it did surprise him to discover that the Tokyo address and fax number at the bottom of "Umeko Takahashi's" *meishi* did not belong to MWE. His repeated attempts to discover the name of the owner of the fax, both in English and Japanese, had gone unanswered until just before he left for the library, when MacLeod had received a short note:

> *Please to excuse poor English. This place is division of Nippon Kokusai Sangyo, largest Japanese corporation. Sorry for inconvenience. I am secretary here for ill secretary.*

A temp, in other words, who apparently had not been told the routine when the other secretary went home sick.

He finished the fiche and put in another, several pages of entries from *The Directory of Japanese Corporations*. He scanned the entry about Nippon Kokusai Sangyo.

> *Among the products Nippon Kokusai Sangyo ships worldwide are routers. These are the boxes that intercept and direct computer messages between systems much in the manner of telephone switching stations. They are the world's largest manufacturer. Their address is 4 Piazza Chondo, Tokyo.*

Machiavelli didn't need Alan Woodrich's counterpart in the hardware division of the NSA. All he wanted was the completed software. How far from completion was Woodrich, truly?

And who had murdered Senator Anthony Beauchard? It was the

top story on every TV news report, every radio station. There were no leads.

Which led MacLeod to his own conclusions. Woodrich was implicated, of course, but it seemed more likely that Machiavelli hadn't liked sharing Woodrich's expertise with anyone. He had to find Woodrich and force him to tell him what was going on.

Samantha came up beside him. She had asked to accompany him to the library while he "did his research on some antiques," citing her fear that "Nathan" might come for her. Casually, he flicked off the fiche reader and asked, "Find anything interesting to read?"

"Just this. I thought you might find it interesting, too." She handed him a copy of *The Prince* and looked hard at him. "It's as relevant today as when it was written."

There was a space of silence between them. This was a message, a step forward, either into a morass of lies or toward the truth.

"Then I'll reread it." Rising, he left the fiche sheets beside the reader and walked her toward the book checkout desk. He handed the book to the librarian, who raised her brows as she stamped the due date in the book.

"How nice," she said. "No one reads the classics anymore."

"Here's another one." MacLeod smiled politely and handed her another book, which he had kept under his arm. *The Art of War,* by Sun Tzu.

Samantha looked at it, looked at him, said nothing.

As they left the library, he gripped her arm. She tensed as if he had hit her, and he was sorry for it. "Be careful," he said, indicating a sparkling patch of ice.

"Thanks." She allowed him to help her across it, his right hand under her forearm, the left clasping her hand. A surge of warmth crept through his body, shielding him against the cold.

He said, "We'll have to begin training together. If you don't keep working, you're going to forget whatever you've learned."

"You'll be my teacher?"

"For the time being." For as long as it took to figure out what she was really doing here, and how and if she was connected to Machiavelli's plans.

If? Was he so naive that he didn't believe that she was?

The happiness on her face was undeniable. Confusing, but undeniable. It would be easy to begin to care for her. And possibly fatal, he reminded himself. *Probably* fatal.

"What's wrong?" she asked.

He shrugged. "Nothing I can't handle."

"Good," she replied earnestly. "Let me know if I can help."

He regarded her. "I will."

"Good," she said again.


*"Guri,"* Samantha said, and Duncan smacked her thigh with his wooden practice staff. *"Gori. Gari.* Stop it!"

They were working in his dojo, doors locked, phones unplugged. He wore a pair of sweatpants and nothing else, and the sight of so much bare skin was distracting her.

*"Giri."* Duncan shook his head in frustration.

She rolled her eyes. "For heaven's sake, I was remarkedly close."

He gave her a funny look and smacked her again. Welts rose beneath her exercise shorts. Slowly they receded. Her fingers were itching to raise welts on his thighs. Anywhere on him. Or take this stick and . . .

*"Shiki,"* she said.

"Good." He nodded approvingly. She wanted to slap his smug face.

*"Ansha. Fudo. Doryo. Nangyo."*

Smack.

"What!" she shouted. And suddenly she could take no more. They had been practicing for hours, and she was exhausted and sore. She rushed him, circling her sword above her head like a madwoman. Slamming it down in an arc, she shrieked as he jumped easily back, shrieked again as he deflected her thrust and grabbed her wrist.

Ineffectually she jerked her arm. Then, whipping her leg forward, she hooked him behind the calf and sent him tumbling backward on the mat. He was surprised, and pleased. Then he began to laugh as she launched herself at him, pinning him with her body.

"You . . . are . . . driving . . . me . . . crazy!" she heaved.

He wrapped his legs around hers and grabbed her arms, pulling her flat on top of him all at once, as if she were a jumping jack and he had pulled the string. "What's the correct pronunciation?"

"Of what? Bully?"

"Of what you called *nangyo*. We're speaking of the six virtues of *bushido*. Duty, Resolution, Generosity, Firmness of Soul, Magnanimity, and Humanity. You've forgotten how to say Humanity."

He laughed in her face as she struggled to free herself. "Do it the right way," he insisted. "Get free."

She braced herself against his shoulders and pulled upward, straining until she had no more energy, and flopped on top of him. Sweaty and grimy in a sleeveless T-shirt, jog bra, and Spandex exercise shorts she had purchased at a sporting goods store, she huffed as her breasts flattened against his broad chest.

They lay still, panting.

"Samantha," he whispered.

His hands splayed over the small of her back and the swell of her buttocks, fighting to keep from holding her. Her body responded to his nearness; she closed her eyes, dizzy with the sensation of his body arching beneath her own. They had been alone for two days. She had called Japan innumerable times, and each time Aaron had told her that everything was fine, and that the group had agreed she should wait to come clean with MacLeod until she knew why he'd been in Washington with her contact, Woodrich.

"Things are more complicated now," Aaron had said, to which she'd replied, "No kidding."

But now, her mind was on other complexities.

She kissed his mouth, urging his lips apart.

"No," he said. But he returned her kiss, thrusting his tongue into her mouth, groaning with pleasure as she moved with him, parting her legs. He raised her up and cupped her breasts, pushing up her T-shirt, fumbling with the hooks on her bra.

"Duncan, take me," she whispered, as her blood roared in her ears. "Duncan, please."

He took deep breaths and pulled away. "No."

She grabbed his hand and led it to her lower abdomen. "I want this. I have wanted this ever since I knew of you. I have dreamed of this." She breathed warm air into his ear, tantalizing him. "Don't you want me?"

His heart pounded. She kissed his neck, drawing her tongue from beneath his jaw to the hollow of his throat. He was salty.

He grabbed her hands, and said, "Stop."

She fell into his dark, deep-set eyes. This was it, then, the last moment of choice. Or the illusion of it. Had this been inevitable? Was this her destiny, as she had once believed Machiavelli to be?

She said, "I don't want to stop."

"Then," he said in a hoarse voice, "I won't, either."

He rolled her onto her back and straddled her, kissing her everywhere, running his tongue along the soft swells of her breasts, her flat stomach, catching her hips between his hands and holding her as he rolled off her exercise shorts.

She curved her back. He held her, suspended, as he moved with her. Her lids were half-closed, her lips pulled taut with desire as she breathed heavily through her mouth.

"I have wanted you, I have wanted you." She threaded her hands through his hair, gripped his shoulders, couldn't seem to touch him enough, explore him enough. Her voice was filled with triumph. "I have wanted you."

"But who are you?" he murmured. "Are you my death?"

She meant to answer, but all words, all thoughts left her as he increased his rhythm, allowing himself to be carried away by the deep, primitive urges that consume men and women, even Immortals. All sense of herself vanished. Pushing and joining, meeting, melding, faster, faster still,

moving, moving moving

with a cry, she found release, exploding in a cascade she thought must be like a Quickening, for it was alive and filled with infinite pleasure; it was a revelation, it was a victory. She reveled in the power of her body, and of his, tamed by her. They clung to one another, riding the tide, transforming the drive to ecstasy; meeting one another in a place where names and secrets had no meaning. Where everything shimmered; where they were one, only one.

He fell against her, his lips finding the space between her neck and shoulder for one last kiss. She was drained, utterly. If someone came after her now, she would have no ability to fight, no need, no wish.

A tear ran down the side of her face and onto the crown of his hair. He caught her chin and made her look at him. "Don't lie to me anymore. Tell me the truth."

"All right." Brushing his hair from his forehead, she took a breath. "I'll tell you everything." She dropped her hand to her side and closed her eyes. "But I'm frightened, Duncan. Very, very frightened."

"No need to be, of me. I swear it."

Tenderly he folded his hand over hers. If this was part of a trap, she would mourn the loss of this moment, but she would harbor no regrets. No man had ever treated her like this. Not Dale, not Machiavelli. Perhaps, as one Immortal senses the presence of another, so one loving heart seeks out another.

"Don't judge me too harshly. I was so young."

"Were you sent here to kill me?"

She put down her hands. "Pardon me?"

"Did he want you to kill me?"

She managed a wry laugh. "Duncan, he probably doesn't even know I'm here."

A beat. Then, "Go on."

And then she was afraid, because it was clear he believed that Machiavelli did know she was here. Or perhaps he was sure of it. She reminded herself that she'd seen Duncan with Woodrich, and still didn't know why. She froze, almost hearing Machiavelli's laughter in her ears. What had she just done?

"Samantha, go on."

In his arms, her body still pulsing, she could feel the blade against her throat. She didn't know him. She might believe she was in love with him, but thus far she had been a terrible judge of men.

Panicking, she struggled to get away. "No. Challenge me in a fair fight."

"Challenge? Samantha, I have no desire ever to challenge you."

"But someday you will, if I live long enough."

"That day is not here. And I will never, ever challenge you." He cupped her face. "I swear it."

"Don't. You can't swear that." She pushed at him. "Please, Duncan, let me go."

He released her instantly, shocking her. "Thank you," she murmured.

"I'm not what you're used to," he replied, and looked regretful that he'd spoken aloud. "I'm a man of honor."

"Are you?"

There was no hesitation in his voice. "Yes."

His cell phone rang. Duncan sighed, and said wryly, "We forgot that one."

He stood and crossed to an exercise bar, where he had hung two towels. He pulled up the phone antenna and made the connection as he wiped his chest and shoulders. "Yes?" He smiled. "Joe. Hi. Yes. On my way."

MacLeod was waiting for Joe at the gate with a striking redhead in tow. Joe's mouth fell open. He knew exactly who she was.

"Dawson." MacLeod shook hands with him. "How'd it go?"

"Good."

MacLeod nodded, understanding Joe's shorthand: he had what Mac wanted.

"This is Samantha August," MacLeod said, and looked at Joe expectantly.

Machiavelli's girlfriend. Joe stared at Mac, who clearly wanted him to tread carefully.

"Hello." He held out his hand. "Joe Dawson."

"Oh. Hi." She blinked and looked at MacLeod, back to him.

"How do you do?" She had a slight Southern accent Joe found appealing. That had not been in the Chronicle.

"We need to go to baggage claim," he told MacLeod. He shifted his carry-on, heavy with copies of files on Machiavelli.

MacLeod nodded and turned on his heel. Samantha August trailed slightly after him.

Man, was this strange.

In Mac's loft, Samantha August walked into the kitchen and put the kettle on. MacLeod seemed to take her actions as a matter of course and walked Joe into the living room area, far enough so that she wouldn't be able to hear them.

"Playing some chess, Mac?" Joe asked ironically, as he surveyed not one but five chessboards in various configurations of play.

"Yeah." As he began to build a fire, he asked quietly, "Did you hear about Beauchard?"

Joe frowned. "Yeah. The death of an American senator plays big in Europe, too. What do you think about our chances of finding Alan alive?"

MacLeod's dark eyes were sad. "Not good."

"That's what I think, too. Well." He sighed. "Let's move on."

"What did you get?"

"Lots." Joe opened up his carryon and flashed him a look at a thick file. "What's with Ms. August?"

MacLeod tensed. "You tell me. Is she with him?"

"Has been for thirty years. I think her Watcher's dirty, Mac. Her file's full of bogus information. I wouldn't be surprised if Machiavelli himself has been writing the reports. And speaking of that—"

He stopped. MacLeod looked stricken. Obviously, he hadn't known she was Machiavelli's longtime lover.

"Mind if I intrude?" Samantha approached with a tray containing a teapot, three cups, sugar, and cream. She set it on an inlaid table from India and began pouring, putting nothing in MacLeod's, some cream in her own, and paused at the third, smiling questioningly at Joe.

"Nothing, thanks." He glanced at MacLeod, who was lifting his cup off the tray.

"You're Duncan's Watcher," she said.

MacLeod almost dropped his cup. Had the Highlander told her? How much did she know about what *he* knew?

"I'd like to know who my Watcher is."

"Oh, ah," he fumbled.

"What about Nathan?" MacLeod asked savagely. "Samantha, what's his last name?" The Immortal set his jaw and balled his fists, as he did when he was angry.

Samantha flushed to her red roots. "I suppose you know that was just a story."

Everyone fell silent.

"You two have a lot to discuss," Samantha said, standing up. "I think I'll go soak in the tub."

MacLeod followed her with his gaze as she crossed the loft.

When she was gone, he sighed. "You remember Venice? Maria Angelina? She and Machiavelli concocted a scheme to lure me to him by making me think she was in danger." His voice grew soft.

For an instant, MacLeod looked shockingly old, worn down by cares and worries. Joe had often wondered how he withstood the stresses and strains imposed upon him by his way of life. On occasion he had watched Richie Ryan lose his cool, storming around the loft, shouting, "I didn't ask for this! Good God, how am I supposed to have any life at all? Guys looking to whack me, I have to hint to every girl I get serious about that I have, uh, reproductive problems, plus that I've got great genes and I'll never age even when we're both ninety-eight. This is too weird, man!"

MacLeod rarely, if ever, lost his cool. And when he did, it was generally because someone else had lost their head, or a mortal had been mistreated. Maybe that was what kept him going, worrying about other people so he wouldn't have to worry about himself.

MacLeod hesitated. "I don't know how to explain what it's like, Dawson. One day you're the son of a Highland chieftain. You assume you'll live your life, marry, father children, die, and go to the afterlife. The next, you're playing chess with control freaks hundreds of years old."

That made Joe laugh. "Yeah, well, I never figured on losing my legs in 'Nam, either."

"Life's full of surprises."

"No matter how long it is." Joe took a breath. "Is she in danger, Mac?" he asked gently.

"Yes. Anyone involved with Machiavelli is, whether they realize it or not." He put down his teacup. "Now that she's politely taken herself out of range, show me what you have."

"Machiavelli has a big group of Immortals in Japan."

"His Beauties," MacLeod said grimly.

Joe nodded. "They have Watchers, but their reports tend to lack a certain veracity. We think they've been identified and bought off."

"Or killed." MacLeod swirled his tea. "Your secret organization isn't very secret these days."

Joe held out his hands. "It's all this modern technology. Secrets are hard to keep." He reached over and unzipped his carry-on bag, extracting not one but five files thick as phone books. There were leather-bound books in the bag, too. Original Watcher Chronicles. MacLeod looked impressed. "Here's the most recent one. He's been a busy boy."

Setting up feuds between Immortals, cutting corners in his manufacturing businesses. Tremendous numbers of meetings with Iwasawa and known figures of the *yakuza,* the Italian mob, and the American Mafia. The Chinese. Russian reactionaries who wanted to bring back the good old days. Trysts with dozens of women, including Samantha.

MacLeod studied the pictures of her with Machiavelli with a hard, dark expression on his face. Joe wished he was in another room.

On another planet.

"Umeko Takahashi," MacLeod said, glancing at a photograph of a thin, muscled Japanese woman.

"An Immortal. You didn't know her? Yeah. The real one, not your card-carrying trollop." He used the word wryly. "It was some bogus feud with a French Immortal. She was caught completely by surprise. According to Umeko's Watcher at the time, Machiavelli engineered the entire thing."

"Who was her Watcher?"

"Mari Iwasawa, who got transferred to Machiavelli." He made a face. "Machiavelli's business partner is her brother. This sounds like a colossal conflict of interest. I don't know how we kept her on the case."

MacLeod put down the photograph and picked up another. It was a photo of Machiavelli with Samantha and a Japanese man in a suit and a pair of sunglasses. They stood before an immense wooden Japanese building with a thatched roof. Large red paper lanterns with Japanese writing on them hung from the eaves. Blossoming cherry blossoms and pine trees grew in charming profusion on either side. They looked very happy, her two hands gripping one of his. She was laughing.

Joe said, "That's his villa, about a hundred miles outside Tokyo. It used to be a wedding park, you know how they spend tens of thousands on their kids' weddings? Then he set it up as a dojo. Guys make pilgrimages out there. That guy in the photograph works for him. Satoshi Miyamoto." He frowned. "Wait a minute. Let me see that."

He leaned close into the picture, "Mac," he said, "that's one of the guys who jumped me at Alan's place."

"Miyamoto? You're sure?"

Joe nodded. They both looked at each other.

"Well," MacLeod said quietly, "it's getting harder to deny she's involved, too." He cleared his throat. "How old is Machiavelli? How long has he been Watched?"

"We believe he's a couple of hundred years older than you."

"He told me he was a thousand years old. I think he must be a pathological liar."

Joe marveled at the way the Immortals one-upped each other: who was better at swordplay, who had taken more heads, who was older. Even Immortals who were friends spent a good deal of their time together sizing each other up. You never knew whom you would face next in a fight to the death.

"Did you know he was a tournament-level chess champion in the nineteenth century?"

In response, MacLeod gestured lazily to the many chessboards. The light dawned. "You're in contact."

"Via e-mail. The game on that big board is the one we're actually playing. P-K4, P-K4, P-KB4, PxP, B-B4, Q-R5ch. What part of the nineteenth century?"

"I don't remember. It's in there, though."

"What does Machiavelli want from you, Mac?"

"I was hoping you could tell me. He wants me to go to Tokyo, for one thing. I don't know why. I'm certain he wanted me to know about his connection with NKS and Ken Iwasawa. He's the CEO."

"Ah, so you know about the alliance with NKS, too. Maybe you could tell me where Mari Iwasawa is? They're worried about her at HQ."

MacLeod cocked his head. "You talked to them about this? You told them what's going on?"

Joe imitated MacLeod's lazy sweep of the chessboards. "Relax, Mac. I told them a cock-and-bull story about research and cross-referencing. You're not the only one who's good at strategizing. Although poker's my game, not chess."

Joe pulled out a folder. "Here. Look at this. This is Mari Iwasawa's most recent report."

*Subject took girl friend and others to dinner. Dinner remarkedly uneventful.*

*Mari Iwasawa.*

Joe pointed to her name. "She goes by Mari, but she always refers to herself as Mary in Watcher correspondence. I don't know why. And this entry isn't like her others. She's usually very thorough. She would have put in the name of the restaurant, every person who attended, and what they ate, that level of detail." He looked at MacLeod. "Machiavelli must have written it."

MacLeod shook his head. "Samantha wrote that. See the word, 'remarkedly'? She uses it when she means to say 'remarkably.' She did it earlier today. I almost mentioned it, but she was already plenty mad at me for correcting her Japanese."

MacLeod pointed to the file. "What about the rest of the reports?"

"They sound like Mari, but they don't say anything. He runs a major multinational corporation, and all of a sudden he might as well be bird-watching for all the activity she's reporting." He sighed. "Something's going on, Mac."

MacLeod regarded him. He nodded slowly. "Something very bad."

"Tell me what to do, and I'll do it."

"I'm going to try to handle it privately. But if I get in trouble, Dawson, you're going to have to bring in a lot of people. FBI, CIA, NSA."

"What if they find out about you guys in the process?"

MacLeod said nothing, but Joe could read the turmoil in his hunched shoulders and tight features. MacLeod literally had the weight of the world on his shoulders.

"And I tell them what?" Joe asked.

"That you believe Machiavelli has installed a way to capture and alter any kind of electronic messages relayed on any system in the world. That Nippon Kokusai Sangyo is providing him with the hardware he needs, and Alan Woodrich is, or was, the one who gave him the software. That he had the senator killed." MacLeod looked speculatively at Joe. "Because Woodrich told the senator what he had done."

"That's a good guess," Joe said. He wiped his face. "This is bad shit, Mac."

MacLeod sighed. "What frightens me is that if he can do it, someone else could. So even if he dies . . ." He shrugged. There seemed to be something more he wanted to say. But MacLeod, being MacLeod, kept it to himself.

Maybe it was about the girl. What a powder keg that was. Joe leaned forward, concerned. "What are you doing with Samantha August, Mac? You should be treating her like rat poison."

MacLeod sighed. "Don't worry. I'm not the same wide-eyed boy I was in 1655." But his expression said otherwise, and he must have known it, for he laughed and put his hands on his knees. "I wish I could tell you it's all a ploy to get her to trust me so I can use her to get to Machiavelli and take both their heads."

There was the sound of a door shutting. It had to be the bathroom, since it was the only door in the house.

They looked at each other. "She'll have to learn to be quieter if she's going to improve as a spy," Mac said. He sounded disappointed.

Joe was sorry for him. He started to put the file away. A photo fell out. "Oh, this is Mari," he said.

MacLeod looked at the beautiful woman who had brushed past him in the lobby bar of the Capitol Hilton.

"No," he said, "she's the card-carrying trollop with 'Umeko Takahashi' on her business cards."

They looked at each other. Joe asked, "Why is he doing this?"

"It's all about the thrill of the game for him," MacLeod answered tiredly. "He believes he'll win, so that holds no interest. What he enjoys is moving the pieces across the board. The elegance of his victory is all-important."

"What are you going to do?" Joe asked.

"I have to get to Japan," MacLeod replied.

"Mac, no. It's what he wants you to do. We don't know enough yet."

"Samantha will tell me."

"She'll lie to you, Mac."

MacLeod shook his head. "She'll tell me, Dawson."

Joe knew better than to press.

Moving numbly, Samantha stood in the center of the bathroom and shook. *"It's all a ploy to get her to trust me so I can use her to get to Machiavelli and then take both their heads."*

That was all she had heard. But it was enough.

# Chapter Fifteen

---

*"Cause division among them."*
——**Sun Tzu,** *The Art of War*

MacLeod and Dawson talked for hours, trying to sort out what was going on, watching another news report about Senator Beauchard's murder. There was oblique talk of a newly discovered fingerprint at the crime scene, but no other information. Dawson wondered aloud if it might have been planted.

"This is creepy, Mac," he said as he left. "I can't help but feel he knows everything we're doing, and he's counting on us to do it." MacLeod nodded. "You have to take his head."

How could he tell Dawson that he couldn't because he'd made an oath three hundred years ago? That his honor required that he find another way, when the necessary solution was so obvious?

Dawson finally left after three in the morning. MacLeod cleaned up the tea things and put away the bottle of Macallan they'd opened.

"Yeah, right," he muttered. He needed to focus, and then he needed to sit Samantha down and make her come clean. He needed whatever information she had.

But he was going to hate hearing from her own lips that she was working for Machiavelli.

He crossed softly to his sleeping area and looked down on her. Her eyes were closed but it was clear she was not asleep. Huddled beneath his blanket, she looked as if she were waiting for someone to shoot her.

She opened her eyes.

He raised his brows, said, "Samantha? Are you all right?" Wordlessly, she fingered the edge of the blanket. "We need to talk."

"Yes," she agreed, staring at him with huge eyes. "Let me have a minute."

Restlessly he walked back to the kitchen. Her terror had been palpable. Was she afraid he would take her head, now that Dawson had told him about her?

He laughed harshly at himself. Had he learned nothing since Venice? Thirty years she'd been with Machiavelli. She must be a consummate actress. She was probably plotting her next move. For all he knew, she was on a cell phone to Machiavelli right now.

There was a noise at the window. He looked across the kitchen. A man stood on the fire escape. *Woodrich*.

MacLeod grabbed his sword and flew through the loft and into the freight elevator. Praying that the noise wouldn't spook the man, he lifted up the door as soon as possible and raced outside.

Woodrich was still on the fire escape, either looking into the window or trying to break into the loft.

"Down here," Duncan called.

Woodrich whirled around. From his vantage point, he gazed down at MacLeod and held out his hands.

The man was terrified. MacLeod said tersely, "How did you find out where I live?"

Woodrich almost smiled. "MacLeod, give me some credit. I work for the NSA." The weak smile faded. He raked his hair with his fingers. "Please. You've got to help me. They're after me."

"I told you they would be."

"I know, I know. They killed Tony. They're making it look like I did it. My fingerprints are at the scene."

"Come down. Now."

"Yes." He scrambled down the stairs and joined MacLeod on the ground. "Okay." He took huge gulps of air. "Okay, I'll have to trust you."

"You're right." MacLeod waited.

"I'm sorry I bolted. I just panicked." He paused. MacLeod kept silent. "After I, ah, left you and Joe, I went to my apartment. I was followed but I waited them out. It was the same two guys who beat up Joe. They eventually left. I went inside and got this." He held up a shiny CD-ROM. "They had torn my place apart, but they didn't find it."

*Too easy*, MacLeod thought, a frisson of tension dancing up his spine. They would never have allowed him to get the disc. They would have burned the building down first.

Machiavelli's men must be nearby. He had no doubt they'd allowed Woodrich to get the disc and lead them to him. Killing two birds with one stone.

"Where was the disc?" MacLeod asked, and then realized that that was the wrong question. "What's on it?"

"The software update Macchio needs. I lied to him. And you. It's ready to go. We've beta- tested the hell out of it, and it's nearly perfect."

"If you've got a disc, it's on a hard drive somewhere. That means it's accessible. He's probably already got it."

"No." Woodrich actually smiled. "It was created on a laptop that ran only off batteries. It was never, ever linked up with anything else, including a modem. When I downloaded it onto the disc, I destroyed the laptop. This is the only copy in existence."

"You've lied to me before. I have no illusions that you're telling me the truth now."

"All right." Woodrich shrugged. "There is one more copy."

"Why did you bring this with you?" MacLeod demanded. "So you'd have something to bargain for your life with?"

*Someone was here.* An Immortal.

"Run," he told Woodrich.

## Outside Tokyo

Mari leaned back in the *ofuro* and sighed contentedly as Nick coiled himself around her like a snake. The villa's bathhouse had been featured in several international architectural and design magazines. The size of an Olympic pool, it looked like a tropical lagoon, with lava rocks, palms, orchids, and *pikake* flowers, and two waterfalls that cascaded over love seats carved from the rock. Nick loved to lounge here, unwinding from the pressures of his life.

She kissed his cheek, his mouth, and rested her head against his shoulder. "Are things going as you had hoped?"

"Yes, my love. You've done so well." He stroked her wet hair. "When you came to Japan, you were so right to suggest the creation of a conspiracy to kill me. We've ferreted out everyone who was disloyal." He sighed happily. "Only a few remain, and they'll be dead soon."

"She, as well?"

"She as well." He chuckled. "She never learned who her last

Watcher was, did she? Some no-account mortal who would write whatever I asked?"

"No, she never knew. She hated having a Watcher."

"Well, he's dead. And she will be, too. They all will."

Mari closed her eyes. "And then?"

"Yes, then."

She shivered with anticipation and a little fear. "And I'll have everything I deserve?"

"Yes, everything. Riches. Power. Everything Ken kept from you. And of course, your place at my side."

She knew he could see the eagerness in her eyes. The love for him, too.

She was the one who had come to him, approaching him when she was Umeko's Watcher. Arranging things so he would do business with her brother. She knew he had killed Umeko because the Immortal had been helping Sammi. But he had also killed her so that she, Mari, could be his own Watcher. She had served him well, deflecting all interest and all suspicion from him. Now it was her turn to be served. "I can't wait."

"Be patient, my angel. All things come to she who waits."

The hot water cascaded, the flowers bloomed.


Woodrich began to run. MacLeod watched him, then turned his attention to an approaching figure. The man was not Immortal. MacLeod pulled his sword.

"Good evening, sir," came the voice, as the figure walked from the shadows. He began to lift off his hood.

"Duncan MacLeod of the Clan MacLeod." Barefoot, and in his bathrobe.

"Satoshi Miyamoto." The hood was off. In his right hand he held a revolver. "One of Machiavelli's knights."

"Don't come any closer," MacLeod said.

There was a sharp crack like the breaking of a stick.

MacLeod looked down at the bloom of blood on his bathrobe sleeve. Miyamoto had shot him in the arm.

Miyamoto said excitedly, "Get him."

The other figure was Immortal, and he was not masked. He made a courtly bow and smiled at MacLeod.

*"Buona notte,"* he said.

"Ruffio." MacLeod raised his sword with difficulty. "It's been a long time."

Ruffio, the cruelest and most vindictive Immortal, Machiavelli's favorite of his Venetian Beauties. MacLeod should have realized he would still be alive.

Miyamoto raised the revolver again, but at that moment, someone shouted in the distance, "Woodrich's getting away."

"Go help them," Ruffio said to Miyamoto. He drew his sword. "I'll take care of MacLeod."

MacLeod said, "I don't think so," barreled forward, ran Ruffio through, astonishing Miyamoto, then raised his sword to take Ruffio's head. Miyamoto raised his revolver again, shot again.

And missed.

Ruffio rolled to the right as MacLeod arced down his sword, wounding Ruffio severely in the shoulder. Ruffio shouted with pain.

"Stop," Miyamoto ordered, brandishing his revolver. He pulled the trigger. The gun was empty.

MacLeod ran toward him.

Ruffio and Miyamoto flew into the shadows.

Woodrich screamed, and MacLeod increased his pace.

*There was nothing more beautiful than a Japanese sunset at cherry-blossom time.*

*Umeko and Samantha rested beneath a canopy of snowy-white and frosted-pink blossoms, toasting spring, their friendship, and the fact that Samantha had bested Umeko in battle for the very first time.*

*"Soon, you'll take your first head," Umeko crowed.*

*Samantha was silent. The thought chilled her. She had lived passively for so long; standing in Machiavelli's shadow had definitely had some advantages. No one dared come after her. No one thought she was worth the danger. Though Machiavelli called her his queen, in reality she was a lowly pawn.*

*"Jails can be fortresses," she said quietly.*

*"Not for you." Umeko regarded her fondly. "Your wings are unfurling. Someday others will notice the regard you have for yourself, and then they will want you."*

*"Want my head," Samantha said bitterly.*

*"Or your heart." Umeko sighed. "I know you don't love me in that way, but I wish you did."*

*Samantha nodded and covered Umeko's hand with her own. "In my way, I'll always love you."*

*"But you have yet to love, in your way."*

*"Yes."*

*In the sunset, in the spring, among the cherry blossoms.*

Ruffio was nowhere to be found, but Woodrich was inside the abandoned bakery on MacLeod's jogging route with at least two other mortals. The ghost-scent of bread permeated the night.

MacLeod surveyed the building, fully expecting Ruffio and his henchmen to leap out at him.

*Samantha,* he thought with a chill. Ruffio had gone after her. To rescue her, or to take her head?

"No, no," Woodrich begged in the distance.

They would be watching all the entrances. He must go in by another route.

There was a tall fence that stretched between the main building and a Quonset hut about twenty yards to the left. MacLeod jumped onto the fence and climbed quickly to the top. Using the tightrope skills Amanda had taught him long ago, he negotiated the length and reached the bakery exterior. He shinnied up a drainpipe until he reached a row of broken windows.

There he stopped and, protecting his fist inside the sleeves of his robe, pushed slowly but firmly on the nearest broken pane, pushing the shards inward. He hoped they didn't make too much noise as they fell.

When he was satisfied that he had cleared enough glass away to prevent serious damage, he climbed through, grimacing as the remaining pieces sliced his legs and hands. He landed softly on more glass and clenched his jaw, holding in the pain.

Below, there was a muffled cry, followed by the unmistakable crunch of bone. Staying focused, MacLeod moved through the darkness, feeling for walls, a door, stairs.

Another cry.

A door. He gingerly walked through it, trying to imagine the layout of the bakery. Conveyer belts? Stairs left or right?

There was a thud.

He moved left for about two minutes and hit a wall. He retraced his steps and nearly fell down a flight of stairs.

The stairs were warm. He stopped and inhaled a vague hint of smoke.

The bakery was on fire.

Venice. 1655. The *palazzo* of the Calegri.

The attempt on his life.

The futile attempt to save anyone else.

He took two more steps. Flames crackled beneath him. Tiny flames like a burning garden poked through the next stair.

He rushed back up the stairs and across the floor, and climbed back out the window. He leaped to the ground, intent upon entering at the ground level.

But the bottom floor was engulfed in flames. He threw a hand protectively over his face and took a step backward, shouting, "Woodrich!"

"Freeze!"

MacLeod whirled around. Two police officers, guns drawn, sprang from a police unit, its lights an odd counterpoint to the glowing shadows of the flames.

MacLeod pointed to the building. "There's a man in there!" At least one. Or had they taken him away? Taken him to Machiavelli?

One of the police officers pointed his weapon directly at MacLeod. "Stay right there."

He raised his hands. "Has the fire department been called?"

"Don't move."

The police officer unslung a pair of handcuffs from his utility belt. MacLeod huffed in frustration. He didn't want to do this, but he couldn't allow himself to be detained.

Feigning compliance by holding out his hands, he executed a knee wheel, throwing the officer off-balance, and knocked the man's gun out of his hand. The other police officer fired, but MacLeod rushed him and pushed him down without being hit. He backhanded the man across the face, knocking him out, and ran.

Through the alleys, back to his loft, he leaped into the elevator and crashed into his home.

"Samantha!" he cried.

But he knew she was gone.

# ENDGAME:
# CHECKMATE

# *Chapter Sixteen*

=====

*"Tire them by flight."*

—Sun Tzu, *The Art of War*

En route to Narita Airport, Tokyo

*The sunset.*
*The cherry blossoms.*
*Umeko . . .*

Samantha came to with a gasp. She pulled at the straps that bound her and tried to think through the throbbing in her head. Ruffio sat across from her, reading an Italian men's fashion magazine. They were on one of Nicky's private jets, either the *Augusta* or the *Angela*. She had been tied into one of the plush gray seats that were more like chaise longues than chairs. Many times, they had flown to Venice for dinner, to London for a rock-concert benefit. Now she was a prisoner.

After Duncan had left her, she'd pulled on her black jeans and sweater by the time she had heard him running outside. Grabbing her sword, she'd darted into the center of the loft to investigate.

Ruffio had been waiting for her, and gave her no quarter. With one stroke of his sword, he had disarmed her. As he swung her around, someone else had rushed her from behind, grabbed her by the hair, and yanked a cloth bag over her head.

Ruffio looked up from his magazine. "You're awake."

She said nothing.

"It's been a long time, *cara*. I have been very patient. Machiavelli promised me I could take your head myself. Although you won't produce much of a Quickening, I'm afraid."

She steeled herself not to shrink from him. "In a fair fight, I could take your head."

He sneered. "What do you know about anything? He only took you into his bed because you were useful."

"And he only—" She bit off the rest of her childish insult. Perhaps he meant Duncan, and not Machiavelli. *"It's all a ploy to get her to trust me so I can use her to get to Machiavelli and take their heads."* She might die without ever knowing how far he would have gone to achieve his ends.

"Only one more hour before we land," Ruffio announced, obviously enjoying the sense of drama. "Given the amount of writhing Woodrich is doing, he might be dead by then. No matter." He showed Samantha a shiny computer CD-ROM. "He'll live on in the hearts and minds of our private global network."

"Your what?"

He slapped her. "Don't play stupid with me. We know you know everything."

"Yes. She does."

"No," Samantha gasped, as Satoshi Miyamoto stepped from the shadows. "Sato, what are you doing here?"

"Taking care of my master's business." He laughed. "You should be proud of me, 'Sammi-san,' for I have learned duplicity at my master's knee. You never once suspected me, did you?"

"But you died!"

*"You* died. I only pretended. Machiavelli-*sama* would never have put me in real danger. We've been laughing so hard. Every time you called Tokyo and spoke to any of us, Machiavelli-*sama* was on the line. Did you know that?"

She was devastated. Of course she hadn't known.

"Satoshi, you're mortal. Why?" she asked.

"There is a saying in English about hitching your wagon to the proper star. Do you know it?"

"Yes," she said, despairing.

"You should have done it."

"Is . . . what has happened to the others?"

"Our spies are fine, of course. But all your earnest coconspirators are dead." Miyamoto turned to Ruffio. "I called on the plane phone. The bread factory burned to the ground. Those men we used to help us get Woodrich are nothing but ashes by now."

"Oh, God," she murmured.

"Indeed," Miyamoto said, and then his eyes bulged and he fell forward, splaying across her as she screamed.

Ruffio picked him up and dropped him to the floor. There was a knife hilt pushed deeply into the base of his skull.

"*Madonna,* he was a bore," Ruffio said, and leaned into her.

"How will you feel if you see your beloved Duncan seated with our master, watching you die?"

She said nothing. She would not cry.

And no matter what he did to her, she would not scream.


"Mac," Dawson said as they drove into the airport parking lot, "we talked about this before. This is exactly what he wants you to do."

"I know." MacLeod looked left, right, surveying the scene for police, for Immortals, for any of a number of other potential enemies or obstacles.

"She probably hopped into a cab and trotted on down here. My God, MacLeod, he's done this to you before. He almost killed you last time. What's going to stop him this time?"

"I could always hold him hostage again." MacLeod flashed a wry smile at Dawson, but his mortal friend was buying none of it.

MacLeod scratched his chin and started to duck as a uniformed woman sauntered by. She was an airport parking-lot "security officer," whose main function was to deter the local gang kids from breaking into parked cars.

MacLeod got out of the car and hefted his overnight bag from the backseat.

"I'm flying under an assumed name," he reminded Joe.

Dawson groused, "That won't help at all. He has spies everywhere."

"I'll be all right." He began to walk away from the car. Joe followed. Mac shook his head. "I'm less recognizable apart from you. Machiavelli knows we're friends. Besides," and now he chuckled, "the police are looking for a man wearing a bloodstained *yukata.*"

"Damn it, Mac. Be serious. You could get killed."

"Then you'd be out of a job." MacLeod meant it to be funny, but he saw at once that to Joe it was not. Dawson cared about him beyond Watching him for history's sake. It was a startling thought to him; he wasn't used to thinking of himself in terms of how other people felt about him.

Unless they simply wanted to kill him.

Dawson put out his hand. "Take care, Mac. And come back.

I . . . a lot of people do care what happens to you." As if he had read MacLeod's mind. "Wish there was more I could do for you. Water your houseplants. Feed your cat."

MacLeod shook with him. "I travel light." They had already agreed that Dawson would check his desktop computer every day, collect the mail, and look for any other communications from Machiavelli. They had also agreed that if MacLeod didn't report in or come back in three days, Dawson was to let the world know what he knew.

"Have a good flight," Dawson said.

They regarded each other. MacLeod replied, "Thank you, my friend. If we'd had a Dawson at Culloden, perhaps the clans would not have fallen."

Dawson smiled, clearly pleased by the compliment. "No doubt of that, MacLeod."

MacLeod headed for his plane, and Dawson stayed behind, Watching from afar.

There was another Immortal on the plane.

On alert, MacLeod moved down the gangway with the rest of the first-class passengers. The Japanese flight attendant at the entrance of the plane bowed deeply, oblivious to MacLeod's intense scrutiny, then dismissal. She was not Immortal. Nor were the crew members in the cockpit.

Could it possibly be Samantha? He studied the faces of the other passengers as he put his small suitcase in the overhead compartment and located his seat. Then, as the first-class attendants passed out warm towels and took drink orders, he checked the coach cabin. Next the lavatories. The presence persisted.

The captain requested that everyone take their seats. Knowing his absence would only cause a delay, MacLeod complied, every sense on alert, laying his seat belt across his lap so that it looked fastened, although it wasn't. He would not be restrained in the vicinity of a potential adversary.

"Is this your first trip to Japan?" an elderly woman in an elegant suit asked as she sipped a flute of champagne.

"No," he replied, "although it's been some time since I was there."

"Ah," she said, and finished off the flute. She held it up. The flight attendant glided efficiently toward her and gave her a fresh one. She downed that one, too. Turning to MacLeod, she smiled uneasily. "May I hold onto you?" she asked. "I'm so terrified of flying."

Was she working for Machiavelli? Warily, he nodded. She wrapped her hands around his biceps.

"Oh, my, you're tenser than I am." She waved a hand at the flight attendant. "My friend would like something to drink." She smiled at him coyly. "Something strong."

"Scotch," he said, and drank it when it came. The plane taxied down the runway and took off. The woman clung to him. He looked left, right, saw nothing and no one move. Would the other Immortal honor the Rule about fighting in the presence of mortals?

For an hour he waited. Another, another. His seatmate became quite drunk and prattled on about her grandchildren and her Pekingese dogs. MacLeod got up several times to scan the aft cabin and the cocktail lounge, returning in frustration to his seat.

Then finally, they reached the Sea of Japan, and MacLeod rose. He would be at a disadvantage when getting off the plane. He had learned never to make himself vulnerable, if he could help it. He thought of Samantha, and smiled grimly.

The woman, barely able to lift her head, looked enquiringly— the seat-belt sign had been turned on—and he smiled and pointed to the lavatory.

Inside the cramped space, he found a book of matches in his pocket and pulled a wad of paper towels from the dispenser. He wadded them in the sink and lit them, ducking quickly out. Then he jimmied the door to make it difficult to open.

He was halfway to the first-class galley area when the smoke alarm went off. Two flight attendants barreled down the aisle; he stepped aside, then ducked into the galley, and into the crew elevator that led to the lower level.

He stepped out into the bowels of the plane, the area known as "the pit," by the time the smoke alarm went silent. He knew that the other Immortal would have been alerted, and standing ready.

Drawing his sword, he burst into the small lower galley, hemmed in on all sides. Slashing furiously behind himself, he forced his way into the cargo area. It was dim, but not dark; he was caught in a maze of large metal containers. Along the bulkheads, large tarp enclosures held piles of luggage. At the nearest of these, he slashed large X's, searching for his adversary.

There was no one there. Yet the sense of another followed him through the labyrinth as he slashed at the tarps.

He moved forward, *katana* raised upward like a shotgun, inching his way to a room filled with switches and lights. A sign read "AVIONICS." He stepped inside.

And his adversary leaped at him from the shadows.

He was Japanese, dressed like a businessman, and hopelessly inept. MacLeod deflected his parry and took a step back.

"My name is Taro Honda," the man said. He held his sword in classic kendo style, looking frightened but determined. He lunged; MacLeod had nowhere to go, so he angled his sword and caught the other's blade. The man, seeking the advantage, attacked again. His style was a strange amalgam of kendo and épée, effective in its way but sloppy, with too many sword strokes.

The man was doomed, and appeared to know it. MacLeod thought of the havoc a Quickening could cause on the plane: the navigational systems gone amok, the hydraulics frozen, the plane slamming into the sea.

"I have no quarrel with you," MacLeod said in Japanese.

"You have with my master." The man flew at him, slicing left, right, aiming low, high. MacLeod deflected his blows and tried to hurt him, if only to stop him.

"Machiavelli?" MacLeod asked.

The man looked surprised. "Yes." Again he attacked; again MacLeod held back. He was hampered by the smallness of the room; as he attempted only to defend himself, and not to take Honda's head, his blade slammed into a bank of lights. Sirens went off, startling the other man.

"You knew from the beginning I would take your head," MacLeod shouted. "Why did you hide down here for so long?"

The man looked abashed and uncertain. MacLeod narrowed his eyes. "You didn't know what to do, did you? You didn't even know how to challenge me."

"That's not true." Taro Honda slashed ineffectually. They were near the main seal. A Quickening might blow it. MacLeod backed up, leading the man out of the room and into the cargo area.

"How long have you been Immortal?"

"My master, Machiavelli-*sama*, gave me eternal life four months ago."

"*Gave* you? That's what he told you?" Farther he moved back, farther still. He would wound him only, cut him down and kill him, then tie him up—

"He gives us life." The man was perplexed as he advanced on MacLeod. He was not hampered by his fear for the passengers on the plane. "He gave you life. He told me so. But you betrayed him. You left him. Therefore, that life is forfeit."

MacLeod seethed. Good old Machiavelli, lying to get his way, throwing people in his path like pieces of furniture to give himself the merest advantage in the chase. "He didn't give me this life. And he didn't give you your life. We were born this way."

The man pursed his lips. MacLeod couldn't tell if he believed him or not.

"It's the truth. I bear you no ill will. Let me spare you. Lay down your sword."

"I cannot." The man steeled himself. "I have sworn."

MacLeod tried again. "I'm telling you, he lied to you. He did not give you this life. He's an evil man who knew I would probably take your head if we fought. He only sent you to inconvenience me." Not very polite, but there it was. "If there's a Quickening, all the people on this plane may die."

"There is no such thing."

Oh, God. "There is, Honda-*san*. And it will be your Quickening."

The man shook his head. "I'm obligated to keep my word."

MacLeod thought of his recent dream of Hamza. He thought of himself as a young man, dooming another to death for the sake of honor. He thought of his pledge not to take Machiavelli's head.

"Don't do this," MacLeod said. "Walk away."

"I cannot." He began to swing and swing, almost blindly. He practically leaped on MacLeod's blade. MacLeod parried and retreated, parried and retreated. Honda was wild. MacLeod remembered the Duke d'Fabrizi, and said, "Have a care."

Honda actually looked pleased, as if he thought he was winning. "I have sent many to their deaths for the sake of my master." He smiled crookedly. "I know where the woman is. I betrayed her. I betrayed all of them. He has dealt with the disloyal ones."

Samantha? MacLeod advanced on him. "Where is she?" he demanded. "Tell me!" His anger rose. "Tell me."

"We will win." Chuckling, the man raised his sword and sliced an overhead cable.

The cargo area went dark except for a sign that lit up immediately, reading "CARGO EXIT." The plane rumbled.

MacLeod slashed.

The man screamed.

*Damn,* MacLeod thought, as the man's head loosened from his body. He hacked at the sign and pushed the body out, leaped after it.

They fell in the darkness, plummeting to earth like huge comets; the tail that emerged from the other man was the Quickening; it enveloped MacLeod like a thundercloud and shook him, shook him with its lighting and savagery; primeval, earth-shaking, earth-changing

*I am more*
*more than I was*
*I am*
*I remain*
*eternal*
*I am a prince of the universe*

He was on fire from head to foot, twisting and dropping, that which was Honda melting into him; the poor, foolish man; they were all poor, foolish

*pawns*
falling
falling
into the sea.

Dying there, on the huge, frozen waves of gray, as the whales called; as memories sucked him under

*Tessa*
*Debra*
*Maria Angelina*
*all the others, so many,*
*all his loved ones*
*Samantha.*

Pulling him beneath the currents as the water rushed in and he died, gasped, died, looked overhead at the silhouette of a plane against the moon and raised a fist as if to push it up, to hold it in the sky.

The fist unfurled; the hand sank.

He died again.

Again.

Again.

His clothes, his passport, and his wallet were soaked with stinking harbor water, but everything appeared to be in good working order. He had lost his cell phone.

When he got to shore, it was raining hard, but not hard enough to clean his clothes. The eerie feeling of déjà vu of Venice swept through him again. He ducked into a row of harbor shops and got outfitted in French jeans and a black turtleneck sweater. The young girl who helped him told him how sorry she was that he had been drenched by the rain. She told him to go next door to buy a phone card and an umbrella, complimented him on his excellent Japanese, and wished him a good day.

He used the phone card to call Dawson at a pay phone. It was possible Machiavelli's routers would be programmed to capture any calls sent to Dawson's phone number, but it was a chance MacLeod would have to take.

"It's me," he said, when Dawson picked up.

"Jesus, Mac, thank God. What happened? Your flight's been on every channel."

"Did it go down?" MacLeod asked, deeply concerned.

"No, the pilot pulled it up in time. Everyone's fine except one passenger, who wasn't accounted for. It's you, of course."

"Good," MacLeod said, relieved. "Machiavelli sent someone after me. Taro Honda."

"I figured there'd been a Quickening," Dawson said. "I just didn't know whose. Thank God it wasn't you. But why did he put Honda on you, Mac? I thought Machiavelli wanted you to go to Japan."

"It's like I told you before," MacLeod said angrily. "It's his way of playing with me. In chess, sometimes you sacrifice pieces to put your opponent in check. I think he's trying to wear me down. Toy with me." He clenched his jaw. "Before Honda died, he told me he had betrayed 'the others.' Samantha included. He's trying everything he can to throw me off-balance."

"No Watchers in Japan have reported in, Mac. None. I'm worried that there's a bloodbath going on."

"Then I'd better get moving," MacLeod said. "I'll catch you again later."

"GRAND MASTER sent another chess move via e-mail. K-B1."

MacLeod closed his eyes, imagining the board. "Tell him P-QN4. Although why he's persisting, I have no idea. Maybe to see if Honda killed me." Surely Machiavelli couldn't have thought that young Immortal would have prevailed. Then again, it would be unlike him not to cover all his bases.

There was an hourly milk run to the outskirts of Machiavelli's compound. MacLeod let a number of them go by, then took a commuter into central Tokyo simply as a diversionary tactic. He hated wasting the time, but he was one against who knew how many. He had to stay alive.

Tokyo was another large city linked by subways and trains, and it, too, had fared better than Washington, D.C. The Americans had been generous to the Japanese after World War II, rebuilding their nation and asserting the rights of the individual, particularly of women, in Japan's first constitution. The Japanese had done everything they could to make use of these gifts, including battling ruthlessly to reenergize their economy. But the Americans, lagging far behind, regarded the Japanese's "enthusiastic" business tactics during the Reagan era as out-and-out treachery: dumping artificially cheap products onto the open American market, forbidding competitive foreign products, including American, from being sold in their country.

The Japanese were dumbfounded by the fury of their benefactors: were they to hold back in some way, pretend they weren't as successful and strong as they were? Commerce was war, was it not? The Americans should be proud of them, and instead they were so livid there had been private conversations behind the closed doors of the Japanese Diet regarding the likelihood of the Americans starting a new war.

Ottomans and Venetians. Americans and Japanese. The Japanese economy was shakier now than it had been in the seventies and eighties, mirroring the Venetian situation in 1655. No wonder Machiavelli had moved here. It was the kind of situation in which he could flourish. Soon, however, it wouldn't matter where he lived. He would be able to control all the economies of the world from a computer so small he could fit it in his pocket, if he chose.

He could shut down Tokyo.

As if on cue, the train brakes screamed and the train began to skid. MacLeod held on as passengers shrieked. Mothers grabbed their children. The people standing in the aisle fell against each other and crashed to the floor, sliding forward. A black leather briefcase flew across the compartment, smashing into a man's forehead. His head whipped backward and his body went slack.

MacLeod pulled a woman holding a child onto his lap as she began to go down. He held them tightly as the train gradually slowed. Then it ground to a halt.

Ambulances screamed in the rain as MacLeod held the mother and child. Surrounded by weeping and shouting, the woman murmured her thanks. MacLeod asked, *"Kodomo wa ii desuka?"* Is the child all right? The little girl was sobbing hysterically.

"I don't know!" the woman cried, examining her daughter. MacLeod assisted her, looking past the bruises and cuts for more serious injuries.

Emergency crews boarded the train like assault forces. MacLeod stayed and helped until a man with a bleeding forehead looked at him, and said, "I saw your picture on television. This man has been missing," he said to a paramedic who bent over him. "He's missing."

"Yes, uncle," the paramedic replied politely.

"He is! He's missing."

MacLeod saw that there was no more he could do here. Now, having been recognized, it was time to leave.

He exited the train, looking over his shoulder. He had a feeling Machiavelli had successfully uploaded Woodrich's demonic software.

Machiavelli's seizure of the global network was starting, and he was the only one who could stop it.

# Chapter Seventeen

---

*"He who causes another to become powerful ruins himself, for he brings such power into being either by design or by force, and both of these elements are suspect to the one whom he has made powerful."*
—Niccolo Machiavelli, *The Prince*

The rain shot frozen needles into Samantha's body as Ruffio half dragged and half flung her toward the abandoned Shinto shrine on the grounds of Machiavelli's country villa. He had brought a kimono for her and forced her to wear it, and a traditional *obi*, or sash, which she'd learned to tie at a class at the New Otani Hotel years before. Machiavelli used to say she looked like a fabulous Kabuki lion in the Japanese traditional dress with her red hair flowing.

In the distance, she heard the guttural cries of men practicing their *kata* in the dojo. She was certain that today, this uneventful, dull day for so many, she would die forever.

He took her to the side stairs that led to the shrine. The statues of the gods were gone; the gilt lotuses and snails had weathered to nubs. Time was fleeting for all things in the universe, except Immortals. And at this moment, it appeared she had no time left at all.

"Sammi-*san*," a voice jittered out of the shadows. A handcuffed man in a suit was pushed forward. Her eyes widened. It was Ken Iwasawa. "They're going to kill me."

"You?" she said in surprise.

Two men appeared on either side of him. She didn't know them, but they appeared to be *yakuza*.

"My usefulness is over," he said bitterly. "The American senator is dead, and my *yakuza* connections wish to replace me with someone who has ties to the new candidate, Jeffrey Thurman.

Nick-*san* has what he wants from me. Thus I am more of a liability than an asset."

"Surely you can save yourself," she said, for a moment more frightened for him than she was for herself. He was a brilliant businessman; he had much to offer Machiavelli.

"I know too much," he replied. "The senator had promised us many things, including the items we needed for various weapons illegal to possess in Japan."

"Nuclear weapons?" she asked, astonished.

"Perhaps. But now he is dead."

One of the *yakuza* drew a gun and pointed it at Iwasawa's chest. Iwasawa was aware of his action. He focused directly on Samantha, staring into her eyes, and was thrust backward as the bullet slammed into his body. Blood splattered across the temple walls.

Stifling her scream, Samantha turned and retched.

"You're next, you American bitch," Ruffio said.


Mac was at another pay phone. After telling Dawson about the train crash, he said, "You told me Machiavelli was a chess champion in the nineteenth century. What name was he using?"

"Staunton."

MacLeod sighed. "It's familiar, but I can't bring it in. Okay, transmit my move. I'll call again when I can."

Dawson cleared his throat. "Mac, I didn't want to tell you this, but . . ."

"What?" MacLeod tensed. It had to be bad news, the worst kind of news: that someone he loved had lost his or her head. Samantha . . .

"A plane went down in the Atlantic. Navigational error's being blamed on an onboard computer."

"Yes?" he snapped. "What, Joe?"

"Mac, Richie was on the plane. He called from the airport to tell you he was racing in Amsterdam. You two were going to meet somewhere?"

MacLeod was chilled. "For his birthday."

"Mac, he'll survive."

Unless the gods were very vicious. Not Richie. He had lost so many friends.

Not Richie.

"Capturing messages," MacLeod said. "Altering telemetry. He

can do those things, Dawson. I'm leaving for the compound. I've run out of time."

"Mac, no. Play out the game."

"How many people is he going to kill to get to me?"

"It might be kind of a clue to something. Knight to Queen Five."

MacLeod forced himself to think. "My chess is rusty, but it does sound familiar. If I think of anything, I'll let you know." MacLeod hung up.

He checked the rail schedule. There was a train due in ten minutes.

Not Richie.

Not Samantha.

He decided to rent a car.


Samantha's kimono was askew, her hair disheveled. Her wrists were tied to the headboard of her bed, her ankles to the posts. Ruffio stood beside Machiavelli, leering.

"Tell me now, Sammi Jo," Machiavelli said. "What did Woodrich tell Duncan?"

"I don't know." She was perspiring heavily. He had haunted her with agony today. "Ask Woodrich."

"Unfortunately, he died." He slapped her. "What does Duncan know?"

"I thought maybe he was working with you."

"Duncan MacLeod? Oh, that is rich! And a very bad lie." He hit her again, this time with a closed fist. She grunted but otherwise showed no weakness.

"I'm impressed, darling. I thought by now you'd be whimpering and sniveling. Umeko taught you well." He whispered into her ear with deadly quiet, "Did you ever doubt I killed her?"

She shook her head.

"Did you ever doubt I would have spies among your conspirators? Didn't you find it interesting that my own Watcher wanted me dead?"

Samantha opened her bloody mouth, but at that moment, Mari Iwasawa appeared on the threshold. She sauntered in and put her hands possessively on Machiavelli's shoulders. Leaning forward, she kissed his cheek.

"It took years to put everything in place," she said. "Niccolo never dreamed you would turn against him. I was the one who doubted you. We set the trap for Umeko together, but I engineered the creation of the conspiracy."

"But . . . but he poisoned you with fugu," Samantha said hoarsely. "You trusted him that much?"

Mari laughed. "The pieces for Satoshi and me were fine. We needed room to work without your interference. It was fun to hear how rattled you were about my disappearance. But it sent you straight to MacLeod, as we had hoped."

"What did he promise you?" Samantha asked her.

Machiavelli put his arm around Mari. "Some of them still believe I give them eternal life. Can you believe it? Just like when you overdosed on drugs, Sammi. Remember that?" He sighed theatrically. "But this is another time. Mari is more like another woman I used to know. Maria Angelina. She wanted riches, and power." He beamed at Mari. "And me, as a lover."

Mari kissed Machiavelli's temple. "Hit her again. Hard."

"All right, my darling."

He reached around, yanked Mari forward, and thrust a stiletto into her chest. Blood gushed from the wound.

"What . . . what . . . ?" Mari said, gasping.

"You stupid cow." Machiavelli pushed her to the floor. She grabbed his ankle.

"Nick . . ."

"This time you'll die, *cara*. So sorry."

"But you love me," she gasped.

"Do you really think you thought of anything? That you came to me first? Who do you think got you assigned to Umeko? How could you be so naive as to believe I would work with your brother unless I had control of you both? And as for dreaming up the conspiracy, cast your mind back, Mari. I gave you that idea. You're just too stupid to remember it." He gave her a savage kick.

"If you had loved me, perhaps I wouldn't have done this. But you didn't. You only wanted something from me. As everyone has, all through time."

It took a few minutes for her to die. Samantha heard the death rattle, the last exhalation. She closed her eyes.

"Don't feel too sorry for her, Sammi Jo. The intensity of her hatred of you astonished me."

"You wouldn't be able to tell if someone did love you," she said. "I loved you, once."

He sneered at her. "You? The sad little orphan? You had no love to offer me. You're incapable of it." He must have seen that he had hit a nerve, for he pressed on. "You only needed me. And when that lesbian convinced you otherwise, you tried to kill me. Is that love?"

"Nicky," she said, looking at him. "I found much to admire in you. Your brilliance, your charm."

"Stop!" he shouted, raising his hand. He froze. His hand was shaking. "Stop! I will not have your lies."

"That's what you're afraid of, isn't it?" she flung at him. "That someone will love you? That it will soften you?"

"Afraid?" Though he laughed, his voice quavered. "Ask Taro if I was ever afraid. Ask Satoshi. Ask Aaron. Remember how he asked you if you actually saw Satoshi die? He told me later he had to fight not to laugh in your face."

Her eyes widened with shock as she realized he was telling her how many had betrayed her. How stupid could she have been?

"Don't worry about Taro, *belissima*. MacLeod killed him. And once they've served their purpose, the rest of them will die as well."

Ruffio leaned his head into the room. "Another chess move came in on your computer, *maestro*."

"Good. MacLeod's still alive. Keep an eye on her." He stood and passed Ruffio on the way out. "Don't go anywhere, *cara*." To Ruffio, who was pulling out his sword, he added, "Don't do anything permanent. I want that pleasure."

A stream flowed across a dip in the private drive to Machiavelli's compound. It was too deep to cross in the sedan MacLeod had rented; the water would flood the tailpipe and kill the engine.

MacLeod inspected the stream for a shallows, even a hydraulic bridge, reminding himself that this was not the time of his birth, when warlords had fortified their keeps with moats. As he walked along the bank, he recalled his entry into Venice. Carnival and stinking canal water. This water stank, as well.

Well, there was nothing for it.

He took off his duster and his boots, rolled up his jeans, and forded the stream. The water reached to his kneecaps. He thought of bear traps and land mines and other things that could be hidden underwater. He thought of train crashes and ruined economies, and Richie downed in a plane crash.

He would not let himself think of Samantha.

He thought of all the other things Machiavelli could do. They would have to be subtle and untraceable. That meant that everyone who might know would have to die. Woodrich, Joe, Iwasawa, Samantha, all his Immortals. MacLeod himself.

Was that the purpose of this whole mad scheme? An elaborate challenge? It was so pointless.

He finished crossing the stream, put his boots back on, and rolled down his jeans. He hadn't sufficiently rested; he was in no shape for battle. His warrior's heart, forever young and vital, insisted that he was ready; his mind, now very old and seasoned, knew he could be in trouble.

Samantha's face loomed in his mind.

He moved into a grove of bamboo and rested a moment, concerned at how tired he was. He hadn't realized it.

He began to step forward, but something made him pause. Dropping to a crouch, he saw two thin posts set approximately two feet from each other, two more spaced the same distance. It was a motion detection system. The entire perimeter must be monitored.

He examined the posts. Unless Machiavelli had angled the beams, they appeared to cover an area about six feet in height.

Again he removed his boots, held them in his mouth, and shinnied up the nearest stem of bamboo. He flung the boots down first, thinking again of traps and mines, the evils of the forest Cambodia had taught him.

When nothing happened, he followed after.

He proceeded to the next set of posts.

He climbed another piece of bamboo.

He dropped to his knees.

He was tiring.

It was almost a relief when Machiavelli's voice echoed on a public address system over the grounds:

"Duncan! *Caro mio!* Welcome."

Two men dressed in black ninja garb approached with submachine guns in their grips. Two more followed them. MacLeod turned and ran into the path of the beam. A shock wave shot through him; he shook violently, and fell to the ground.

The ninjas surrounded him. He pushed the barrel of one of the weapons aside and got to his feet.

Without speaking, they all began to march deeper into the grove.

Was this her second death?

In her bedroom, Samantha felt her old self wither as Ruffio pawed and tormented her. Fury had almost completely obliterated her terror. Goddamn him, God *damn* him and every single person she had allowed to hurt and victimize her. Starting with her mother and all her men, and Dale, and the worst offender of them all, Machiavelli. It was her fault that she had let him cajole and bully her, but she would not waste her anger on herself.

Changing, seething, transforming, building, it would be frightening if she let it be so, but she took all the emotion, all the energy, and used it for the strength that this rebirth required.

I ain't no damn dog.

I'm not a damn dog.

*And I never was.*

*Duncan.* If he had betrayed her, she'd kill him.

*No. Never.*

Yes.


As Machiavelli's guards threw MacLeod to his knees, he drawled, "I expected you here days ago."

The Highlander said nothing. With the dignity Machiavelli remembered so vividly, the man got to his feet and stood. Another fighter, such as Machiavelli himself, could detect the energy coiled inside him. The modern age suited him. The hair drawn back, the clothes. Duncan MacLeod was timeless, ageless. He bore his centuries with grace.

He extended his hand. "I welcome you." MacLeod only looked at him. Machiavelli shrugged, dropped his hand to his side. "You know what I have accomplished."

MacLeod finally spoke. "I know you must be stopped."

"The gambit paid off. A few pawns sacrificed. Let's jump ahead to your last move. NxQ."

MacLeod remained silent.

"You should play. NxQ." He frowned at the bruise fast disappearing on the Highlander's high, chiseled cheek. He looked at his men. "Which of you struck him? I gave orders that he not be harmed."

No one answered, but one man—a mortal—reddened. Machiavelli reached forward, grabbed the man's submachine gun out of his hands, and fired at least twenty rounds into him. The man fell to the ground. Machiavelli, face impassive, fired another twenty and tossed the weapon on top of the bloody body. Shocked, the others drew back slightly, but regained their composure within seconds. He was proud of them.

"That was not necessary," MacLeod said angrily.

"Oh, but it was. Did you never read *The Prince*? If you cannot be loved, be ruthless. NxQ. Oh, come. You must know what I want."

"My head."

"I thought so as well. I've been waiting for this day for so long. No, not waiting. I never wait." He smiled. "Planning. I knew I'd have only one opportunity to get you. But then my disloyal Beauties started making their own plans. I figured I'd take advantage. Besides, it would be better to have you out of the way before my system was in place."

"Why? Why do you do this?"

"Why not?"

MacLeod shook his head. "That's not a good enough reason, not for you."

Machiavelli walked languidly to a ruined statue of the Goddess of Mercy and touched the ravaged base. "I was made for this time, when so many things can be done, and so easily. The little bad men, they're hampered by computer data bases that reveal their secrets to the FBI and Interpol. The age constrains them. But I am Machiavelli. I was outfoxing governments before most of the nations on the globe were founded. My name is in the dictionary, friend Duncan, and it means manipulative and cunning."

He shrugged. "Why do I do these things? Because I can. Because the more power I have around me, the more invincible I become. There is no power on earth greater at this time than the corruption and control of computer systems. You can manipulate reality with computers—send out photographs of events that never occurred, file reports of events that never happened. Heretofore, altering the world at such a basic level has been the provenance only of God, if you believe there is one. Surely a man in your position—

an Immortal—can grasp the attraction." He spread his hands. "Don't *you* want to win the Game?"

"How will any of this accomplish that?" MacLeod demanded. "Harming hundreds of innocent mortals, causing misery—"

Machiavelli felt almost sorry for him. "How entangled with them you are, *caro mio*. We sent Sammi Jo to you because we knew you wouldn't be able to withstand the charms of a wounded dove, but I see it wasn't really necessary. Your heart bleeds for anyone in trouble. It's very weak and shortsighted of you. You really need to toughen up."

He folded his arms. "Duncan, once my knight, always my pawn, this world as you knew it is finished. There is no way you can protect these people any longer. Those who are not for me are against me, and I will brook no enemies. I'll be the only authority on this planet."

"You will be dead."

"Ah, so focused. Such a hero. You know that's a hollow wish."

"Draw your sword. I'm challenging you."

Machiavelli pursed his lips. "Perhaps we could join forces. I need someone I can almost trust."

"I'm not that man."

"Ah, but you are. You always keep your word. I'll tell you what." He made a show of holding out his empty hands. "Our girl is waiting like a princess to be rescued by her handsome knight." He made a courtier's bow to MacLeod. "There's a lock on her door. In one hour, I will signal the other person in the room, an Immortal you have never cared for, to cut off her head. You may spend the hour looking for her, or fighting me." He chuckled. "And you swore, many centuries ago, never to take my head."

*He was right.*

MacLeod raised his sword, hesitated. Machiavelli was right. He had sworn.

"I never said I would not harm you," MacLeod said slowly. "I only swore I wouldn't kill you."

"Then what's the point, Duncan?" Machiavelli crossed his arms and smiled condescendingly at MacLeod. "If you're not going to stop me, why bother slowing me down?"

"There are other ways to stop you."

Something crossed Machiavelli's face—a strange, simmering fury—and MacLeod advanced.

"The sand stopped me," he whispered. "And I hated you for that, Highlander. I hated you every day that I suffered."

"What are you talking about?" MacLeod asked harshly. "The sands of time? What?"

"You don't even *know*?"

MacLeod waited. He had angered Machiavelli, and that was good. Anger threw an opponent off-balance. The truth was that he really didn't know what Machiavelli was talking about. He had left Algiers for Europe and—

—Ah. Ali had told MacLeod he would detain Machiavelli. He had never said how.

"The lady is not sufficient incentive, then," Machiavelli said, his voice rising. "But she'll slow you down. You're worried about her. You'll worry about how much time she has. You'll wonder if she'll survive."

"She'll survive." But MacLeod wasn't sure of that. Machiavelli was right; he would worry. He was worried now.

"She?" Machiavelli snorted. "She's a frail little blossom."

"No." Of that, MacLeod *was* sure. "She's like us. She has a warrior's heart. She just hasn't had to use it."

"High praise from the laird of the Clan MacLeod."

MacLeod assumed a fighter's stance. "I'm taking you on."

"On holy ground? I think not. This is a Shinto shrine."

MacLeod looked at the ruined place, then back at Machiavelli. "Is it your intention to hold me here an hour then? Make a mockery of your challenge?"

"It's all a game anyway, is it not? Perhaps a grand one, but a game nonetheless?"

"Not for those you've killed."

Machiavelli waved his hand. "Mere pawns, Duncan."

"No. They are people. With lives, and dreams. Living beings you have no right to murder!"

And suddenly, MacLeod was filled with rage. As if they were back in Venice, and he stood before the grave of a small boy, killed for sport.

He stood before Maria Angelina, who had been exploited, battered, and bruised.

He stood before Richie's crashed and sinking plane.

"You bastard." He advanced like a snake, slow, sure. He aimed his sword. "You are going to die today."

Machiavelli's eyes widened. "Holy ground, MacLeod."

MacLeod came closer.

"*Madonna,*" Machiavelli breathed. "You mean to do it." He looked wildly at his men. "Take him!"

But there must have been something in MacLeod's face that frightened them; they kept their distance, white faces looking from Machiavelli to MacLeod and back again.

"They don't care what happens to you," MacLeod said through his teeth. He was so angry; he was seething. 'Tonio, popes, kings, Richie, Samantha.

Machiavelli would not touch them. Not the ones he loved.

With an inhuman shout, he flung himself after Machiavelli.

The other Immortal turned and ran.

It was the most foolish thing Machiavelli could have done, MacLeod told himself as he flew after him. For who would fight on holy ground, truly? Who could?

But now, out of the shrine, the bastard was fair game.

"Is this how you hunted 'Tonio down?" he shouted after him, pushing people out of the way.

Then Machiavelli's guards began to realize what was happening; one of them drew a gun. Before he could fire it, MacLeod lunged forward and ran him through. Another aimed. MacLeod dispatched him.

Machiavelli saw, and stopped.

"They're loyal to me," he said with a hint of relief.

MacLeod didn't hear. He dived at him, slashing. He had never fought so fiercely in his long life. Death; he would deal the final blow to this evil on the earth, this smiling jackal—

"I'm unarmed," Machiavelli shouted.

MacLeod ignored him, coming hard, whirling his sword over his head like the Highlander he was.

Then Machiavelli pulled his weapon, and in his left hand, a short, sharp stiletto. He had lied; he had been armed all along. He was the Prince of Lies.

And suddenly, MacLeod was in a black, hard place he had never been before. Icy fury propelled him forward; he was racing against time, through it; he was a blade forged in the pit at the beginning;

he was inhuman; he was nothing but the desire to kill this treacherous moving target, this prey.

Machiavelli saw the transformation, and said desperately, "Forty-five minutes until she dies."

But MacLeod scarcely heard words. *Kill him, kill him,* his blood commanded, for all the innocents he had been unable to save. *For ancient Scotland, and the modern world. For the tyrants you have watched rape, plunder, and murder. For the death of the evils that assault the world daily.*

*For yourself, for the pain and the loss and the inability to stop any of it.*

*MacLeod, you are fierce. You have always been fierce. Though you cast away your warrior's role, you have never cast away your warrior's heart. You fly at me; you terrify me. But I fight back now. I pierce your shoulder socket; you stagger, chancing a thought for your sweet darling.*

Across the compound, dodging bullets and the vain attempts of Machiavelli's men to cheat him of this triumph. Across a field and into a cave, as Machiavelli looked at him with eyes vacant with terror.

He came at him, animalistic, atavistic, a killing machine—*Such we must have been, to survive; I will cut you down, bastard, killer, menace, you will never hurt anyone again. You will bend to my will and you will die.*

Thirty minutes.

*I am on you, Machiavelli. I slash and slash, answering your lightning parries, your riposte, your lunge. I cuff you with the hilt of my katana. I hit you with my fists, I knee you. I will beat you. I will destroy you, body and spirit and soul.*

Fifteen minutes until she died.

*But Duncan, you have sworn not to take my head.*
*What measure of a man are you, if you break your oath?*

"Check," Machiavelli said, as he sliced MacLeod's arm and laid bare the bone, and the Highlander slipped to the ground. Then, without a moment of warning, he was on his knees with Duncan's sword across his throat.

Duncan hissed, "Stand." When Machiavelli did not, MacLeod pressed his blade.

"Take me to her. Now."

"She's as good as dead." Machiavelli was terrified, outraged. Yet his terror was exhilarating; he had not known such depth of passion in all his long life. "But I'll humor you, if you renew your oath here and now. You will not kill me."

MacLeod was silent. "You swore to me, Duncan. And though your Turkish friend caused me unbearable agony, I must concede that you kept your oath. And have, all these centuries." Machiavelli made a show of looking at his watch. "She has ten minutes. I will show you where she is if you swear once again that I am safe with you."

MacLeod struggled. It was over. Again, he was defeated. Tersely he said, "On my honor. But throw down your weapons."

Machiavelli obeyed. MacLeod dragged him into the house threatening anyone who approached with Machiavelli's death. Again the eerie sameness made him wary; where before he had rescued a friend, Ali, now he was to save a woman who may prove to be as faithless as Maria Angelina.

There were five minutes left. MacLeod said, "What now?"

"She's in the most dangerous part of the house."

MacLeod thought for only a few seconds. "Her bedroom."

Machiavelli smiled. "Ah, *bravo*."

"Show me."

They moved through the house. Machiavelli's people fell away, stunned at the sight of the great man held at sword point. One or two darted forward, but he told them to desist. They marveled that he was smiling. He was fearless. He appeared overjoyed.

They were awed.

An alarm sounded. Ruffio looked at Samantha.

"Your time is up."

Slowly, deliberately, he walked to her. Hoisting the sword over his head, he took a deep preparatory breath.

Her heart pounded, yet a portion of her mind remained calm. If she was to die, she would die. If she was to survive, she must remain in possession of herself.

"At least uncuff me," she said.

He paused. "I thought you'd be screaming by now."

"Yes, I imagine you did." Did it hurt when the Quickening took your force and gave it to another? Would she be aware? Or would she be nothing at all?

She made fists to hide the fact that she had started to shake. But Ruffio saw her fear, and smiled.

"All right," he said, "I'll uncuff you."

"And fight me."

He shook his head. "A nice attempt, but there's no advantage to me, *carissima*. Let's get it over with, *si*?" He brought his sword down on her wrist and ankle cuffs.

"Oh." She raised her hands to her face and burst into tears. "God, help me."

"There is no help for you. Not even Duncan MacLeod can help you." He swung.

Screaming like a banshee, she dropped her pretense of tears and rushed him, toppling him to the ground. He jumped up and slapped her hard, sending her flying across the room, and charged toward her.

"You bitch! *Strega!* You'll pay for that."

It didn't matter too much. Better to die this way than the way she had been. To die a warrior.

Better.

They reached the door. Machiavelli said, "Hear them? He's killing her." The keypad was prominent beside the doorknob. "A few buttons separate us from them."

"Open the door."

"Oh, no, I didn't promise to do that." Machiavelli pulled himself away. MacLeod punched in some random numbers. "And now, I'm finished with you for today. I have a helicopter to catch."

MacLeod whirled on him. "Open the door!"

"I've done as much," Machiavelli said. "If you weren't so stupid, Immortal, you'd know the code. *Madonna*, you're such a terrible player."

Immortal. A player.

Chess.

The chess moves.

Machiavelli had been a chess champion in the nineteenth century. As such he had been present at many ground-breaking matches, many written up in chess history books.

Suddenly he remembered: They had been playing the famous game won by Adolf Anderssen in Berlin in 1864.

The game known to history as the Immortal Game. A man named Staunton had been his adversary.

MacLeod punched in the last play: B-K7.

The door opened. Machiavelli cried, "*Bravo!*" and took off at a run.

Ruffio whirled around on MacLeod and knocked him to the floor. As Ruffio moved back, Samantha launched herself at him, pummeling him. MacLeod threw his own sword to Samantha.

Their gazes locked. She was battered and bruised, and his fury rose again at what had been done to her. She nodded, and for the oddest moment, he thought she was going to swing against his own throat. Then she attacked Ruffio, shouting as she brought down the heavy blade.

As soon as the man's head fell from his shoulders, MacLeod grabbed Ruffio's sword and flew after Machiavelli, wheeling his sword around his head, ululating a Highlander war cry.

Machiavelli half turned as he ran from him. He shouted, "You swore!"

"Aye, I did. On my honor," MacLeod replied, launching himself at the Prince of Lies.

Machiavelli went for his sword. MacLeod caught it with his blade and flung it out of Machiavelli's reach.

The Italian was shocked. "At least let me fight like a man."

"No."

Machiavelli stared at him openmouthed. He had poisoned kings and popes; he had promised to dominate the earth. And yet, he was just a man.

Who had thought to live forever.

"Duncan, I'm unarmed. And you took an oath."

MacLeod replied, "There can't be another chance for you." He took a breath and swung.

In the distance, Ruffio's Quickening overtook Samantha.

*Highlander, where is your honor?*
*Where is the foundation of your word?*

*You have lied. You have deceived.*

*You have sinned.*

*The Quickening rocked him; it dragged him under, and above; it killed him, revived him. It transformed him.*

*It became him.*

*Machiavelli, dead for all time. And yet, as MacLeod shook like thunder, a memory separated from the others like a feather, and trailed into the calm at the center of the tumult:*

*A little boy with foxlike eyes, standing hopeful and eager in a doorway. It was a school. And the other boys laughed, "You puny little girl! Get away. Go away."*

*Unloved.*

*Sobbing home, to seek the arms of his mother. Comfort there, understanding there:*

*But his father was home, drunk, beating her. Her hands vainly covered her face. She begged, "No, per favore, per favore, amore mio."*

*Unloved.*

*Niccolino stood helpless before his father's anger.*

*Ashamed before the laughter of the other boys.*

*Humiliated.*

*Unloved.*

*Never again, the little boy vowed. Never again. Better never to care.*

*Never to love.*

*Mortified and suffering in the desert where MacLeod had left him; MacLeod, whose power and vitality he adored.*

*And MacLeod, rising weakly, opening his eyes, whispered, "Rest peacefully, Niccolo Machiavelli. It's done. It's over."*

Samantha crawled to him, and he lifted her into his arms. She was wrung limp, but triumphant.

"It was your first," he told her. "Next time, you'll know what to expect."

"You are my first," she replied softly, and kissed him.

# Epilogue:
# The Kata of The Victor

<hr>

*"All things that are born must die. Work hard for your own freedom from sorrow."*

—**The Buddha**

The Quickening of Niccolo Machiavelli turned the compound into a pile of burning rubble. Glass and metal was fused. It looked as if a bomb had gone off.

Miraculously, MacLeod located the original CD-ROM. It had melted into an unreadable glob. The second, Dawson told MacLeod by phone, was reported destroyed and unreadable in the bakery fire. He didn't tell MacLeod how he had found this out, but MacLeod believed him.

Yet no one could be certain it was over. The routers were still in place. They would have to wait and see what happened next.

Richie was safe; the plane had gone down, but most of the other passengers had been rescued. Most. Some had died.

Of the conspirators, only Samantha was alive. She grieved, and MacLeod held her, knowing the pain, knowing it would be part of both their lives until they were killed, or left alone to be the one.

Now they checked into an old-fashioned country inn, a *ryokan*, in the peaceful countryside. She was different. More confident. Stronger. She moved like a fighter. There was a radiance about her.

She didn't need him anymore.

He was very happy for her.

But after steaming hot baths and long, sensuous massages, they were alone again. She fell into his arms, and he carried her to bed.

Eagerly, she opened herself to him. Her skin was silky, her flesh soft and yielding, her muscles steel.

"Duncan, I can be yours now," she whispered. "I have something to give you, because I have more than I need. Machiavelli was wrong; I was able to love him. He just couldn't accept it. I have more than enough for both of us."

He held her tightly. *Then restore me,* he wanted to tell her. *I've lost what was inside. I've sacrificed the value of my word. I've lost who I am.*

*If I had not placed such a high value on my honor, I would not have lost Debra. I would not have lost Hamza. I would not have lost myself.*

*I would not walk so alone.*

*I wouldn't have dreams that make me weep.*

"You saved us all," she whispered. "You did it."

What other choice was there? Permit Machiavelli to continue his scheming and domination? The Immortal had adapted to this century, as he had to all the others, but in this modern, high-tech world the harm he could wreak was numbing. He could have been anything he wanted. He would have been unstoppable. He would never have developed a conscience. He had no code except that he must control; he must dominate; he must *be.*

And so, he could *not* be.

But what of the next time, the next adversary? Would he, MacLeod, find a way to justify breaking his word to save his own life? Would it become easier now to build his morality on shifting sand, rather than the age-old rocks of his beloved Highland hills?

"I thought you were going to sacrifice me to get to him," Samantha murmured. "And I think I would have killed you for that, because I didn't know then just how evil he was."

He didn't answer. He had promised never to challenge her. Would he break that promise, too, someday?

"Duncan?"

"I'm lost," he murmured under his breath, thinking she wouldn't be able to hear him.

"No. No, I know where to find you." She laid his hand over her heart. "In here."

Could that be so? Could it be enough to save him? Was he yet a man of principles and honor? If sometimes those principles required that he sacrifice a tiny part of his soul to save others, did he still have a soul?

"Hold on tight," she said. "We'll go together this time. The path isn't so narrow when you share it with someone else." She cradled his head. "Someone you walk beside, not in front of."

"Aye," he said, releasing himself from too much pain, and sorrow, and disappointment. The *katas* of the last adversaries.

Going with her, his eyes closed, hoping.

Perhaps if he held on tightly enough, trusted enough, hoped enough, and loved, he would always be Duncan MacLeod of the Clan MacLeod.

An Immortal.

A Prince of the Universe.

The Highlander.

# IT'S A KIND OF MAGIC . . .

## On sale in July 1997,
### *Highlander: The Path*
### by Rebecca Neason

Duncan MacLeod learns of an international peace rally, but he is reluctant to attend, for the guest of honor is to be the Dalai Lama, and his appearance stirs painful memories 200 years old . . .

In 1781, growing weary of Immortality and The Game, Duncan wanders into Tibet, where he meets the eighth Dalai Lama. The Dalai Lama helps Duncan to find the path he was meant to take, and during his stay in Tibet, Duncan falls in love with a beautiful young woman. When Gurkah soldiers attack the sacred monastery, Duncan is forced back into battle—but with the help of the Dalai Lama's teachings, Duncan now understands the true use of his special nature.

# HIGHLANDER™

## THE CARD GAME

---

## FREE UNIQUE CARD OFFER!

Now you can play an Immortal in the fast paced card game that lets you pit your sword against others in the quest for The Prize.

In celebration of the new series of original novels from Warner Aspect, Thunder Castle Games is making available, for a limited time only, one Highlander™ Card not for sale in any edition.

Send a stamped self-addressed envelope and proof of purchase (cash register receipt attached to this coupon) to Thunder Castle Games, Dept. 119, P.O. Box 11529, Kansas City, MO 64138. Please allow 4-6 weeks for delivery.

---

Name: _____

Address: _____

City: _____ State:_____ Zip: _____

Age: _____ Phone: _____